THE TIME OF MAGIC BOOK II

THE CATALYSTS

AMIR SHEVAT

CONTENTS

CHAPTER ONE

Valor sat in the dark.

He closed his eyes. The mountain cave air pressed cold and damp against his skin. Water dripped somewhere in the darkness, each drop echoing off stone. He needed to meditate, to rest. He was so tired, but his mind kept yanking him out of serenity's hold.

"Don't get used to it. This is the calm before the terrible storm," a voice in his head said.

He tried to quiet his thoughts by focusing on Brenda and how her face grew younger each day.

A horrible picture flashed in his head of Brenda screaming as she fell to her death.

Enough!

Valor refocused on his people and how they were thriving in their new village. He should feel proud. He made this happen. He had saved them.

A vivid vision of death and war haunted him now. Dead elves and burning cities.

Enough with that! Why was he so anxious?

"Because you know this calm is short-lived. You are afraid you won't be able to protect your loved ones when the time comes," the pesky voice in his head answered.

He sighed, took a deep breath, and tried to meditate again and bring his mind to the now. Didn't he deserve to enjoy some tranquility?

"*How can you experience joy knowing you might lose everything you care about at any moment?*" the voice accused.

Isn't that the meaning of life? To enjoy things while they last? he answered himself.

"Perhaps. Well, time is up!" the pesky voice said with a hint of vindicated glee.

The air in the cave suddenly turned frosty. His attention snapped back from meditation as he felt his mother's presence in his mind.

"My son, your immediate presence is required by your father." Her voice resonated through him.

A command, not a request. He knew it required no response, just compliance.

Behind him, the heavy door scraped open by itself, stone grinding against stone. Even with his eyes closed, he felt the change. Still cave air gave way to a gentle breeze from outside. Sunlight warmed his body.

He opened his eyes, stood, and walked into the light.

VALOR DESCENDED the winding path from the meditation cave as the warm breeze lifted his hair. Saplings dotted the settlement's edges below, their leaves bright against the desert landscape. The scent of turned earth and growing vegetables drifted up from green fields stretching between tents conjured of vines and leaves. An elf's voice rose in magical chant, promising an apple sapling strength and good yield. Even in the desert heat, the young plants thrived with the power of their magic.

Three months. It had been such a short time since they had started building their new home, yet it already felt like they had been living there forever. Magic was still weak and unstable, but the village rose anyway. Just yesterday, he'd walked past the fifth completed longhouse, its roof beams carved with protective runes. He and his people had transformed a desert into a flourishing village.

He spotted the white tent that was the village infirmary, and his thoughts went straight to Brenda. The elvish healers marveled at her progress. "We've never seen such a quick recovery," one had told him the day before.

Brenda was much less impressed. A smile tugged at his lips as he recalled her impatience with the healing process.

"I've been stuck in this bed for three months!" she had griped at him the last time he had seen her. It was good to have the familiar feisty Brenda back.

"Good morning, young prince." General Baliz's baritone voice pulled Valor from his reverie.

"Hello, General. Good to see you. How is the perimeter defense project progressing?"

The king was waiting, but if Valor brushed off the general now, the old elf would sulk for weeks.

"Very well indeed, my prince. Today, we finished placing the wards all around the village. They will protect us from anyone with bad intent, anything from spying eyes to an army of undead. Nothing will get close to our village now or even spot us from afar. Come, let me show you th—"

The general was settling in for a long talk, but the king wouldn't tolerate delays.

"Pardon me, my good general, but I am on my way to the

king. I have been summoned." Valor used the most official voice he could manage.

"Oh, yes. Of course, of course. Do not let me keep you waiting." The general reciprocated the official tone, though he did look disappointed.

Valor continued walking quickly between the smaller tents, keeping his gaze low and trying to avoid running into more officials. Being next in line for the throne made him a celebrity of sorts, and important people always wanted his time.

A gust of wind passed through the tents, long black strips brushing his shoulder. Each strip bore the names of family members who had died because of the plague. Memorial ribbons were everywhere. Many were still mourning their dead.

Valor walked to the big central tent, nodded to the guards, and entered the first chamber.

His mother waited for him there. Her moonlight dress seemed to be woven from white rays, making her look out of place anywhere other than inside a magical crystal tower.

Brenda had told him a few weeks back that she was "scared shitless" of his mother. "She is always so official, so commanding, so royal," Brenda had explained.

Standing here now, he understood exactly what she meant.

"My son," she greeted him. "Thank you for coming. Your father is expecting you." She used her royal voice—booming, clear, and commanding.

"Thank you, Mother." He bowed lightly. "I trust all is well?"

His father was not the kind of king who called upon his son for small talk or family bonding. The king was always extremely busy and had many other priorities. Most of his life, Valor was the sixth of six sons, so definitely not a priority...but now, he was the only son and heir to the throne. Maybe things had changed? What was so important?

"No. All is not well," his mother said softly. Her eyes exposed a rare glimpse of sorrow and worry. "Your father is having visions again. He is haunted by them. The Royal Curse is draining him."

Valor had known about the Royal Curse since he was a child. The phenomenon was shared by the royalty of all magical races. Ominous possible futures would often haunt their dreams. Kings and queens throughout the generations would know to gather food for drought, prepare for war, or evade assassinations. However, it was far from a useful tool, as it was very hard to tell the difference between ordinary nightmares and the Royal Curse.

"He will tell you all about it." She gestured toward the king's hall entrance. "Valor, please listen to your father very carefully. This might be one of the last times you will have the chance to..." Her voice trailed off, as if she wasn't willing to finish the sentence.

"Why? What do you mean, Mother?" Valor kept his voice steady despite the clench of fear spreading through his gut.

"Your father is old, Valor, much older than any Elvish king before him. His time with us is not long, and soon, he will retire to the forest. All things come to an end. Praise the force of all living things."

His mother was barely a thousand years old, so much younger than his father. Her composure never cracked, but seeing her husband fade had to be tearing her apart.

Valor said nothing. She was too proud, too regal. Instead, he nodded and bowed again.

"I will go in at once."

Without another word, he entered the king's hall.

The "king's hall" was the glorified name for a large tent. The place was modestly arranged, with a bed in the corner, a simple wooden dresser in another, and the reception area in the middle.

His father was sitting on a throne made of vines and leaves and was reading a scroll with fascination. His left hand made signs in the air, and his lips silently vocalized a chant.

He lifted his gaze and studied Valor. A smile came to the king's face, and he lowered the scroll and extended his hand. "Son, thank you for coming."

Valor kneeled and kissed the ring on his father's hand. "Of course, Father. I came as soon as you called."

His father grasped Valor's chin and examined his son's face.

A cold shiver tripped up Valor's spine. The physical touch of his father was startling enough, but his father looked so much older, as if the last three months had aged him three hundred years. The king's skin had become almost transparent, and his face seemed unhealthy and slim. His father's eyes struck Valor the most. They were yellowed and less clear than Valor remembered.

The king frowned in puzzlement. "Why are you so worried, my son? Did your mother tell you I am dying? By the forces of life! That woman is so worried about the future she can't enjoy the moment!" His laughter rumbled deep but held a childlike brightness. "Everything that lives is dying. That is the way of all things. I have walked most of the path, but I still have some road left to cover." He took his son's hands between his own.

Valor managed a nod. Words stuck in his throat.

"Now, let's talk about the present for a bit." The king's voice warmed. "How are you?"

"I am well, Father. Trying to help our people build our home anew."

"That is good, my son. I am in awe of our people's ability to overcome and rebuild. Being a leader is sometimes the art of observation and discernment, letting people do the best they can without standing in their way."

"Indeed, Father."

These were probably the most words his father had ever uttered to him in one breath, and Valor felt like he was basking in the sun, but a small voice whispered, *Why now? After all these years of distance, why this sudden warmth? What did his father need from him?*

"And how is Brenda?" the king pressed.

"She is recovering better than expected. Thank you for inquiring, Father." Valor blinked. His father not only remembered Brenda's name but had bothered to ask. Of course, the king knew Brenda had been afflicted with premature old age, a complication of the time spell Valor and Brenda had co-cast to bring the elves forward in time, but he'd never thought his father cared for her.

"Good! You need her for what happens next." The king's face was now serious, his tone somber. "I called you because I have seen a vision of burning cities, of fire from the skies, of death and loss." His voice was sad, and his eyes turned glassy from unshed tears. "So much destruction of life force, so much pain."

The king's gaze moved from Valor's face and stared into the empty space in front of his makeshift throne. His expression looked tormented.

"There are many paths that lead to this terrible future and very few paths that do not," the king whispered as if talking to himself now. "I have made many bad choices that led us to this future. Driven by fear, ego, and lust, I let a horrible path come to fruition, one that cost me so many sons, but I still have hope. Valor can finish the quest I failed, the only quest that matters. I will call Valor and send him."

"I am here, Father." The words came out rougher than intended. Watching his father drift in and out like this, haunted by his past, made something cold and heavy settle in Valor's stomach.

"Oh, yes! You are here. I told you that your mother is worried about the future. I, too, am worried, but not for myself. For all life." The king's voice was urgent, almost pleading. "I have spent the last three months looking for a path away from my horrible vision. I only found one. The path involves you, my son. I know how it begins but not how it ends, and that actually fills me with hope." His father's voice became strong again.

Valor leaned toward his father, remaining on his knees, saying nothing.

"It starts with a quest for a union." The king peered at Valor intently and drummed his fingers against the armrest. "Magic is coming back to our world, but too slowly and too weakly. If we wait for nature to take its course, it will take hundreds of years for magic to return to full force."

"We are elves. What are a few hundred years? We have time," Valor said.

"No!" The king's voice was sharp. "There are forces of destruction at play, and they will be fast and furious. For life to have any chance at all, you need to bring magic to our world in full force before they become too strong."

Valor's stomach dropped. He nodded, hiding the doubt that crept through him.

"Look at this spell." The king held up the scroll he'd been reading. "It is an extremely powerful incantation that can instantly reverse all the effects of Kador's spell to eliminate magic and more." He paused, his thumb running along the edge of the scroll. "I held this scroll once before, found it on a quest a lifetime ago. I was not ready then. I lost it soon after. Three days ago, it found its way back to me." His voice dropped to a whisper. "I thought I would never see it again."

Valor reached for the scroll and eased it from his father's weakened grasp. The paper was warm to the touch. The words seemed illegible. How strange. Usually scrolls were only illegible until the wizard had reached the correlating casting proficiency, but Valor was a master wizard and should have been able to read the words. Unless...

"This is the most powerful spell I have ever laid eyes on." The king's eyes blazed. "Casting it might fix it all. It must. But it requires all four magic types in order to read it—air, water, fire, and earth. You know the song."

Valor chanted the childhood song that every elf knew by the age of ten:

"Elves are the water that gives life.

Humans are the fire that powers it.

Dwarves are the earth where life resides.

Fairies are the air that all life breathes."

"That is true." The king looked at Valor. "We all have each of the magic types, but can only truly control the magic type of our species. For this spell, you need all four."

"Why didn't Kador need all four for the destruction of magic?" Valor asked.

"I do not know, my son." The king's eyes glazed again. "But it is my observation that it is easier to destroy than to build. This spell you are holding in your hand will bring back magic in full force and even fortify it. I have sacrificed much to put this powerful magic in your hands." The king's gaze drifted beyond Valor to something only his aged eyes could see. "I have found the scroll again, my love. I promise not to make the same mistake. The spell will be cast. Fear be damned. No, it is not too risky. You are wrong. It is a good idea! It must be done." He uttered it sharply, almost snarling.

"Father, are you well? Who are you talking to? Who do you see?" Valor started to rise, to call for his mother, but the king's fingers locked around his wrist.

"Yes! I am here. Listen!" The king focused on Valor again. He sounded frantic now. "I need to tell you about the first step of your quest. Your path starts with the dwarves. You must go to the mountains and seek them. They have been hiding in their mountain shelters for six hundred years. Wake them. Find a dwarf wizard willing to co-cast this spell with you. That wizard will be your land. Take Brenda with you. She will be your fire. I do not know where the fairies are these days, but they have the tendency to find you when you need them, so do not worry about that just now." The king smiled when he mentioned the fairies, as if recalling something.

His father produced a hard leather pouch, which must have been tucked into the throne beside him, and placed the scroll inside. His hand hovered over the bag, and the bag faded until it completely disappeared. The king then passed the invisible object to his son with trembling hands.

"This scroll holds the future we want but also the danger we fear. Guard it with your life." The king's jaw tightened. The lines around his mouth deepened as he gazed into Valor's eyes.

Valor took the pouch and tucked it in his pocket.

"Once your company is assembled and accepts the quest, you will have everything you need to cast this spell." The king leaned forward. "This will be your Quest of Ascendance."

Valor froze. Even his heart seemed to stop beating. The Quest of Ascendance.

"Yes." The king nodded. "This quest will be the last step required for you to become the next king of all elves."

Valor said nothing. What could he possibly say to that?

CHAPTER TWO

"We know where they are," James Webber announced, settling into his desk chair. The leather gave slightly under his weight. "We have ninety-five percent conviction that the elves are in Redstone Springs, Arizona."

Mike Stone, a US Army intelligence general, filled his chair, his chest straining against the buttons on his uniform. Scott Radcliffe, the head of the National Security Agency, sat beside him, his lean frame sharp in his black suit.

James had positioned both chairs exactly seventeen inches from the other side of his desk. The room was small and gray, designed like a bank mortgage office. James had chosen every detail, from the fluorescent lights and the temperature set two degrees too cold, to the hard chairs. The message was simple: *Get your business done. Sign the papers. Leave.*

"Bullshit," the general said, dismissive. His thick fingers drummed on the armrest. "Our intelligence officers combed through all the satellite images. There is nothing there. You are wasting our time."

The general had fallen right into it. James pressed his lips together, fighting the smile.

Without comment, James clicked a large button on the remote. The screen behind him hummed, then blazed white before resolving into satellite imagery. Arizona's high desert stretched across the display, nothing but bare canyon and rock. A small black label at the right bottom corner of the screen indicated that they were looking at a compiled video of the area over a month, with photos taken every hour.

"Well, General." James kept his voice flat. "That is correct. Your people have reviewed the same material we did and completely missed the fact that this area is the only one with zero change over the month. While all the rest of the imagery shows change over time, due to weather or other factors, the Redstone Springs area shows no change throughout the entire month."

The video zoomed in on several areas demonstrating seasonal change, but Redstone Springs remained the same. God, James loved an effective presentation.

The silence stretched. General Stone blinked at the screen, his mouth agape.

James said nothing about Mary Drechsler's phone. Its last signal had pointed them to Redstone Springs before going dark, together with its owner. The NSA and the Army didn't need that detail.

"It can't be..." The general's face flushed red, then drained to white.

Radcliffe leaned forward. "I have heard enough."

James had never seen him cut Stone off before.

Now let's hear true power speak.

"The president needs results, and the Kildare Organization is clearly delivering better than our own intelligence," Scott said. His tone was stripped of emotion, purely factual.

Say it! Call the game. James's mouth watered.

"I have been authorized by the president to deputize the Kildare Organization as the NSA's contractor responsible for intelligence around all unnatural phenomena," Scott continued with the same bureaucratic tone.

James's skin tickled with an almost sensual pleasure. He loved bureaucracy—its predictability, its efficiency. His predecessor, Roy Valemont, had been a psychopath who had lied and killed his way to the top. Mary Drechsler, his security officer, had been a zealot who thought she was invincible. Both were dead or presumed dead. James's superpower was being boring and consistently effective. This superpower yielded the role of the head of the Kildare Organization and now top contractor for the NSA.

"This is unheard of!" The general's face flushed again.

His eyes cold and unblinking, Scott stared down the general. "Do you want to open this here? Very well." Scott leaned back. "This is the third time Kildare has outperformed your organization using your own data. They've helped identify, stop, and clean up after unnatural incidents."

James noted that Scott did not use the word magic, as if it was tainted or unprofessional. He felt the punchline coming.

The general's voice rose. "The Army is responsible for protecting the US from—"

Scott cut him off. "The president has had enough, General. We are bombarded with media scrutiny, international pressure, and national panic combined with loss of trust. We have had enough of your excuses for your failures while the Kildare organization has been delivering results."

Finish him. James licked his lips.

"From now on," the head of the NSA said, pointing at James, "he will be running point on all intelligence operations. He will be reporting to me and me alone."

They all fell silent.

Time to play the good cop, as planned.

"The Kildare Organization will of course collaborate with the Army intelligence on an ongoing basis." James kept a pleasing voice and his middle finger hidden under the table.

"Of course, we must put the president's wishes and our nation's safety first," Scott said with a polite smile and a nod to the general. "Understood? Agreed?"

James glanced at the general. The man knew he'd lost.

"Yes. Understood." The general's voice was low, subdued.

Checkmate.

Time to pivot the conversation.

"Thank you for your vote of confidence, Scott. Our top priorities right now are to contain all unnatural phenomena that are happening in the US and prevent them from spreading and generating more harm and panic. We need to understand why and how this is happening and stop it at all costs." James moved back to his business-as-usual tone of voice. He clicked the clicker, and the next slide came up showing media snippets covering incidents of magic across the country.

"Agreed. I want a progress report on a weekly basis. This is a top priority for the president. We will leave you to do your important work." Scott stood, signaling with his hand for the general to join him.

"Scott, prepare the president for what is coming. This could get much worse before it gets better. We might need to use extreme measures here." While James's voice was calm, he knew his words were going to keep Scott awake at night. The meaning was unmistakable—we are facing war.

Scott frowned but said nothing. He nodded, and the two men both left quietly.

James leaned back on his chair and put his legs on the table.

That had gone as well as expected. He allowed himself three minutes to relish this success.

He took a deep breath. That was the easy part of his agenda today. What came next sent shivers down his spine.

Then he stood, straightened his gray suit, and marched out of his office.

"Your next meeting is in thirty minutes, Director Webber," his executive assistant reminded him as he came out.

"Thank you, Timon," James mumbled while walking to the elevator. His mind was focused on the task at hand.

He waited for the elevator, walked in, and removed a key from his pocket. Inside the elevator, next to the door, was an electric panel showing floors from ten to minus ten. He slid the key into the slot above the panel and turned it. Metal scraped metal. Another floor appeared on the electronic panel, the numbers blood-red against black. Minus thirteen. He pressed the button, and the doors closed.

He had been procrastinating on this task for too long. It was not like him. He was a man who did things right away. Early was on time, on time was late, and late was unacceptable. Still, he had waited three months to do this.

As the door opened, a wave of cool air hit his face, the type that kept museums cool and dry.

Samuel, the guard of the Kildare archive, did not seem surprised to see him.

James hated to surprise his team. Being unprepared created unexpected results, and James would have none of that.

"Good morning, Director Webber," Samuel said, his voice raspy and deep, like an old jazz singer.

"Morning," James said, not yet sure if it was a good morning or not.

The entry room was well lit, with a big safe door behind Samuel's desk. A small panel was attached to the center of the frame. James walked to the entrance, typed his password, and scanned his retina. The door opened with a heavy dragging sound.

He stepped into the Kildare archive. It looked like a scene from an adventure movie. The walls were lined with shelves holding swords that hummed with residual energy, daggers with runes carved into bone handles, and shields marked with sigils that seemed to shift in the blue light. Strange bodies of all sizes were embalmed on the walls and in glass jars: winged human-like creatures with feathers that graduated from white at the base to obsidian at the tips; horned hominoids, their skulls elongated and crowned with curved rams' horns; and mermaids with translucent fins and skin that still held an iridescent shimmer even in death.

James passed by them and approached a table in the center of the room. A golden chest with delicate embroidery in gold and silver sat on a table. A thumb reader lock was affixed to it.

James pressed his finger to the cold surface of the thumb reader and heard a gratifying ding as the chest unlocked and popped open. He inspected the book in the chest. It radiated faint blue light. Its cover was plain brown leather with three words written on it.

Book of Kador.

His skin prickled as he took the book out of the box. It was strangely warm. The leather was worn soft and brittle with age. James opened the book to the last chapter, read through it, and frowned. Exactly as he remembered from the copy he owned. It talked about The Witness and the danger of enabling her to bring magic back to the world. Why would Mary send him to read what he already knew?

He opened his phone and went through his texts until he got to Mary's last message.

If I am dead. Read the last chapter of the Prime Copy. Through pain and blood. God be with you.

Why would she send him to read this chapter? She wasn't the kind of person to do that. He read through the chapter again, looking for missing or added words, but there were none.

Then he saw it. A page was tucked into the rear of the leather cover of the book.

He tried to peel the leather cover. It felt like part of the blue glow was covering his fingers, burning them. Dropping the book on the table, James backed away, hissing and putting his fingers to his mouth. After a second of thinking, he dove into the task again, ignoring the pain.

Once the cover was off, he examined the page. It was yellow with age, still partly sticking to the binding. Clear writing showed through from the other side, but he could not read it. The page was glued to the hardcover at its top and bottom corners. He carefully peeled it free, the parchment crackling under his fingers. The brown glue was flaking. It seemed like dried blood.

Through pain and blood. *Mary, you sneaky bastard.*

He turned the page. The words were written in gold.

> *If all has failed and turned to dust,*
> *If Witness prevails and all is lost,*
> *Catalysts of fire, water, air, and earth will come.*
> *They'll cast the last spell to end the time of man.*

James's blood ran cold in his veins.

CHAPTER THREE

"W*here are you?"* Valor's voice came softly into her mind. Not words exactly, more like...a feeling. Intent. Question.

Brenda's fingers stilled on the braid she'd been weaving through her hair.

"The infirmary. Where I've been for three months." She didn't add "you fool" even though the impulse rose. He sounded worried.

She abandoned the braid and stood even as her legs protested. Better than a week ago, though. A week ago, she'd needed help just to cross the room.

Three months had passed since the spell that had aged her body and scrambled her mind. During that time, Valor had sat beside her bed until they'd developed this connection. He called it the Bond.

Brenda liked that word. She had never had a bond with anyone before. She felt closer to him than she felt to her family.

Well, that's not a high bar.

"I am coming over. Stay there," he said in her mind.

She crossed to the mirror the healers had brought last week, examined her reflection, and frowned deeply. *Where else would I go?*

The mirror showed gray streaks she'd been trying to braid away and lines around her eyes. She looked to be forty, maybe older, but she was actually just twenty-two. The time spell had stolen years from her body even as it had saved Valor's people.

For a split second, the woman in the mirror reminded her of her mother. Guilt flickered. She should check on her parents. But if she did, they'd drag her back to that life. She couldn't have that. Not now. Not ever. Besides, she was still healing.

The first month had been nothing but fog and pain. She touched her temple, remembering the headaches. The second month, the pain had eased, but her mind had stayed sluggish. Healers had come and gone, chanting in languages that made no sense until the third month when they'd given her that potion. Tongues, they had called it. It had tasted like Cherry Coke. After that, she could finally understand what they were saying and speak their language back.

The last month had been good to her. Her mind had cleared, her body was getting stronger every day, and she'd even started to make friends in the infirmary.

Three months of recovery and kind, gentle, endlessly boring elves. She would go insane if she had to spend much longer here. The problem was she could not share that with Valor in case it hurt his feelings.

Valor! He is coming.

"I look forty! So freaking old!" she exclaimed out loud.

She heard the usual giggles to her remarks from the healers' section, which was separated from the patient section by a heavy cloth. The giggles were interrupted by a knock on the infirmary door.

There was a quiet exchange of soft words behind the curtain

of the healer quarters. Brenda tried to listen in, but it was too low for her ears to decipher. More giggles followed, both from her healer and the visitor.

Are they whispering really low, or is it my damn old ears?

A few moments later, Valor came through the curtain. He was smiling like he'd just heard a good joke. She suspected she was the subject of it.

"What?" she asked with a fake accusatory tone.

"The healers are amused that you think forty is old. You know they are well over four hundred, right?"

His happy voice always made her smile. His grin spread to her face before she could stop it.

"The fact that they all look perfectly well in their fifth century doesn't make me any happier about looking this old," she complained, raising her voice so that the healers would hear her.

A fresh wave of laughter came from the healer quarters.

"You are great the way you are," he said earnestly.

What a weird trait. Being genuinely supportive. Elves. What a bunch of weirdos.

She studied him. His tired eyes darted around the room. His jaw was set, and he clenched his fists by his sides.

"What's on your mind, Valor?" she asked. Luckily, other than her, the large infirmary tent was empty of other patients today.

Valor walked toward her and sat in the chair next to her bed. "My father has asked me to go on another quest with you. He says that magic is coming back too slowly, and it is still too weak. He wants us to cast a spell that will bring back the magic in full force."

She took a seat on the bed, cross-legged. A small part of her brain was thankful her knees were feeling better today.

"Why can't you cast that spell right here and be done with it?" she asked. Sometimes the most trivial things escaped him.

"This is a very powerful spell." Valor stood and started pacing the small tent. "Powerful spells require the four elements of magic."

"Elements?" Brenda shifted on the bed, tucking her knees under her. They protested less than yesterday.

"Each race has a natural affinity, an element they're good at." He turned back to her, his hands clasped behind him, that formal pose he took when explaining things. "We need four casters for this spell."

"Okay." She watched him pace. "So where do you find four casters?"

"That's the quest. We need to find two more." He paused. "A dwarf caster and a fairy, but you can't really find a fairy. They find—"

"Wait, two more?" She counted on her fingers. "So you already have two?"

He nodded, not quite meeting her eyes.

"You're one of them obviously." She tilted her head. "Who's the other?"

"You are."

The words hung in the air for a moment.

"Me?" Her voice came out higher than intended. "I've barely recovered from the last spell we cast."

"Human wizards have the power of the fire essence in their blood, a natural affinity to fire spells." He finally met her gaze. "You don't have to do it, but you're more than capable."

Shit, that sounded so cool. *I have fire power!*

She needed to steer back to the task at hand. "So we're looking for a dwarf and a fairy. What's the catch with fairies?"

"You can't find them. They find you, when they want to, and only if they like you." He grimaced.

"Great." She grinned despite herself. "So we're hunting for magical creatures with attitude problems. This keeps getting better. Where do we even start?"

"Dwarves are in the mountains. They're magical builders and masters of earth essence."

"Earth essence." She repeated it slowly, testing the phrase. "And the fairies? What's their deal?"

"Air essence. They're spirits." His voice changed, taking on an edge of awe. "Powerful. Fierce. Chaotic."

She leaned forward, reading his face. "So you're the fourth element? Water?"

"All elves work with water magic." Pride crept into his voice. "It gives life and makes things grow. Controls things that flow." He met her eyes again. "Like time."

"And I'm fire." She said it out loud; it felt good to say it. "The fourth spellcaster." Her gaze narrowed. "Hmmm."

"Only if that is your wish." His voice took on that no-one-is-forcing-you tone she remembered when her friends offered her a drink in college. "No one can force you to cast magic."

His blue-gray eyes peered back at her. That perfect hair. He stood tall and confident even now when she could see doubt written all over him.

She leaned forward. "So, why not go on this quest?"

He looked away. "I'm not sure we shouldn't just wait it out." His eyes darted around. "My father speaks of dark forces. I feel them, too, but not as strongly. Maybe he's haunted by ghosts of his past. Why not wait fifty years? Let magic return naturally."

Fifty years? Did he really say fifty years?

She couldn't wait another month in this place without going crazy. Three months of the nicest, kindest, most thoughtful people she'd ever met, and she was dying of boredom. Elves had too much time on their hands. For them, meditating for a week was the norm. It was unnerving. Like an endless yoga retreat. Unbearable. Fifty years of this would kill her faster than any spell backlash.

The truth was that she was physically enjoying that magic was getting stronger. She couldn't put it into words, but she *felt* magic. It was palpable. On days when magic was stronger, she was energized, and on other days, she felt weaker. The closest resemblance was the feeling you had after a good night's sleep versus a day after very little sleep. Her body wished for stronger magic. She was hungry for more. No, she was lustful for more.

"Let's do it!" she said. "I want to meet dwarves and fairies. This sounds like a wonderful quest."

He stared past her shoulder, not responding.

Brenda frowned. "What is it, Valor?"

"I'm not sure I'm the right fit for this." His voice dropped. "I don't think I'm ready. My father said completing this spell would make me eligible to be the next king of the elves."

Oh, there is no question about it. We are fucking going on a quest!

Brenda covered a smile. "Valor, this is awesome! You will be such a great leader for your people. We should do this."

Yeah, he is not *listening.*

"Hmm...I think we should definitely wait five or ten years and see what happens," Valor concluded. He stood and brushed off his tunic with an air of finality. "Yes. That is the wisest course of action. We agree, then."

Brenda grinned at him. "Yeah, right. We are definitely waiting another ten years."

She tried to keep the sarcasm out of her voice. She really did.

THEY PACKED THAT NIGHT.

Brenda said goodbye to her friends from the infirmary. She gave a big hug to Anat, the chief healer.

"Do not worry. We will continue your healing when you come back." Anat's voice was always like a warm ray of sunshine on a chilly day. The healer's smile turned mischievous. "How did you manage to convince Valor to take the quest?"

I guess gossiping and rumor-mongering are not beyond any intelligent being.

"I didn't. We agreed just to go and seek the dwarves and the fairy and see if the quest is even feasible in the first place." Brenda couldn't stifle her smirk. Whatever it took to get some excitement back in her life.

Valor waited for her at the entrance of the infirmary, going through his pack. He looked up and gave her that big, easy smile. Even after everything his father had just laid on him, he could still grin like the world was full of wonder.

"Are you ready?" he asked.

She tried to match his energy. "Bring it on! Brenda and Valor on the road again."

Leaving the village's green shade for the open desert felt like stepping through a curtain. Heat pressed against Brenda's skin. Her muscles protested every step, weak from three months in bed.

Valor slowed his pace without being asked. Sand crunched under their feet.

Out here, away from potential eavesdroppers, she could finally ask the questions she'd been collecting.

"Valor, what do the elves want to achieve? Like, what's the end goal?"

He didn't answer.

She glanced at him, wondering if he'd heard her.

"Elves do not think that way, Brenda," he said after a long while. "Humans are short-lived, so they have goals. They want to be remembered. They want power. They want control. Not everyone living wants that. Most animals do not, for example. Elves are very long-lived, and even after they pass and become a tree, they are still conscious. Elves strive for a healthy balance in the world. We want harmony. When we feel an imbalance in the world, we are driven to take action and fix it. That is our end goal."

"Do you feel it now?" she asked.

"Yes, very much so!" Passion flooded his voice. She'd never heard him sound like that before. "The lack of magical creatures is sinking my heart. I feel an evil rising up in the north and a great sleeping power in the south that should be dormant yet is awakening. Nature is screaming for help after years of destruction." He seemed to notice her confusion and added, "Some of these things I cannot explain. This is not a feeling I can turn into words. I can just tell you that I have never experienced such an imbalance in my life."

She sensed he wanted the topic dropped.

They hiked in silence for a while, the sun climbing higher.

Finally, she asked, "Valor, how does magic work? We keep saying it and using it, but I do not really know what it is. You have read the whole Internet, so I am sure you can come up with a scientific description of it."

"It's a good question," he said, "and I have thought about it for a long time. There are some things that modern science cannot define, life force, for example. I thought it might be like that, but I do not think that is the case. I think magic is an attribute of reality like gravity, mass, time, and energy. It most commonly manifests itself as a kind of energy, but the dwarves are masters at turning magic into physical things, so the transformation to mass is logical in the same way mass can become energy, given the right conditions." He looked at her.

She nodded and smiled at him. She was following to some

extent. It was fascinating that he was bridging between his world and hers.

Now for the hard question.

"Am I turning into a magical being?" she asked softly.

"You have always been. It was dormant in your family line's DNA but is now awakened in you. As you unleash more and more of your magical power, you will become more of a magical being. You will probably experience longevity. Most wizards live to be hundreds of years old. You will get sick if magic weakens again and become stronger when it becomes stronger in the world. I think that from humanity's point of view, you will mutate away from the human race into something different, at least according to some modern philosophy I read on post-humanism."

The words hit like a physical blow. Her jaw went slack.

Valor kept walking. It took Brenda a second to start following him again.

No longer human? The thought should've terrified her. She felt the urge to tell him he was full of shit, but she didn't. That restless hunger, that pull toward stronger magic...it made sense now.

She looked down at her hands. They were still aged from the spell, still healing, but changing in other ways too, ways she couldn't see yet.

She was no longer human. She was becoming something different.

CHAPTER
FOUR

"Boris, you look hungry. Can I bring you a fresh young boy to eat?" Tanya asked.

She stretched across the sofa like a cat claiming territory, her black leather pants creaking softly with the movement. She watched Boris through the curtain of her shining blonde hair, her blue eyes fixed on him.

Boris glanced up from his desk, papers scattered before him in organized chaos. The corner of his mouth twitched upward. "I ate three hours ago, but your concern is touching, Tanyushka."

"Mmm." Her Russian grandmother called her Tanyushka; it was comforting. She rolled onto her side, propping her head on one hand. "You look different tonight. Energized. Like you've seen something interesting."

His smile widened. That was answer enough.

"Tell me," she purred, drawing out the words.

He leaned back in his chair, studying her, and she allowed it.

Beyond the door, she could hear the evening stirring of the

den—footsteps in the hallway, voices raised in argument, someone turning up a television. The apartment itself was modest by vampire standards. Heavy curtains blocked the downtown Bucharest evening. A single lamp cast warm light that did nothing to soften the room's cold edges.

"Our den has grown," Boris said, gesturing vaguely at the walls around them. "This entire housing complex is ours. All of it."

Tanya tilted her head. She'd noticed the expansion, of course, more vampires every week, more servants, more rooms claimed.

"The neighbors stopped complaining." She smiled. "Eventually."

"Well, we ate most of them and turned the rest into undead servants." Boris chuckled. "Our version of gentrification."

She laughed, using that low throaty sound men seemed to love. "Very civic-minded of us."

"But that's not why I'm energized." He stood, moved around the desk, and faced her.

Outside the door, someone shouted something in Romanian, followed by laughter.

Boris ignored it. "I had a vision last night."

Tanya sat up straighter, her playfulness fading. "What kind of vision?"

"A Foretelling Vision." He said it like a prayer, like something sacred. "The first I've had in decades, Tanyushka, maybe longer."

She knew what that meant. Every vampire knew. Foretelling Visions were the rarest and most mysterious form of magic. Only kings had them. Boris told her the old stories of how events in the future could be so powerful, so world-changing, that they somehow rippled backward through time, penetrating the dreams of kings.

"What did you see?" Her question came out as a whisper.

"I saw cities burning, Tanya. Fire from the skies. Death on a scale we haven't seen since the old wars." He moved to the window, pulling the curtain aside just enough to see the street below. "And magic returning in full force. Not the weak trickle we've been surviving on. Real magic. Ancient magic."

Her dead heart didn't beat faster because it couldn't, but something in her chest tightened with anticipation.

Tanya thought of Viktor down the hall, who couldn't fly worth a damn. Of Sasha, who failed at charming more often than she succeeded. Of all the vampires they'd turned in the past three months, weak and incomplete, shadows of what they should've been. With real magic...

"We'd be unstoppable," she said softly.

"If it returns." Boris leaned back on his desk, bracing his hands on the surface. "I also saw the elvish king in my vision. May his old bones rot in hell. He's sending his only remaining son to make it happen, putting his boy in harm's way to reignite magic, to bring it back in full force."

"And if the prince dies trying?"

"Then the elves will be leaderless. Choosing a new crown prince can take them years. Years, Tanya." His eyes gleamed. "They'll be weak, distracted, vulnerable."

She uncoiled from the sofa, moving toward him with predatory grace. Her pants creaked with each step. "No matter which way it goes, we win."

"Exactly." His hand found her waist, cold fingers on cold leather. "Either magic returns and we grow strong, or the prince fails and the elves crumble. Either way, this is our moment."

Tanya's smile was all teeth. She pressed herself on him. "How big are you thinking?"

"This den is already large enough to fill this entire housing complex, but that's not enough anymore." He gestured to the window and the city beyond. "I'm thinking continental, Tanyushka, maybe global."

The purr built in her throat before she could stop it, that cat sound that betrayed her excitement. "When do we start?"

"Soon." Boris pulled her closer. "But first, we need to be ready. We need our numbers up, our weak vampires strengthened, our territory expanded."

"The new vampires," Tanya said thoughtfully, "the ones who can't fly or turn to shadow properly. You were talking about banishing them."

"I was, but maybe I was wrong." Boris's hands caressed her. "Maybe they're not weak. Maybe they'll turn stronger when magic returns. Surely the newly minted will be glorious once magic comes back in full force."

"And if it doesn't?"

"Then we'll still have an army. A large one. Large enough to take advantage of elvish chaos." He held her chin, his eyes on hers. "I need you sharp for this, my queen. I need your strength, your cunning, your viciousness."

"You've always had those." She traced a finger along his chest. "What else could you possibly need?"

His smile widened. That was answer enough.

She leaned in for a kiss.

Without warning, the door burst open. Sasha stood in the doorway, one hand on her hip, jaw tight. Her blonde hair was pulled back in a severe ponytail, and she wore the same ripped jeans and tank top she'd been wearing for three nights running. Sasha never bothered with appearances.

"Boris, my king." Her voice dripped with mock formality. "Can you please tell Vadim to get the fuck out of the living room? We're trying to watch TV, and he's been standing there for eight hours, drooling on the carpet."

Tanya watched Boris's expression shift from satisfaction to annoyance. She bit back her own irritation at the interruption.

"Ask him to come in, Sasha," Boris said, "and knock next time."

Sasha's gaze dropped to the floor. She nodded and left, pulling the door closed behind her.

Boris turned back to Tanya and ran a hand through his hair. "I completely forgot I asked Vadim to wait for me." A rare flush of embarrassment crossed his face. "Poor bastard stood there for eight hours without a single complaint. You've got to love zombies. Even the new ones never complain."

"What do you need him for?" Tanya sighed, her lips curling in disappointment. The moment was lost. She returned to the sofa, tucking her legs beneath her.

"To raise the odds the elvish prince finds an early death." Boris's smile returned, sharp and calculating.

A few seconds later, Vadim entered. Drool leaked steadily through the hole in his left cheek. Although surprisingly fast, his footsteps were heavier than a living person's, the distinctive zombie shuffle-stomp that came from joints that no longer bent quite right.

"Master, you summoned me," Vadim said in a lightly accented voice. Romanian, maybe. Or Serbian. Hard to tell with his undead slur. His jaw moved awkwardly when he spoke, the muscles no longer coordinating quite right, but the words came out intelligible.

Tanya had always found zombies fascinating in a clinical way. Most vampires looked down on them and treated them like furniture, but she appreciated their utility. Vadim oversaw hundreds of them now, all the undead servants Boris and his vampires created in the past three months. Despite what humans believed from their stupid TV shows, zombies weren't infectious. You couldn't catch it from a bite. Sometimes their bites caused infection, but that was just bacteria from rotting teeth, nothing magical. To make a zombie, a vampire had to drain someone almost completely, taking away just enough life that they didn't turn into a vampire but didn't quite die either. Boris had compared it to making espresso once—not too bitter, not too sour. An art.

Vadim had more brain capacity than most zombies. He could actually speak clearly instead of defaulting to the embarrassing *"bla bla hgggg"* most of them managed. He was also violent when needed. Tanya had seen him tear a man apart with his bare hands, methodical and emotionless.

"Vadim, you're going on a vital mission for me," Boris said.

More drool leaked through Vadim's cheek. "Yes, master."

"Gather the fastest, most violent members of your army. Pick the top nine. I can't teleport more than ten of you." Boris leaned against his desk. "You'll be going to the desert, so pick members with good legs. None of the crawlers."

"Yes, master."

"You'll be hunting and killing an elvish prince." Boris's voice remained casual, like he was discussing the weather. "Make sure you're armed, Vadim. The prince is a formidable force. Be fast and violent. If you succeed, the elves grow weaker. If you fail and the prince prevails, we grow stronger. Either way, we win. Do you understand?"

"Yes, master," he said in the same monotone voice.

Tanya watched Boris's face light up with amusement. "Always such stimulating conversation with you, Vadim. Go now."

"Yes, master." Vadim turned and left, his movements stiff but determined.

Boris closed the door behind him.

From the living room came the unmistakable sound of the

Twilight soundtrack again. The den had been obsessed with those movies for weeks, and the noise grated even through the walls.

Boris caught Tanya's eye and smiled. "It's a good day, Tanyushka. Everything's falling into place."

CHAPTER FIVE

"Are we there yet?" Brenda half-joked.

Rocks and scrub brush stretched endlessly in every direction, broken only by the occasional stubborn cactus. Sweat glued her shirt to her back, and dust coated everything from her hair to her boots.

She pulled out the water container and took a long sip. The water was surprisingly cool and refreshing despite the heat. Maybe the fact that the container was elvish-made contributed to that?

Brenda still couldn't figure out why they needed to walk. In this day and age, civilized people had travel technology. Hell, at this point, she would settle for a pony. Her bum ached, her legs burned, and the freaking mountains never seemed to get closer. Her forty-year-old body screamed for rest in ways her twenty-two-year-old body never had.

The hike reminded her of eighth grade, trudging through Joshua Tree while Mrs. Glazer chirped about their "great progress." The whole class had reeked of sweat and tuna sandwiches.

Damn, what she wouldn't give for a sandwich right now.

Good progress or not, they would be sleeping on the ground. A passable but endless canyon waited before the mountain slopes even started. As for climbing the freaking mountain itself? *Nope. Not thinking about it yet.*

Valor gave her one of those carelessly happy smiles. He was fresh as a daisy with perfect hair, like he'd just stepped out of a bath. His clothes were somehow cleaner than hers. Yeah, she resented him for that.

"We're getting closer. Tomorrow, we'll reach the mountain, and from there, it's just a quick climb to the entrance of the dwarf kingdom," Valor assured her. A moment later, he nodded toward a clearing. "Perfect place to camp."

He must have noticed she was dragging her feet.

They spent the next hour "setting up camp." Brenda perched on a boulder while Valor did the actual work, his staff drawing arcs of soft green light through the air. Leaves lifted and wove together, forming walls and beds at his whispered commands. Each spell cost him. By the time he finished, he was pale, sweat beading on his forehead despite the cooling evening. Magic was still weak, he'd explained. When it returned in full force, this would be easy. Until then, it drained him dry just to summon them a shelter for the night. He swayed a bit as he lowered his staff.

"Come see the sunset!" Brenda called.

He climbed up beside her, dust-covered and clearly tired, but his expression stayed calm. The sun blazed across the desert, throwing light in every direction and painting the sand gold and orange.

"It's like the Fireball spell but a thousand times over," he said almost to himself.

"What's that?" Brenda asked.

"A simple spell. Entry-level fire magic. You're human, so you'll master it easily."

"Clearly human." She massaged her aching calves. "Why does that matter?"

"Human wizards are creatures of fire. You'll cast fire spells intuitively. Other elements will be harder. Fire spells will be more powerful and accurate than if other races cast them." He paused. "It's in your nature."

Creature of fire. The phrase settled warm in Brenda's chest. It felt right, as if she knew that this was who she was all along.

"What does the Fireball spell actually do?" she asked.

"Let me teach you this spell. Point your finger at that rock there. Picture a ball of fire starting at your fingertip and continuing to the rock. Just like shooting an arrow. Imagine a string jumping from your hand to the target. Like that movie...*Spider-Human.*"

"*Spider-Man,*" she corrected. She closed her eyes, opened them, took a calming breath, and envisioned the string.

"Say '*Valashi!*'"

"*Valashi!*" She tried to sound confident.

The word "Fireball" appeared in her vision like an overlay.

Yellow power exploded from her chest to her fingertip. Her hand whipped back before she could control it, but a small ball of fire shot from where it had been a moment ago. It struck the rock dead center. The stone cracked in half.

"It's useful for entry-level work. Doesn't do much damage, but it never misses a stationary or slow target."

Brenda flexed her sore hand. The recoil had felt like she'd shot a gun. Her shoulder protested too, but *damn.* She'd shot actual fire from her finger. Totally worth it. She'd have to strengthen her core to stabilize her aim.

"You're very talented." He sounded genuinely surprised.

"This takes most wizards days, even weeks. Did the healer teach you anything? The breathing, the visualization?"

"Nope. It just felt right." She couldn't keep the smugness out of her voice. "Natural talent, clearly. Let's skip the baby spells and hit the good stuff."

"Slow down." A half-laugh escaped him. "Maybe tomorrow."

For the first time in what seemed like years, Brenda felt happy. Actually happy, not just distracted or numb. No job interviews going nowhere. No rent anxiety. No wondering what the hell she was doing with her life. No healer poking at her aging body. No one chasing them through the desert. Just this moment with a warm boulder, distant mountains, and magic fire still tingling in her fingertips. Purpose.

They sat at the cliff's edge, the mountains spread before them, the last rays of sun painting everything gold. She drew in a long, deep breath as the sun dipped behind the peaks. The evening air cooled around them. She could get used to this.

Rocks ground together behind them.

Still seated, they glanced back over their shoulders. Ten human figures loomed behind their camp, silent and watching.

Brenda's blood turned to ice. Every hair on her neck stood up, and her throat went dry. The bodies were rotting, in different stages of decay. Jeans and jackets hung from frames that shouldn't have been standing. One wore a business suit. They gripped knives, axes, hammers, and other weapons in rotting hands. They moved awkwardly, their joints bending in directions they shouldn't.

A six-foot, heavily built man stood front and center, staring at Valor. Bone showed through the gaps in his rotted flesh. He spat. Blood and saliva hit the dirt.

Valor was already on his feet, facing the figures.

"Choi blat!" The big man raised a pistol toward Valor's

chest. His jacket sleeve was gone. Bone jutted from his hand, his elbow bent at an angle no joint should make. He fired. The twisted elbow threw his aim off. The recoil wrenched it further sideways. A chunk of rock to Valor's left exploded, tumbling into the chasm.

What the fuck? Zombies can shoot guns?

Action movies lied, Brenda realized. They showed things in sequence because that was what human brains could process, but everything was happening at the same time, too fast to separate.

To her left, Valor shouted, "*Boras Vendi!*"

Glowing text appeared in Brenda's vision. "Summon Sword."

Blue light erupted from his palms, crystalline and brilliant. Between his hands, a sword took shape, a long, curved blade of silver steel. Flowing elvish script ran along its length, glowing faintly. The crossguard curved like branches, and the grip looked wrapped in leather that had never aged. It was beautiful and deadly.

Yet something went horribly wrong. Brenda felt it before she understood it. A sick wrongness hovered in the air, and the magic twisted back on itself. The sword flickered. The blue light crackled and sparked, and it flickered again.

Valor's scream cut through everything else, agony and shock combined. The blade blinked in and out of existence. There, gone, there, gone. Then it vanished completely. The elf's hands clutched at the empty air.

All the figures started screaming as they charged. Fast. Too fast. Nothing like movie zombies. Snarling, spitting, cursing in voices that gurgled and rasped. Heads jerked at wrong angles. Limbs twitched and spasmed, but they didn't slow down.

A woman screamed. Who was that?

The big zombie, the one who was six feet tall and almost

that wide, reached them and pointed the gun straight at Valor's heart. He was so close now, he could not miss.

Brenda raised her hand and pointed at the big zombie's chest. "*Valashi!*" The scream tore from her throat.

In her mind, everything slowed, and time stretched like taffy. Even her own words felt sluggish, dragging through the air. She felt the power burst in her chest, an explosion of energy that took her breath away. It flowed to her hand, blue and radiant. The flame built at her fingertips, tingling, simmering, eager to be launched.

The big zombie rattled his hand until his elbow locked into place, the weapon still pointed straight at Valor's heart. He pulled the trigger. The pistol fired, aiming true. Brenda released the ball of fire.

The zombie's chest exploded as his pistol fired. The gun's muzzle flashed. The fireball tore through his midsection, ripping flesh and bone. Flames spread across his torso, consuming rotten flesh. Through it all, his eyes never left Valor. Focused. Passionate. Filled with hate.

The power of her magical blast threw Brenda violently off of the rock. She was already tumbling down the chasm in free fall.

Valor was within her eyeshot. On the edge of the cliff, starting to fall backwards himself.

A woman screamed in despair. So strange. Who was that?

She finally realized it was her own scream.

CHAPTER SIX

Lixi sat on Jin's shoulder as usual, busy moisturizing her dark arms and face, and fluffing the tips of her wings to look cool.

Jin was brushing her teeth. They were both getting ready to go to sleep.

"No kicking boys tomorrow," Lixi said to Jin.

"No messing up with teachers' eyesight!" the seven-year-old answered back.

Lixi crossed her arms and scowled at Jin, putting on her best scary-fairy face. Three months ago, that look would've made Jin freeze, asking what she'd done wrong. Now, the girl caught her eye in the mirror, grinned, and kept right on brushing. In the last few months, Lixi had watched the shy kid transform into this loud, fearless menace. Jin did what she wanted and said what she thought. It was fucking beautiful.

"What should we paint tomorrow, Jin?" Lixi asked.

"Uuunicon," Jin said, the brush not leaving her teeth.

"Oh." A memory hit Lixi. "I remember I met a unicorn once, many years ago. I would really like to paint him."

"Ooookayyy," Jin said with a mouth full of toothbrush and paste. "But what colo—" Jin froze.

Everything froze.

Water stopped mid-drop from the faucet, a crystal bead suspended in the air. Bird songs cut off mid-note. The washing machine's rumble died instantly. Even the dust motes, lit by the bathroom light, hung motionless.

Lixi frowned and sniffed the air.

Reality smelled wrong.

It was really weird to explain to adults, but kids understood intuitively when Lixi told them what she could do. She was able to sense when this fragile thing called reality was broken or rotten or smelled like bad cranberries. In those moments when Lixi was focused enough, which she would admit were few and far between, she could suss out this "disturbance in the force," as one of her previous kids called it.

It was a common skill. Fairies could smell it. Human reality, in general, smelled like crap most of the time, and most fairies had much more important things to do, like make sure butterflies did not get too cocky or that cupcakes were not left uneaten. Fairies knew that reality was broken by design and most just did not care, but Lixi did care. A lot.

Centuries earlier, Lixi had started to help kids. They were the only type of humans who were smart and fun to be with. Most days, she did not understand why adult humans even existed or where they came from. It was an unsolved mystery. Kids were the most awesome kind of humans. It was a true wonder how sweet kids became asshole adults.

Reality had to be unbroken for the kids so they could stay awesome. That was why Lixi had started to care about fixing this stupid reality. The fact that everything had frozen, combined with the awful stench of just plain *wrongness*, meant that Lixi had to act now...and fast.

Her wings drooped. She touched Jin's still cheek, Lixi's hand seemed so small against the girl's face.

"Bye, Jin. You will only hear this in your heart when time starts moving again, but I love you. I have to go and save the day so that things do not become worse for us all." She snickered. "You know, the usual hero stuff. Have a great life, dear!"

Lixi took off, flying from where it was cold to where it was warm, from where it was wet to where it was dry. She followed her nose, and the rotten cranberries smell became stronger and stronger. She felt very proud of the way she was not distracted by the fourteen hundred and seventy-seven cheeky butterflies and two thousand half-eaten cakes. She only stopped to try out one cupcake, but it was for the energy, nothing else. Two full milliseconds had passed by.

The source of the bad smell was in the middle of the desert on a cliff of a big valley. It was almost unbearable to breathe there. Lixi had to cover her nose, which was extra sensitive after the cupcake's wonderful smell.

On the cliff, Lixi noticed a circle of figures in what looked like a single-tent campsite. Of course, all the figures were also frozen in time. One figure in the middle of the circle was pointing a gun at a tall thin figure on the other side of the circle.

Guns. Lixi hated them. Kids never had guns. At least not the kids she knew.

The end of the barrel of the gun had fire coming out of it. More like sparks and a bad smell of sulfur. That was not the worst smell, though. The next bad smells were the people in the circle, at least all of them other than the tall thin figure. They smelled of malice and rotten meat. Kids never smelled like that. She did not like rotten meat.

Lixi pulled out her wand that was tied to her back between her wings and pointed it at the smelly figures.

"Fuck off," she said the magical words.

Lixi, like all fairies, knew that the actual words spoken did not matter. The power was in the intention, and this was definitely a fuck-off kind of intention.

A gust of wind swept across the desert, collected all the figures other than the tall thin one, and crushed them on the side of the mountain in a deathly crunching sound. The wind then continued to drive big rocks from the mountain and crush the bodies until Lixi was pleased with the job.

This was still not the worst smell, though. It was maddening! Where was that smell coming from?

She continued to fly around and look for it. Rotten cranberries... Rotten cranberries. Rotten cranberries!

Then she found it! The bastard little cheeky oddest thing. A small piece of metal was frozen in midair. It had a pointy part that was aimed at the tall figure.

Bullets. So small, yet so smelly.

Lixi pointed at the object, and it turned to dust and dispersed in a puff of air. The bad smell was gone.

Lixi wanted to go back to Jin, but she knew this was not meant to be. Something was drawing her to the tall, thin man.

She came to have a closer look. An elf! She had not seen elves in so many years. This was a rare delight. He looked young, at most a hundred and ninety years old. Almost a kid. Lixi liked kids.

She fluttered closer to him. His eyes were filled with terror, and he was half falling down the cliff.

Time started moving forward again really slowly. The elf was ever so slowly falling down backward. She studied his eyes. He was so frightened. Was it the fall? Was it the little metal that had been chasing him? Was it the smell? No, she decided it was none of that. Something else was causing that fear, but what? She had to find out what.

She could unfreeze time and ask him, but that was too risky, which meant there was only one other way to find out. Oh man. It was going to hurt like hell, though.

Fairies could bind to a non-fairy and share, well, everything. Lixi would have to bind with this young elf in order to know what was scaring the shit out of him. This meant she had to unbind from Jin. She'd done this thousands of times before, yet it didn't make it less painful.

She pointed her wand to the young elf's head. Her hand shook. "We are one," she whispered.

Time moved slightly faster.

His eyes flickered and met hers. *"Save her. She is falling, behind me off the cliff,"* were his first words in her mind.

Time moved faster.

"Shit, shit! Fuck, fuck, fuck!" Lixi said.

She flew as fast as she could down the cliff.

Time moved faster now, almost at normal speed.

She saw a human female bound to the elf falling to her death.

Lixi felt his terror through the binding. Losing her would destroy him. No way that was happening. Not on Lixi's watch.

She flew as fast as she could, which was very damn fast if she could say so herself, pointed at the falling figure with her wand, and screamed, "Slow down!"

Wind erupted from nothing, howling as it spiraled down. It caught the woman mid-fall, wrapped around her like a net, and slowed her descent inch by inch.

Lixi heard a man scream. She looked up and saw the young elf, Valor she now knew, falling above her.

"Holy shit! You slow down as well!"

Controlling two gusts of wind was no easy task, but Lixi was not a regular fairy. She was a kick-ass boss. The two figures slowly slid down the cliff and landed gently on a pile of sand.

Tired, Lixi dropped at the top of the pile of sand, where they lay, next to their heads. She rested for a few seconds and leaned back, exhausted. She had flown for what felt like ten hours, pulled all this magic out of her ass, and almost lost her bound elf in the first five minutes.

She flopped fully back onto the sand to sleep this crazy ordeal off. "Fuck my life."

CHAPTER SEVEN

It's time to visit a witch.

James Webber walked down the hallway of the gray government holding facility. His footsteps echoed off bare concrete. Emergency lighting strips lined the floor at exact intervals. Security cameras hung at every intersection, their red indicator lights blinking in perfect rhythm. The building stood in stark contrast to the bright, colorful design of the Kildare offices, but he admitted to himself that he actually liked it better here. Yes, the lighting was dim, the gray walls oppressive, and the place smelled of industrial detergent, yet everything here was in its place, and everything worked just fine without any bells and whistles.

He stopped at the fireproof door. Next to it sat a bench with several dirty fire-safe suits. The sign on the door read, *Warning: Put on a protective suit before entering.*

James inspected the suits closely, selected the cleanest one from the bench, and pulled it over his pristine clothes. He opened the heavy door and stepped into the dimly lit observation room.

Doctor Burley was standing by a large glass window, writing in his notebook. The man looked tired, his white coat wrinkled, dark circles under his eyes. He was probably in his fifties, with thinning hair and reading glasses perched on his nose. The doctor was not wearing a fire suit. James hated people who did not follow instructions.

The doctor raised an eyebrow toward James, then looked back at the one-way glass separating them both from the inner holding room.

The inner holding room was lit by harsh white fluorescents. In the middle of the room, a reclined chair sat with a woman strapped into it. Heavy leather restraints crossed her chest, waist, and thighs. Her wrists and ankles were secured with metal cuffs bolted to the chair's frame.

"She keeps waking up every hour despite heavy sedation," the doctor said. The man's tone was too casual.

James let the silence hang in the air, his gaze steady on the doctor's face, the kind of stare reserved for subordinates who'd overstepped. Only after the man shifted his weight and cleared his throat did he say, "Doctor Burley, please present the patient properly. We can discuss symptoms after that."

The doctor flinched, then he looked down at his notes and nodded.

Had James hurt the man's feelings? James dismissed the thought. Directors of the Kildare Organization were not forgiving or gentle with their feedback.

"Of course, Director Webber," the doctor said. "Patient Rosy Underwood, twenty-six-year-old woman. Incarcerated a month ago after destroying a gas station in Montgomery, Alabama. History of incarcerations and escapes following the incident where her partner's head exploded three months ago. Special magical skills appear to be the ability to create and control fire, as well as extraordinary healing abilities. Her body is able to heal from extreme wounds and resist most sedatives, a skill that has improved rapidly in the last few weeks."

The woman in the chair opened her eyes and glared at them. Large frame. Unwashed dark hair. Plain, hostile, unpleasant face. Hospital gown hanging loose on what should have been a powerful build. A month of captivity should have weakened her, but she held herself with unsettling steadiness even with the restraints.

Despite the fact that there was no way for her to see them through the one-way mirror, she looked straight into James's eyes. "*Valashi*," she said.

The word was barely audible through the glass, but it rang in James's head like a bell.

Fire erupted in front of her, a sphere of brilliant orange flame that shouldn't exist. The heat hit him through the glass. The fireball hurtled forward, faster than anything he'd ever seen, and James stumbled back despite himself. The fireball crashed into the mirror with a sound like thunder. Small cracks appeared where it hit, and the temperature in the observation room spiked. The flames were scorching. His face burned, his skin prickling with sudden sweat beneath his fire-safe suit.

"Her fire skills seem to improve with time as well," Doctor Burley said, noting something in his papers. He gestured at the cracked glass with his pen. "She's been doing that all morning. Don't worry. The fireproof glass is state-of-the-art."

"I do not care much about her fire skills. We can easily make fire. I want to understand her healing skills. I heard someone slit her throat and she survived it," James said.

"That is correct, Director Webber. The patient has also completely healed from any injury caused in every altercation after that. We have made zero progress in understanding that skill, as she has not suffered any injury since coming to this detention facility."

"Then cut her hand off immediately," James said dryly.

"Director James, we are in a government facility, and she is a human being with rights and protections," the doctor said, looking frightened but also shocked by the cold-blooded proposition.

James turned to the doctor.

Burley took a step back.

He is afraid. Good!

"Human? She is not human." James stepped closer to the doctor, closing the distance between them. "She is a magical creature. Some might say she is a witch, a wizard, or a sorcerer. I do not care what you call her." He paused, letting the words sink in. "The moment she gained abilities that violate natural law, she ceased to be human. Evolution doesn't work in reverse, Doctor. She's something else now. Something new. She is not a human. Is that understood?"

"Yes, Director, but still..." Burley started to protest.

"As a non-human, she is afforded zero protection from the law. We do not protect non-humans. We only protect humans and their property, and if we are really *open-minded*"—the last two words dripped with contempt—"we protect the environment and protected species." James let the silence stretch. "Tell me, Doctor, is she a protected species? Did Congress pass a law I'm not aware of?"

"No, but sir..." the doctor said.

"Director Webber for you, Doctor," James corrected. The doctor's pen trembled in his hand. "And as she is not a human, or human property, or a protected species, we can do anything to her, and it will be perfectly legal. Have you ever thought you would go to jail for stepping on an ant, Doctor?"

"No, Director Webber." The doctor's shoulders slumped, his eyes focusing on his notes.

"Have you ever thought of going to jail or getting in trouble after dissecting a mouse or a rabbit in your laboratory, Doctor?" James pushed.

"No, Director Webber," the doctor said.

"There is a reason for that. We are humans. We are at the top of the food chain. Our laws define that we have the right to do whatever we want with any other species, and believe me, Doctor, if this changes, humans will be on the dissected end of some other species' knives."

The doctor lowered his head. "Yes, Director Webber."

"So cut her damn hand off, and tell me how we can replicate her skill, how to stop it from happening, and what the limits of it are." James's voice remained calm and businesslike. "The president needs actionable intelligence. Can we duplicate this ability? Can we suppress it? Can we kill someone who has it? I expect a comprehensive report by Friday, five p.m. Is that understood, *Doctor*?" He spat the last word.

"Yes, Director Webber," the doctor said meekly.

"Thank you," James said calmly.

He turned back to the observation window. The woman in the chair stared at them with pure hatred. Sweat soaked her dirty hair, strands clinging to her flushed face. Her mouth moved, forming words he couldn't hear. Profanity, most likely.

James nodded. Cutting her up would definitely not be a big loss for humanity.

He walked out the door, closed it, and was about to take the fire suit off. Why did Burley irritate him so much? James considered it for a moment. It wasn't the hesitation or the moral posturing. It was the weakness. James had no patience for weak, incompetent men.

As he started to pull off the suit, he paused. *"Valashi."* The word echoed faintly in his mind.

He shook his head, dismissing it. Probably just residual anxiety from seeing actual magic for the first time.

Then came the explosion.

A deafening boom shook the building, and the lights flickered. Smoke seeped from the bottom of the fire-protected door, dark wisps quickly becoming a thick stream. After a few seconds, the door groaned open, and the doctor stumbled out. His clothes, face, and hair were all on fire. He took another step into the gray passage and fell down in a heap of ash.

The smell of charred flesh and melting fat flooded the hallway, thick and nauseating. The sound of sizzling accompanied it, like bacon in a pan. James's stomach heaved.

From inside the room, he heard a woman scream, her voice much clearer now, "*Valashi! Valashi! Valashi!*"

James turned toward the exit, his hand reaching for the wall to steady himself. The corridor seemed to grow brighter with each word she yelled. Heat built behind him like an approaching wave. He managed one step. Then the flash came, and everything went white.

CHAPTER EIGHT

Brenda warmed herself by the fire, throwing small scraps of wood into the flames.

Dawn broke slowly over the desert. The sky transformed from deep purple to gold, the color shifting across the horizon. She wrapped both hands around the clay cup Valor had given her, relishing its heat. The fire crackled softly. Everything was still except the light that poured down the mountainsides like liquid.

She peered at the new arrival, the fairy sitting on the other side of the fire while she cleaned her wings. The motion reminded Brenda of birds after a storm, that same attentive preening, that same unconscious grace. Beautiful and natural but also intimate.

Valor sat next to Brenda, smiling warmly. He hummed softly as he, too, fed small twigs to the fire, each movement deliberate, calm, and thoughtful. He'd been humming on and off since they'd made camp. Brenda's heart was still trying to break through her ribcage, and he was *humming*.

When their eyes met, the joy of his smile made her forget

about being angry, though she did not forget about the real-life fairy on the other side of the bonfire.

"We are very lucky," Valor announced.

"Are we now? Really?" she said quietly, trying to hide her skepticism.

"Yes! We have a fairy!" he said. "This is wonderful, Brenda. We needed a fairy, and the only way to get one is to have them come to you! A fairy must choose to join you, and she has! Now, we only need to find an entrance to the dwarf city in the mountain. These are very tricky to find, but I am more hopeful. This should not take us more than two to three weeks."

Two to three weeks? Is he kidding me? There are freaking zombies in this desert. I can't think about his quest right now.

The little fairy was licking her armpit. Now she seemed more like a cat cleaning itself.

She glanced at Brenda and flashed a smirk as if saying, "Let's see you lick your armpit."

Brenda blinked a few times, took a deep breath, and glared at Valor. "Valor, I just had a near-death experience. Can I please ask a few questions before I share your excitement?" she asked in a tone that every male in the universe should understand meant she expected a yes for an answer.

"Yes, of course." His smile faltered. The light in his eyes dimmed, and he shifted his weight on the rock.

Brenda nodded, thankful. Her hands still trembled when she lifted the cup. "Let's start with: What the actual fuck? What happened?" She ran her hand through her hair, feeling the tangles and dust. "Why are zombies after us? Why are there zombies at all?"

Valor sighed. He stared into the fire for a moment, as if gathering his thoughts. "Magic is a power that is the life source of all magical creatures and, to some extent, all living creatures. Like all power, magic can be used for good or for evil. There are many wonderful magical creatures but also many terrible ones, just like there are wonderful humans and terrible ones."

Brenda turned to face him and winced. She'd pulled a muscle in her back during the fall, and the ache flared every time she shifted position.

Valor leaned forward, his elbows on his knees. He spoke faster now, more animated. "The major difference between humans and magical creatures is the Affinity. Humans in general do not have Affinity. They can be good or bad as they wish. Humans usually justify everything they do as good, even when it is very bad."

Brenda nodded. Yeah. Humans were excellent at justifying terrible things. She'd seen it happen many times.

"Of course, good and bad are very relative terms," Valor continued, "but generally speaking, magic has two polar ends—destructive and constructive. The more you are powered by constructive magic, the more you want everyone to flourish and for life to grow. The more you are powered by the destructive side, the more you want everything but you or your kind to be destroyed. Affinity can be weak or strong, but every magical creature has it, and you can cast a simple magical spell or use your species' knowledge to know its Affinity."

Brenda took a sip of tea, using the moment to try to process what he was saying. Affinity. Polar ends. Constructive and destructive. The words started blurring together. It had already been a long day.

"The point is that magic has these poles, and in the same way you have good magical creatures like elves and dwarves, you have evil magical creatures such as zombies and vampires. Magic is all about balance. It powers all sides equally," he added.

The fire crackled between them. A gust of wind sent sparks dancing.

"Why did they attack us? Who sent them? How did they find us?" The flow of questions poured from Brenda.

"I do not know," he said solemnly. "Zombies rarely attack without guidance. Somebody is probably aware of our journey and wants to stop us, or they just want to kill me, which will endanger the succession of the elvish nation."

Brenda gestured toward the tiny stranger. "And this fairy saved us?"

"Yes. She sensed our need from far away and came to our rescue. That is what fairies do when they are focused," he said, looking amused, "which is very rare."

"How can such a small creature stop zombies and save us?" Brenda asked. "Aren't they supposed to just leave gifts under our pillow when we lose our teeth?"

His eyes widened in shock. "No! Fairies are one of the strongest, most magically powerful, and most intelligent creatures in the world. They are part of the spirit world, which makes them sometimes susceptible to losing focus or giving too much priority to things that we look upon as trivial, but believe me, it is us who are wrong."

Brenda glanced at the fairy. She was busy trying to lick her back with her weirdly long tongue. The fairy's dress caught the morning light like thousands of tiny mirrors, sending sparks of red and gold dancing across the rocks. Her black hair fell in tight coils to her shoulders, and when she moved, it seemed to float on its own, like she was in zero gravity or underwater. Her skin was a deep, warm brown that seemed to generate blue light rather than reflect it. She was maybe four inches tall and perfectly proportioned, but her brown eyes were older than anything Brenda had ever seen.

Brenda studied the fairy and then the elf and back again. The silence stretched. Finally, she asked, "Are all fairies African American?"

Valor and the fairy exchanged looks as if Brenda had said the funniest thing. Valor's belly laugh was genuine, and the fairy fell to the ground and laughed her ass off as well.

Brenda frowned at them both. They were laughing *together.* Not just at the same time. The exact same laugh, the exact same rhythm, the exact same pause for breath. Like they were connected by invisible strings. Brenda's skin prickled. Somehow, they were magically in sync.

"American? The entire US history is a blip in the timeframe of a fairy! Fairies are immortal. They have lived through endless generations and civilizations across the universe," Valor finally said after catching his breath.

The morning light grew stronger, warming the chilled air.

"Fairies do not have their own earthly figure. They usually adopt the figure of an earthly being they like or were bonded to in the past," he added.

The fairy flew and landed on Brenda's knee. She had no weight, but still, Brenda felt her presence there, a warmth, a tingle of magic against Brenda's skin. The fairy's wings twitched, almost like a hummingbird. Brenda held perfectly still, afraid to move.

The fairy considered Brenda with her big brown eyes. "Lolla was a good friend. She died of cancer shortly after I bonded with her. She was the kindest, smartest, funniest, most beautiful girl who ever lived. She died alone in a hospice before she lost her second tooth. That did not smell right to me. We had a week together, but I will never forget her. I promised her that I would always carry her figure the way she was at her prime."

Something in the fairy's voice made Brenda's throat close up. The fairy's wings stopped their constant flutter. Her face went long, and those brown eyes held ancient pain so heavy that Brenda had to look away from the weight of it.

"I have no shape and many shapes," the fairy whispered as if gently sharing a secret with a child.

Brenda returned her gaze to the fairy, whose form shimmered like heat waves off the desert sand. A Black girl. A Japanese boy with straight dark hair. A pale Nordic-looking girl with ice-blue eyes. An Indian boy with a gap-toothed smile. Each form lasted less than a heartbeat. Each one was complete, real, and impossibly vital. Then Lolla's face returned, grinning, despite Brenda's slack-jawed expression.

The fairy cheerfully reached with her tiny hand to shake Brenda's hand. "Nice to meet you, Brenda. I am Lixi, your lover's bonded fairy." Her smile widened.

Valor's face turned red.

"Lover? Oh, no!" Brenda's whole body recoiled, and her stomach did a sickening flip.

She couldn't explain why the thought made her skin crawl, why imagining Valor's face close to hers felt fundamentally wrong, like mixing oil and water.

For a split second, she could have sworn she saw the faintest words as an overlay in her vision. *The Great Treaty*. What was that all about?

"Oh, you did not have sex yet?" Lixi asked, turning to Valor. "Why not? Does she smell? I do not smell it."

"No, Lixi," Valor said. "Elves and humans are not meant for each other. It's unnatural." He was really turning red now.

"Unnatural my ass, Valor," Lixi responded, giving Valor a reprimanding look.

Valor's gaze held firm. "Lixi, no."

Brenda had never seen the elf look so desperate. Valor's whole face pleaded with Lixi to stop.

"Oh, Valor, don't be a prude. One day, Brenda, I will tell you all about why y'all think the birds and bees don't match." She spat the words toward Valor, shaking her head and squinting at him. Lixi was a very cute angry fairy.

Brenda laughed. She couldn't help it. An elf and a fairy were bickering about sex around a campfire. This was her life now.

Lixi glanced at Brenda and winked. Then she glared at her own hand still in the air. "Are you going to shake it or keep me hanging, girl?"

Brenda shook Lixi's small hand with her little finger. "I like you, Lixi!"

This tiny, ancient creature had saved their lives, licked her own armpit, and carried the face of a dead child. Lixi was real, raw, and powerful. It made all the horrors of the night seem less terrible since they had her on their side.

"If you like me now," Lixi said, "wait until I tell you that I know where the entrance to the dwarf kingdom is." She let that hang in the air, looking very pleased with herself.

CHAPTER NINE

Pain.

James's entire body hurt. His chest felt packed with concrete. His throat was raw.

There was a beeping sound. Repetitive. Irritating.

Why would something be beeping?

He tried to open his eyes, but his eyelids were so heavy.

Is this a dream? I smell smoke and burnt meat.

His mind went back to the dream he just had. It was so vivid. Visions of burning cities and the smell of ashes and dead bodies. Big cities. Seattle and San Francisco both burning. Kids screaming. Mothers holding charred babies. Men walking, half their skin gone, mouths open. No sound coming out.

Why do I smell it? Am I dreaming? Maybe having a vision?

His mind raced. The Kildare book foretold that the head of the Kildare might gain visions. It talked about how being at the top of the human race granted the ability to foresee the future, to be able to deal better with what's coming. Blasphemy. Magic. But if this dream was true, the future of humanity was very grim.

Maybe this was a sign to be more diligent? To make magic extinct, to save humanity... Maybe it was a sign he was not doing enough.

Pain. That was real. All across his body. He tried to open his eyes again.

The beeps continued. More annoying in his head. *Beep...wait. Beep...wait. Beep...*

"Patient coming back to consciousness. Nine twenty-six p.m.," a female voice said.

James finally managed to open his eyes. Heavy. Everything was heavy. Big white bed. Tubes in his arm and his nose. Plastic tape pulling at skin. Monitors to his left, glowing numbers he couldn't focus on. The beeping. Still beeping. Everything white and light blue. Large sterile room. Two empty leather chairs by his bed. He was in a hospital.

"Hello, James, I am Nurse Bane. How are you feeling?" She was a short, heavy woman with a strong Southern let's-be-friends accent.

He did not want to be her friend. He resisted the urge to correct her about his title. His breathing hurt like hell, and assessing the situation was a higher priority.

"What happened?" he asked. It felt like a super mundane question to ask when coming back to consciousness, but that was all he had. His brain was mush.

"Oh, dearie. You were in an explosion. We did not get a lot of details, but apparently, you were in a government facility that had a gas leak. You suffer from smoke inhalation but have no serious burns or other major injuries. You should be fine by morning. You were very lucky. Some of your coworkers were not so lucky. Some of them..."

James looked away. Her voice continued, a steady stream of unwanted information and unneeded sympathy. He focused on the monitor instead. The beeping. The numbers. Heart rate, oxygen saturation, blood pressure. Anything but her voice.

She stopped talking eventually. She probably noticed he wasn't listening.

Beep, beep. That monitor was getting under his skin.

"I need to be discharged immediately," he said in a commanding voice.

She scowled at him, her mouth tight with unease. "I would discharge you right now, dear, but we got strict orders to have you stay in the hospital, in this bed to be precise, until midnight tonight. There are government officials that wanna talk to you. It seems like they are high-ranking, because you are the only patient on the entire floor. Other patients were forced to move to other floors in the hospital. It took us hours to clear the..."

She was insufferable with her talkativeness. He closed his eyes, blocked her voice out, and fell asleep again.

"Wake him up," a distant voice said.

Something hit his nostrils like a punch. Chemical burn, sharp and acrid. His eyes watered. Smelling salts?

He coughed, and his lungs screamed with pain.

He opened his eyes again. The fully lit room hurt his eyes. He blinked and looked around. Four men in black suits. Two by the window, two by the door. Earpieces. Hands clasped in front, the classic ready position. Not Kildare security. Wrong posture, wrong suits. Secret Service maybe, or private contractor.

Who were they guarding? He looked around.

The President of the United States of America was sitting next to his bed. Next to him sat Scott Radcliffe, the head of the NSA.

Scott resembled a beaten man who'd been screamed at for the last hour. His collar was damp with sweat. His hands gripped a tablet so hard his knuckles were white. In the three months James had worked with him, he'd never seen Scott Radcliffe rattled. The man had built his career on unflappable competence. Not anymore. Whatever the president had done to him before they got to this hospital room had stripped that away.

The president, Paul Rogers Junior, was a tall and heavy-set man. James randomly remembered reading somewhere that most presidents were tall. *We are all stupid monkeys looking up at the tallest alpha male,* he thought.

"How are you feeling, James?" asked the president.

Again with the first names! *What am I, his cousin?*

"I am well. Thank you for asking, Mr. President." At least James knew how to keep protocol. "May I ask—"

"I don't think we have ever met," the president cut him off, "but Scott here tells me you are the guy in charge of making all the Unnatural Phenomena shit show go away."

James looked at Scott and back again at the president. *Of course we've met.*

"I present in your security briefing every Monday, sir. We meet week—" James started, not sure if the president was joking or not.

"Who fucking cares? A million people like you present to me every week. What matters is the fact that you fucked up, James. You fucked up really hard," the president uttered.

The hair on James's back stood up.

"How so, sir?" he asked. He did not like the profanity and intentionally kept his voice even.

"Scott, would you care to explain to James here how he totally and utterly fucked up in making this problem go away quietly?" The president's voice was full of venom.

"Yes, Mr. President." Scott's voice cracked on the first word. He cleared his throat. "Well, James, CNN caught footage of one..." He fumbled with the tablet, nearly dropped it, and caught it. His hands were shaking. "...Rosy Underwood, who was apparently reported as dead in the good state of Mississippi a few months ago, walking buck naked out of our burning government facility."

That witch!

James's chest tightened. She was Doctor Burley's patient. Fire manipulation, regenerative healing. The one he'd ordered dissected and studied. The one who'd screamed that word and blown up the facility. She'd killed Burley and nearly killed James.

Scott looked at James with an accusatory stare before he carried on. "Miss Underwood then continued to shoot fireballs from her fingers, on video broadcasted live by CNN, mind you, and blew up a Starbucks."

James chuckled. Which was weird. He never chuckled. The drugs they'd given him for the pain were probably strong.

"She didn't like the coffee?" James regretted the stupid comment the minute he said it. Not professional.

"This is not fucking funny!" Foam came out of the president's mouth. His eyes raged, veins bulging at his temples.

The outburst caught James off guard, and he kept perfectly still. The tubes pulled when he breathed. His lungs ached. He would not let his face show it.

"Sorry—" James started.

"The mother of all fuck-ups! The entire press is all over this. All the videos, stories, and rumors that our administration denied in the last few months have all gone to shit! Shit! You hear me? My defense secretary resigned. My press secretary is about to resign soon. This is an enormous giant freaking shitstorm." He was now red and sweaty.

The president stood and pointed at James with an

accusatory finger. He loomed over the hospital bed, close enough that James could smell his cologne and see the spit on his lips.

"...and *you* promised us to keep it under wraps, under control! The UN is calling, and the bloody UK government has already shared a statement that they have been asked by the US administration to keep the fact that we are experiencing paranormal phenomena all across the globe from the public eye. This is the absolute worst thing that could ever happen! Don't you understand how bad the timing is?" More spit covered the president's lips as he fired the words.

Out of the corner of his eye, James saw Scott shift in his chair. The NSA director's discomfort was almost imperceptible, just a slight adjustment of posture, but James caught it. Scott knew the situation was more complicated than the president understood. He wouldn't say so, though. Political survival trumped honesty.

A long silence followed.

James raised an eyebrow at Scott, who gave him an unreadable stare back. It was as good a time for a stupid question as ever.

"Why is the timing so important, sir?"

The president's eyes widened, his mouth hanging open for a beat. "You know nothing? There are primaries coming up in three months!"

"That is not the *most* important—" James started.

"No, no! James." The president cut him off. "It is your turn to say one thing. You should say, 'I am sorry, and I will take care of this, Mr. President!'"

James peered at the president with a flat look. *You fuckwad! You piece of self-serving shit. You do not care about humanity or even the American people! A government facility was destroyed, a business was blasted, people are dead, humanity is scared, and you are worried about the primaries!*

His hands wanted to curl into fists, but he kept them steady against the sheets. James took a careful breath. Even that hurt. His voice came out perfectly level.

"I am sorry, and I will take care of this, Mr. President," he said instead.

CHAPTER TEN

Confused, Brenda stared at Lixi.

They'd been climbing steadily for the last mile, and now, the path had flattened into a small clearing surrounded by similar gray boulders.

"Ta-da!" Lixi said, pointing to a big, ordinary-looking rock. She flew excitedly like a child waiting for candy. She looked at Brenda's unsure face and frowned. "Ta-da!" she said more pointedly, gesturing with both hands at the boulder.

"What? I don't see it," Brenda said finally.

The last two days had been much more cheerful despite the fact that Lixi kept complaining they weren't going fast enough. She asked at least seven times why they couldn't just all fly there. When Brenda said humans couldn't fly, Lixi waved her off.

"I knew a young kid who could fly. His name was Peter. I taught him to fly myself," she had said.

"Are you sure you haven't seen it in a movie? Was his last name Pan?" Brenda had asked.

Lixi had looked at her suspiciously. "Where do you know him from?"

"He's a fictional character in a book, Lixi!" Brenda had replied, laughing. "We're real, Lixi! There's a big difference."

"Girl, you need a reality check ASAP!" Lixi had said, putting her hands on her hips as she'd angrily flown away.

She'd returned a few minutes later as if the conversation hadn't happened, chattering about something else entirely.

Lixi seemed carefree and happy, never taking anything too seriously. Brenda envied that spirit. She herself would've replayed the argument in her head for hours, but Lixi had just moved on.

In contrast to Valor, who rarely said more than necessary, Lixi was always fun to talk with at length. She had many crazy stories, from elves to dwarves to a fairy tree friend called George, as well as ridiculously lengthy descriptions of cupcakes throughout the ages.

"Ta-da!" Lixi said a third time, looking at Valor hopefully.

Valor studied the rock for a moment before turning to Lixi with a warm smile. "Thank you, Lixi! If you say it's the entrance to the dwarf kingdom, we are forever in your service." He bowed.

Lixi batted her eyes and waved a dismissive hand. "Stop it, hon. You're going to make a fairy blush. You are most welcome, young dear." She curtsied midair. Lixi's eyes unfocused, and her head tilted. Her little nose wiggled on her face. She looked at them both with a surprised expression. "They're making cupcakes inside!" she said in a voice filled with delight. She danced in the air and zoomed toward the rock.

Before Valor or Brenda could say "How do we open the door," Lixi vanished straight into the block of rock.

There was a long moment of silence.

"Wait, how do we open the door?" Brenda asked slowly, her mind still trying to catch up, staring at the solid wall before her.

Valor looked at her with a smile that said he'd been waiting for a long time for the right time to say stupid shit. He handed her the water container he had in his hand, started walking toward the rock, and said, "Hold my beer."

"The fact that you've seen all the YouTube videos ever created doesn't give you the right to repeat ridiculous phrases," Brenda said after him, grinning despite herself.

Valor stepped closer to the rock. He closed his eyes, took a deep breath, put his hand on the rock, and said, "Makat Patishos!"

The words "Hammer Blow" appeared in Brenda's vision.

A big gong echoed through the rock and bounced around the surrounding rocks.

They waited a full minute. Nothing happened.

Valor did that another three times. His jaw tightened on the third attempt, and his hand pressed harder against the stone. Brenda watched him take a controlled breath before stepping back.

"Maybe they're not home?" Brenda suggested, half-laughing.

He took another deep breath and kicked the rock really hard. "Moger Shek'tar!" he spat, immediately grabbing his foot.

The words didn't translate in Brenda's ear or mind, but the meaning was clear enough. Brenda winced but couldn't hide her smile.

"I need to meditate on this," Valor said, lowering himself to the ground.

Half an hour crawled by. The only sound was the wind moving around the rocks. Valor had settled into stillness, his eyes closed and completely motionless.

Brenda picked through their food supply. She ate some of

the elvish loaves of bread, turning one over in her hand. They still looked fresh, as if they'd been baked that morning. Magic, probably, just like her childhood Wonder Bread.

After a while, Valor's eyes opened. The frustration from earlier had left his face. He smiled and stood up with the kind of purposeful energy that said he'd figured something out.

"I know what I can do! A royal elf can summon a same-level royal of another race if they are close by. This is an uncommon spell, as it's not very useful, but I think I remember it's rather effective at events and banquets," he said.

"Yeah, those pesky banquets," Brenda said with a mouth full of berries.

Valor stood and put his hand on the rock. He said the word "Bokan," and the word "Summon" flashed in Brenda's vision.

"I hereby summon a royal dwarf prince to come to my aid," Valor said in an official voice.

A shining blue light appeared on the rock surface with what looked to Brenda like a hammer and chisel insignia.

"It's working," Valor said, smiling. "I can feel a bond, and it's getting stronger."

After a few seconds, the rock started moving outward with a low grinding sound. A draft of cool air escaped from the widening gap, carrying the smell of earth and stone.

"Step back, please, Brenda? I don't want them to be scared by seeing a human with me," Valor said.

"Why should they be scared of a human?" she asked.

"Well, your race did kill most of the magical creatures in the world. I think the dwarves might be sore about it," he said while gently placing her a few paces behind him.

A lot to unpack there, but the door was almost open, and Valor started pacing forward toward the entrance.

The figure on the other side of the heavy stone door was massive. Three hundred pounds, easily. He stood half Valor's height but was at least three times as wide, built like a barrel with legs. His massive beard hung to his belt and was braided with dark beads, and his eyebrows were so bushy they nearly hid his eyes. He wore a blacksmith's tunic, the leather apron over it marred and stained. Everything about him, from his thick arms to the iron-banded boots, radiated strength and weight. He was built like he could easily deadlift them both.

"I am Prince Valor, son of Valor the Third, King of the Elves," Valor said, voice deep, royal.

"I am Prince Odel, son of Dumble the Great, King of the Dwarves," the dwarf said. His voice held none of Valor's enthusiasm. "Now leave."

This is awkward, Brenda thought.

"There is a grave matter that we must discuss," Valor said. "Please allow me to come in and consult with you and your father. This is of utmost urgency." The edge in his tone made Brenda's chest tighten.

Odel's eyes darted back and forth between the darkness inside and Valor.

Was someone back there? Brenda leaned to the side, trying to see past the dwarf's broad frame into the darkness. She couldn't make anything out, but Odel's nervous glances made her certain they weren't alone. A cold shiver went down her back.

"Please leave. We're busy." Odel looked inside again and started walking back into the dark mountain entrance. Valor started taking a step toward him, but the dwarf shook his head and cried out, "No, no, no! Go away! It's not safe!"

Valor started to say something but then raised his hand to his neck and cried out in pain. He fell to the ground, shaking violently as if he were being electrified.

"No! What the fu—" Brenda screamed as a horrible pain stung her neck.

Fire shot through her veins. She tried to reach for the spot, but her arm wouldn't respond. She fell, twisted, on the ground, an electric shock filling her entire body with burning pain. Her muscles locked. She couldn't blink or swallow. A few seconds later, she was lying on her back, staring at the darkening sky, unable to move a muscle.

Time passed, and she heard the sound of something being dragged on the gravel. She shrieked in her mind, but her throat remained frozen. Her eyes couldn't even locate or focus on the origin of the sound. What were they doing to Valor?

A few moments later, two iron fists clamped around her ankles and dragged her over the gravelly surface. Small rocks drove into her back and arms as she was pulled into the entrance of the mountain, into darkness.

CHAPTER ELEVEN

"Hold endless love for humanity and no love for any single human."

James loved that verse from the Kildare book. It expressed his feelings toward the world perfectly.

He bit his lower lip as people started pouring into the meeting room he was in, in the West Wing of the White House.

It's show time.

The plan he'd outlined had been simple—rattle the top executives of the government in the middle of the night; create uncertainty, fear, and doubt; get everyone in the same room before they had time to think, coordinate, and build alliances; and strike while they were disoriented.

They had all been woken in the middle of the night—the heads of the CIA, FBI, Chief of Staff of the Army, NSA, DOD, and other lesser-known government branches. Phone calls at two a.m., no explanations, just addresses and time stamps. Twenty minutes to dress and get in the car.

The Secret Service had escorted them all to the White

House. Black sedans formed a convoy through empty DC streets. No sirens, no lights. Silent urgency.

They were placed in one of the big conference rooms. The officials clustered together, their voices low, postures defensive. They smelled of hastily applied cologne and stale coffee. Some had missed buttons on their shirts. The CIA director's tie was crooked.

James watched from his position in the corner. He sat alongside a few other unimportant people—note takers and interns, the people who became invisible the moment someone more important entered the room.

He preferred it this way. Invisible meant underestimated, and underestimated meant that all these backstabbing political animals in this room wouldn't see him coming.

The chatter continued, speculation, complaints, confusion. James said nothing. His notepad was open, his pen ready. He looked like he belonged in the corner.

For now.

The president entered the room. They all stood up.

"Please be seated," the commander-in-chief announced. He took the empty chair at the head of the table.

The president acknowledged a few people. James got a quick nod, and an answering smile tugged at James's mouth.

James glared down at his notepad, annoyed at himself. That was pathetic.

"I will be short, gentlemen," the president began. "I have declared war. The enemies in this war are what some call colloquially magical creatures or, more formally, unnatural phenomena." He paused.

Some nodded. Others looked stunned.

"The attack on a government facility in Virginia represents the most significant assault on American soil since 9/11." The president glanced around. Voice firm. "You are all ill-equipped to deal with this situation." The man didn't mince words. "So I sourced someone who leads an organization we have been working with for a while secretly, an organization with years of experience."

The room blew up with questions and comments. "Why were we not told?" "Who gave you the authority to hide this from the American people?"

"Silence!" the president bellowed. "For hundreds of years, the Kildare Organization has been preparing for the return of these creatures." He glanced around. "Yes, you all heard me right. The return. They had been on Earth hundreds of years ago, and we 'took care' of them. These dedicated people made this problem go away last time, and I am confident they can do it again. The Kildare Organization is an international private corporation that does not owe us anything. They are here to help us, frankly, because you are all clueless when it comes to managing this shit show."

It was political magic at its best. The president who'd chewed his head off for the attack in Virginia was now totally confident in James's ability to deal with the entire, fucked-up situation. *How quickly these people pivot when it serves their needs.*

The room burst into "We can handle it!" and "My department owns the..."

The president glared around again. "Do any of you want to be foolish enough to commit the political suicide of leading this war? Speak now, or shut up and let him run this shit show without objections!"

The room went quiet.

James despised the theatrics, but he had to admit the man knew how to work a room.

He scanned the room slowly, watching for objections, for someone brave enough or stupid enough to challenge him. No one moved.

After a quiet full minute, the president continued, "Well, then, that settles it.

"Let me introduce you to my special director for this operation, code-named Pandora, who will represent me in all things related to this matter and will report directly to me. For the sake of this operation, you report to him. If you have doubt whether something should or should not be under his authority, I am telling you now that he has full authority. If you need to take a shit that is longer than five minutes, ask him for permission. In case I die, he will report to my successor. I will immediately fire anyone who disobeys or works around him. He is the boss. Do I need to make myself more clear?"

The room was deathly quiet.

These rules were James's price, and he made sure to spell it out to the president when they had finished the conversation in the hospital a few days ago. He needed the authority and freedom to act as he wished to stop magic. This administration's desperation had been obvious in the hospital negotiations. The president admitted he couldn't handle this. More importantly, he didn't trust anyone else in his administration to do better. That was why he'd agreed to James's terms.

"Please welcome Director James Webber." The president clapped.

A few more polite claps echoed through the room. Most officials kept their hands folded, exchanging glances.

James stood up. Every eye in the room turned to him. He felt their assessment, their confusion, their envy. The bureaucrat from the corner. The nobody. Most of them had never heard his name before this moment.

He'd rehearsed this. Not the speech itself but the posture. The confident voice. The measured smile that said "I belong here" without arrogance.

He nodded to a few of the government officials he knew. The

CIA director's eyes narrowed with recognition. The NSA chief still looked beaten. James inspected them all, small people with a big task at hand.

It was his turn to be the good guy.

"Thank you, Mr. President. Your trust will be met with action." His eyes went around the table. "The United States has the strongest military in the world. We have the best Secret Service and policing force in the world. I am proud of you all. We are facing an unprecedented war, a conflict that began with a successful invasion and occupation of US soil, an action that cannot go unanswered."

The room exploded, voices over voices. The CIA director half stood from his seat. The FBI director's face flushed red.

James clicked the remote. The screen behind him flashed to life. A map of the United States filled the display. Red dots scattered across it like a rash, with clusters on both coasts and a heavy concentration in the Southwest. Each dot represented a reported encounter.

He let them gape. Let the pattern sink in. Let them count.

"We are seeing ten to twenty reports a day of magical-creature encounters. In twenty-five percent of them, humans are injured. In sixty percent of these, the magical creature is injured or killed. We also note that a growing number of humans are transforming into magical creatures. This extremely concerns me, and we need to understand how to treat these individuals."

James stared at the president's legal counsel, who was sitting in the corner. This was the last but most important part of the agreement with the president.

The legal counsel, Drew Kensington, glanced at James with a flash of anger before dropping his gaze back down at his notes. His jaw tightened.

"From a legal perspective," Kensington started, looking at his notes, saying what had been rehearsed over the past few days, "I want to make our administration's point of view very clear."

The room went still. Even the quiet shuffling stopped.

"Humans who possess magical traits stop being human beings in the eyes of the law. Their DNA changes. Their thought processes change. Their brotherhood with other humans diminishes. They are considered by our administration's interpretation of the law as outside the protection law-abiding humans receive from it."

James watched faces around the table. Some nodded immediately. These were the practical men who dealt in threats and eliminations. Others shifted in their seats but stayed silent.

"We'll be issuing an executive order within the next two weeks," Kensington continued, his voice steadier now. "It will be called the Protection Against Unnatural Powers Act. It will outline this administration's legal framework and our intended actions going forward. Every agency in this room will receive detailed guidance on implementation."

Nobody objected. The generals and heads of departments nodded. They were used to having designated terrorists and other hostile foreign detainees "enjoy" fewer rights than American citizens. The nods came easily, just as the president had said they would.

"Gentlemen, we are taking these measures to protect humanity and to protect America," James said. "This is not a theoretical situation."

James clicked the remote again. The national map disappeared. Arizona filled the screen, a red circle marked over a remote area.

"Redstone Springs, Arizona."

Silence.

"An encampment of elves has taken over that area. They're preventing satellite imagery and blocking air and ground traffic.

We also believe they've already established defenses against missile attacks."

The Army Chief of Staff leaned forward. "What kind of defenses?"

"We don't know. We sent reconnaissance drones. However, signal loss occurred when they converged. Furthermore, we dispatched a patrol helicopter." James paused. "It didn't come back. All hands presumed lost."

Someone muttered a curse.

"America has never successfully been invaded...until now." He waited for his words to sink in and watched them register. The implications spread across their faces like cracks in ice.

His final line would be pure theater. The president had insisted on it during rehearsal. James hated it, but the man knew his audience.

"Now, let's get to work to return America back to us!"

James delivered the missive with conviction he didn't feel, his voice loud, his fist on the table for emphasis. The performance was complete.

They all clapped and cheered.

It worked. Of course it worked. People were predictable. Give them an enemy, give them a mission, wrap it in the flag, and they would march wherever you pointed them.

James gathered his notes while they applauded. The meeting was over. Now the real work could begin.

CHAPTER TWELVE

Colors. Psychedelic colors.

Brenda opened her eyes. The colors that filled her vision faded a bit, but the room kept spinning around her. It reminded her of that one experimental night in college. Only today she woke up in a dark chamber, seated, with her hands tied behind her back and her mouth gagged.

Why wasn't she panicking? Her mind was so sluggish. Her tongue felt like sandpaper, and when she blinked, her eyelids moved through molasses. Everything looked a bit wrong, edges too bright, shadows too deep.

A vast stone chamber surrounded her. She could barely make out the walls. The air was damp and cold, carrying the mineral smell of deep earth. Somewhere in the darkness, water dripped with a steady, hollow plunk.

Brenda peered upward, saw a big stone column, and realized she was tied to it. The column went all the way to the roof of the chamber. Three feet above her, attached to the column, was a light source. She couldn't tell if it was a torch or an artificial light. Her ass felt cold and numb from sitting on the cold floor.

A muffled noise came from beside her. Brenda turned her head to check it out. Valor was sitting on the ground to her left with his hands tied to another big stone column behind him.

She tried to move her feet and was able to wiggle them around. The rope bit into her wrists. Her shoulders ached from the unnatural angle, and her left foot had gone completely numb.

Valor opened his eyes and stared at her. Despite her foggy mind, she now realized that his mouth was gagged as well.

It was not an effective gag. It was like someone had done a half-ass job shoving a paper napkin into her mouth and put some kind of slack band around her head to hold it in place. Brenda worked her tongue a little and chewed on the piece of thin fabric that was stuck in her mouth. After a few minutes, she was able to spit it out beyond the loosely tied band that was wrapped around her face. A few jaw movements later, and the band dropped to her neck. Finally, she was able to speak her mind.

"What the fuck was that, Valor?" she asked. Her voice came out too loud and echoed in the chamber.

"Dou dou machik," Valor said, still trying to get his mouth gag off.

Brenda's head still spun. What was the stuff they had put in her body that had made fire in her veins? She felt like the entire world was turning around her.

Her gaze focused for a second on Valor's face. His eyes were wide, the whites showing, darting frantically between her face and her bound hands. She found it odd that he wore a new necklace tight around his neck. The necklace glowed with a sick greenish light. When she studied it, a low hum vibrated in her skull, and she could swear she felt the same pressure on her own neck. The black pearls seemed malevolent.

"Since when did you have that necklace?" she asked. Her voice sounded weird, slurred, and muffled. These drugs were strong!

"Dou dou machik!!" Valor said with more urgency.

Was he asking her to do magic? She tried to focus. What type of magic could she do to save them from this mess? She knew how to shoot a fireball. Would she be able to release his mouth gag? Or maybe release herself from the rope that tied her hands behind her back? Her mind spun again. Was she drunk?

"Bredaa, peeese, pleeese, dou do machik!!" Valor cried out.

Okay, it was time for magic. If she could only get her head to stop spinning, she could burn through the rope, save Valor, and stick a knife in that horrible, horrible dwarf that had captured them. She would be able to save the day! They would name a holiday after her! Maybe write a song!

The world spun. She slowed her breath and tried once more to focus.

Valor wiggled violently, his whole body convulsing as he tried to get closer. His chest heaved with each ragged breath, and muffled screams tore from his throat. He was sliding lower on the floor, using his legs to push himself, his bound hands scraping against the stone column, getting his feet closer to her. He was yelling something, but she would hear his thank-yous later, after she saved him and the day.

Warmth bloomed at her fingertips and spread up her hands. The spell words formed on her tongue, familiar and ready.

White-hot, sharp pain exploded in her shin and cut through the drug haze like a knife, bringing the world into sudden, sharp focus.

She squinted and saw Valor raise his ankle and hit her shin with full force again. Sparks filled her vision from the pain.

Why? Why was he doing that? Didn't he know she needed to concentrate?

Spit and blood edged the corner of his mouth as he worked to chew his gag cloth. He finally spat the torn cloth. His face was red, and parts of torn cloth covered the lower part of his mouth. He was still royal, but this was definitely not his best self.

"Brenda! Do *not* cast any magic! You will die! You have the Necklace of Brathloom on you. It will explode your head off your neck if you cast any magic." He spat blood and ran his tongue across his inner cheek.

Oh, that is not good. I don't want that, thought Brenda, although she might have said it out loud. She wasn't sure. The drugs were messing with her. The heat at the tips of her fingers subsided.

"No, you don't," he answered.

Yeah, she probably had said it out loud. She tested her mouth, opening and closing her lips deliberately to see what happened. Which thoughts were staying inside? Which ones were leaking out?

Her mind went back to Valor. Lines of sweat dropped from his forehead. She imagined him thinking of her blowing her head off in front of him. Something in her chest twisted. He'd hurt himself trying to save her. Her eyes teared up.

Oh, Valor, you really care if I blow up my head or not, don't you?

When he did not answer, she guessed she'd kept that thought inside.

Then it occurred to her.

"Wait. How...how do you even know it is the Necklace of Brathloom and that it will blow up?" Her words came out slower, suspicious.

"You have the Detect Magic ability. Look at my neck and focus on the necklace for a few seconds," he answered.

She almost laughed. Of course he'd turn a hostage situation into a magic lesson. That was classic Valor.

She focused on his necklace, the same black pearls she'd noticed earlier, and ignored the hum. After what seemed like five seconds, words started to appear in her vision. "Necklace of Brathloom, magical artifact, explodes when magic is cast by the wearer."

She was both proud of her ability and freaked out by the menacing device.

"What a shit show." She sighed quietly.

"What happened?" Valor asked, his voice tired. "The last thing I remember is..."

"That fucking dwarf kidnapped us!" Brenda said. "He fucking drugged us and tied us up and is probably going to violate us in his horrible dwarfish ways." Her head started spinning again from her agitation.

Valor stared oddly at her for a while and then awkwardly toward her right-hand side. He was glancing behind her. Why wasn't he paying attention?

"Valor, listen to me! If I find that fat-ass dwarf, I am going to strangle him!"

Valor's eyes kept darting to her right, then back to her face, then right again. He opened his mouth, closed it, and opened it again. The panic in his expression had shifted to something else. Was that...embarrassment? Amusement?

"Brenda, I do not think—" Valor started.

She cut him off. "No, Valor, give me a break. I know you need their help, but you were courteous and nice, and he was a mean bitch. I know mean bitches. They only respect power."

It was invigorating to be angry. She needed to vent. Valor was bound to be good. She was not.

"He will pay. I will fuck him up. No dwarf will ever mess

with me again after they learn what I did to this unhospitable fool Odel." Her loud words echoed through the chamber.

"Brenda." Valor's voice was quiet, almost resigned. "Please. Look to your right."

She did.

Oh, shit.

There was a big third stone column on her right. Sitting on the ground, tied and gagged, was the dwarf prince.

Odel regarded her with his big brown eyes behind his big bushy eyebrows. He was bruised, bloodied, and tied up just like them. She noted his judgmental expression around the gag.

"Rewee?" the dwarf said through the fabric.

This time, her mind did not have a hard time translating it.

Really?

CHAPTER THIRTEEN

Tanya curled on the sofa next to Boris, both of them watching TV.

She'd once learned that the Danish had a word for this—hygge. It meant coziness, warmth, and comfort. Back when she was human, the concept had seemed impossible. Warmth? Safety? Not for girls like her.

Now, here she was, her head on Boris's shoulder, sipping a warm glass of blood from their latest shared victim. The apartment was quiet except for the TV and the heavy rain beating the window, the Bucharest autumn weather hitting hard. Wrapped in warmth beside Boris, she felt safe.

The TV showed a news anchor getting overly excited about "The War to Save America from Unnatural Phenomena: Witchcraft, Wizardry, and Ungodly Creatures Attacking Peace-Loving Humans."

The screen cut to footage from prison camps, rows of humans suspected of having magic power all caged together, and riots being suppressed violently by mounted police.

Boris was transfixed by the TV. She was more transfixed by him.

After three months of feeding on humans, he now looked no more than thirty years old. He had a strong, handsome Slavic visage, with pale blond hair and light blue eyes. His muscles bulged beneath his buttoned shirt. The simple, elegant clothes she'd chosen for him—pressed pants and fitted shirt—gave him a modern European look instead of the ancient thing he was. She felt tiny next to him, her ballerina figure pressed against his big arm.

"Weak humans," Boris said. "Hateful, fearful, greedy, and prejudiced. It's good that they are divided."

Tanya nodded against his shoulder and took another sip of the warm blood. She'd need a refill soon. Perhaps their source had another round left in her.

"They are putting the only people who can protect them from us in their camps." He gestured to the TV. "Gathering all the wizards together where they can organize, unite, and grow stronger. The fools are building armies against themselves." He shook his head. "Vampires would never be that stupid, or as evil to their own kind."

Tanya smiled at Boris. Not agreement. Just affection. His warmth, the nightcap, and the sofa's comfort were making her sleepy.

The TV broadcast switched to a pale and sweaty bureaucrat standing at a podium with American flags behind him. He looked extremely unhappy to be there in front of a crowd of news reporters.

Boris sighed and turned off the TV.

"We need to act." Boris's voice shifted to that passionate tone of his. "These humans think they own this world. They believe that God gave it to them to use and abuse. The fools assume they are at the top of the food chain. No more! We will show them who is at the top of the pyramid. They will be cattle, as they were always designed to be. No other species is this evil," he spat. "They confine other creatures in cages just for entertainment. They kill just for amusement. They manipulate other species to suit their taste. Worst of all, they treat their own kind with similar evilness."

Tanya nodded again. For years, she'd suffered at the hands of men, passed from one abusive man to the other, treated as a discarded commodity. Disposable trash.

"It is our turn now. I am done waiting," he concluded.

She looked up at him. He was going to do it.

"Boris, please, don't tease me. You know I am bored out of my mind here. Empower me. Give me a challenge. Unleash me! I am so done with easy targets. So weak, so timid, so frail."

She spat at the human girl sitting on the floor at their feet. Late teens, maybe eighteen. Blonde. Pretty once. She still had baby fat in her cheeks, though her eyes were half-dead now. Blood was leaking from two punctures in her neck onto her white dress, staining the fabric dark red. She'd stopped whimpering an hour ago, long after they'd refilled their goblets.

Boris looked at Tanya, his old blue eyes in a young face. *That gaze*. The one that made her feel like she mattered. After a long while, he finally nodded. "Okay, Tanyushka, it is time. I need to expand my power, and you do look absolutely ready to go on a killing spree." He smiled, showing his sharp teeth.

She cocked her head. Waiting for it.

Boris's smile deepened. "Tanya, I need you to establish your own den in North America. By the end of the year, I want you to conquer the United States of America for me."

Her jaw dropped. Her own den. America.

"I want you to control the population there. Turn as many as you can into vampires and the rest to zombies. Keep enough fresh humans to sustain our population, all right? We do not want to start a humanitarian disaster that will hurt our food supply." He chuckled. "Is that a big enough adventurous killing spree for you?"

She jumped on the sofa with joy. "Finally!"

The bleeding girl on the floor sneered and stared up at her. Tanya knew that expression—mean girls judging her. She'd seen it her whole human life. This bitch thought she was better than her?

Tanya went to the wall and picked up a short sword that hung above Boris's work desk. The blade was dark with carved red runes. She brushed her fingers over it gently—it was warm to the touch. Perfect. She unsheathed it and walked menacingly toward the girl.

"Tanya, we do not waste food in this house," Boris said with a serious tone.

"Oh, Boris, I am so happy. Just this once? Please? I'll be good after." She smiled mischievously.

He looked at the girl sitting on the floor. The girl's breathing was shallow, her skin gray. She had minutes left, no more than that, and they both knew it. He nodded to Tanya.

Without waiting another second, Tanya lashed out with the sword and beheaded the girl. Tanya then kicked the girl's head straight between the legs of Boris's work desk. The body stayed up for another second, blood oozing from the neck, while the head rolled perfectly into the imaginary goal.

She raised her hands in victory. "She shoots. She scores!"

Boris's laugh was so pure and joyful that it made her chest swell with delight.

She jumped onto his lap. Her breath caught with excitement. Her own den. The first outside of Boris's in thousands of years. Her arms hugged his big chest, and her mouth moved toward his neck. He smelled of power.

"When can I leave?" she whispered in his ear.

She ran her finger along his arm, tracing the muscle. She was so eager to start.

But then her hand slowed. She'd miss him desperately.

He took a deep breath and placed his big hand over hers, holding it there. "I can get you there today," Boris said, "but you will need to work carefully. No crazy parties, at least not at the start. I will send a few other vampires with you, but you can send them back once you create your own den. I need you to establish your stronghold of power carefully, because the humans are vulnerable but also very wary these days."

Vampires were loyal creatures. Their first loyalty was to their creator. Tanya would forever be a member of Boris's den and utterly loyal to him in every essence of her being. The vampires she created would be loyal to her and, by proxy, to Boris. This was also a big win for Boris, making him the first vampire king, the ruler of multiple dens, since Dracula the Great.

She looked at him with renewed passion. "Thank you, Boris. I will not fail you," she whispered.

"Tanya, I trust you," he said simply.

Her throat tightened. She glanced down at her hands, then back at him. Girls like her didn't get trust. They got used. They got promises, but trust? Real trust?

She nodded once, uncertain her voice would remain steady. This was more than she'd dared to hope for.

"Pick your crew, up to five vampires and five zombies." He leaned back. "I will land you in a small town up north where it is dark and cold, just the way you like it."

Excitement made her skin tingle. She knew exactly who to

pick. She'd been planning this for months, every detail mapped out in her head, every scenario worked through. She was ready.

She couldn't stop smiling. Her face hurt from it. Desire, anticipation, and violence all flooded through her at once. Tonight. They would celebrate tonight with blood and music and bodies until dawn.

CHAPTER FOURTEEN

Brenda's face went hot. "Well, I am such an idiot," she muttered. She did not feel proud of herself. "Shit, I am truly sorry."

The dwarf was clearly bruised and roughed up. Blood had dried on his large forehead, and one of his eyes was swollen. He glared at her for a long time. Then, to her surprise, he nodded as if he totally accepted her apology.

His gaze shifted from Brenda to focus on Valor. Opening his mouth to speak produced nothing except a muffled grunt. He worked his jaw, as if grinding his teeth against the cloth, trying to get purchase on the fabric. He fought with it for five minutes, his face reddening with the effort, while Brenda offered increasingly desperate encouragement.

"Prince Valor," the dwarf said once his mouth was finally cleared. He had a deep voice that matched his barrel chest. "I am deeply ashamed of the lack of hospitality I have shown you. I assure you my people are forever in elvish debt. We are prisoners in our own mountain. My intention was to save you from this fate." He studied his bruised legs. "I am deeply, deeply ashamed," he repeated.

"Prince Odel, son of Dumble," Valor said in a formal voice, "the dwarves should never be ashamed in the presence of their friends, the elves. We are forever in dwarfish debt and grateful for our camaraderie."

Odel's entire bearing shifted. His back straightened, his chest swelled, and he sat proudly despite his bindings. His beard seemed to bristle outward.

"Tell me how it came to be for the dwarves to be prisoners in their own mountain?" Valor asked.

Odel frowned and stared at the ground for what seemed like forever.

The silence stretched. Brenda shifted her weight, her bound hands going numb. Was the dwarf falling asleep? Despite her discomfort from the awkward quietness, Valor seemed to be very comfortable with the dwarf's long pause. Valor kept waiting patiently as if he had just asked the question. As Brenda was about to yell at the dwarf to get on with it, he finally started telling his story.

"In the first weeks of the big plague, our nation was a haven for many magical creatures. We built a double-sealed chamber that protected our people from the sickness while still letting others take shelter in the mountain," Odel said. "We let halflings, leprechauns, winged lions, centaurs, and so many more inside. We took care of them and provided them with shelter and food." He sounded proud again. "But then we received a convoy from the gnome king, Kirchuk the Tall. He asked that we host him and his people as refugees. They were dying in droves, and we could not let them all die. We let in the healthy and strong that Kirchuk picked himself." Odel almost spat Kirchuk's name.

Valor frowned. "You know gnomes are borderline evil and

chaotic at best. How could you let them into your home?" he asked.

Odel stared at Valor for a long while, as if summoning the courage to say what he said next. "Valor, dwarves are not elves. We are not purists. We are pragmatic. The magic in our hammers was starting to fade, and Kirchuk's magical machinery did not show signs of slowing down. We needed these machines to gather ore and to plow our underground fields. Basically, we understood we would need them to survive." His voice turned hollow. He dropped his gaze, and his shoulders curved inward in shame, as if the weight of the story were crushing him. "That was also our downfall. Kirchuk the Tall had a son called Kirchuk the Great. He used their machinery to change the balance of power, and we found ourselves in debt and working for the gnomes. Kirchuk the Great's son, Kirchuk the Vicious, basically enslaved us after we tried to rebel and take our mountain back."

He raised his eyes now and met Valor's. "They have war machinery now. They do not abide by the promise they gave your father after their last war. They use their machines for death and destruction. They kill every dwarf who does not bow to them. We are in ruins. The gnomes treat us like they are our superiors at best, but most of the time like our slavemasters."

"Because slaves you are!" The voice was screechy in Brenda's ears, like an engine that had run out of oil.

She heard the scrape of metal on stone before the screechy stranger came out from behind the stone pillar. He did not seem like the cute creature Brenda had in mind when she had heard Odel talk about gnomes. This one was a short, skinny, and filthy human-like figure, red sores weeping on his face and very oily hair that hung in strings. His hands glistened with the same grease which covered him. He wore dark leather and boots with metal spikes. He looked like a little punk suffering from a seriously disgusting skin condition.

The funky gnome kicked Odel hard in the leg. The wet smack of boot against flesh echoed through the cavernous chamber. The motion was surreal, like he was kicking a football or something much more mundane. Odel's whole body jerked against his bindings. He bit down on a scream. Blood started dripping from his knee, dark and thick.

Brenda's stomach twisted. Her hands curled into fists despite the rope, and her nails dug into her palms.

"Let me introduce myself," the gnome said. "My name is Zig the Vanquisher. I am the cousin of Kirchuk the Vicious. I am your temporary master until my cousin decides what to do with you. I say *temporary* because I do not think there is going to be much left after he is done with you."

Brenda's jaw clenched involuntarily. Her pulse hammered in her temples, and the world spun around her again. This little gnome asshole pissed her off in a way she had never experienced before, some primal reaction she couldn't control. She wanted to strangle him for kicking Odel.

"Let the human and the dwarf go, and I will negotiate with your king," Valor said with a calm voice. "Your past king broke the promise given to my father."

"Shut up!" the gnome screamed in Valor's face, leaving dirty spit on the elf's cheeks. "You are a dog. A flea on a dog. We do not negotiate with you. You and all your kind will bow to us when we come out of the mountain and conquer the world again."

"Again? Did gnomes ever conquer the world?" Brenda asked Odel, genuinely curious.

"No," the dwarf said.

"Not even close," Valor said with disdain while looking at the gnome. "They didn't even own their own lands. They only lived in the swamps and shallow caves because no one wanted to live next to them. They magically rub people the wrong way. Humans are most prone to their natural Taunt ability."

Valor gave her an intense look. His eyes seemed to be saying something important, but the residual drugs in her system made it hard to focus on anything except that horrible, grating voice. Was Valor warning her?

"Shut up, I tell you!" the gnome screamed.

He looked at Brenda and moved toward her. His smell hit her first. Not just sweat. Something sour and chemical, like eggs gone bad mixed with rotting vegetables. Her eyes watered.

"We did conquer the world. Elves, dwarves, and humans bow to us every day. You humans surely still have songs of our glory." His voice was doubly irritating and increasingly antagonizing.

"Glory, my ass. Maybe songs of your yearly showers!" she mumbled, not caring she voiced her thoughts outright.

There was silence. Then Odel started laughing quietly.

"You are driving me angry! I will have your head!" the gnome screamed.

"I am okay with that as long as you don't ask me to give you head. You are disgusting," Brenda snapped.

The gnome's face turned red.

Valor tried to look serious but shortly after gave up and joined Odel, who was still laughing out loud.

The gnome's face flushed crimson. His hands balled into fists. "My cousin will skin you alive. He will boil you in oil."

Brenda's mind warned her this was not the right direction but also told her pissing off the gnome was a lot of fun. The influence of the drugs in her veins made it seem like this was all happening to someone else. What really got to her was this little creature's voice. It was unnaturally irritating. Magically irritating. Was this the Taunt ability Valor mentioned? Some natural gnome power to crawl under your skin?

The gnome raised his leg to kick Brenda's thigh. She saw the boot coming. The pain exploded in her upper leg, white-hot and deep. Not the sharp pain of a cut but something duller, spreading like a shockwave through muscles. Her anger at the little bastard grew more intense. The blood boiled in her veins now.

"Leave her alone!" Valor cried with renewed worry.

Brenda started, "Did you smell like this when you came out of your mother's—"

The gnome's boot hit her inner thigh again, and she lost consciousness in great white pain.

CHAPTER FIFTEEN

Lixi regretted eating the last cupcake. Actually, she kinda regretted eating the last five cupcakes. They were so good, though, that she was torn between sorry and not sorry.

The kitchen was full of dwarves. Heat radiated from the ovens. Pots clanged and wooden spoons scraped against iron. She vaguely remembered they had come to see them, although for the life of her she did not remember why. Maybe it was because of the cupcakes? It must have been that. This world didn't have enough magic to support the proper memory and sound mind of a fairy like her.

This place was boring. Her wings drooped as she stared at the stone walls. Not a single flower. Not even a sad little grasshopper to talk to. Just rock and more rock and cooking dwarves. She was lying on a table with a dozen half-eaten cupcakes around her.

Three dwarves carried a massive pot between them, passing within inches of where she lay surrounded by cupcake carnage. Their eyes stayed fixed ahead, never flickering toward the glittering fairy sprawled across their workspace. She was awesome that way. They would notice her only if she decided that they needed to.

Something buzzed in the back of her head, like a bee going back and forth. That feeling she had when she forgot something again, though she was sure it wasn't important. She always remembered the important stuff. She knew from experience the feeling usually faded after a few days or... years.

"Okay, enough with the sugar," she told herself. She was all about enjoying her life and not giving a shit about body shaming, but health was a concern, right? Or maybe that was something she heard from someone else?

Away from the fairies' home world, everything felt like a confusing dream. Events phased in and out all the time. Time stretched and contracted. Had she been here an hour or a week? Was it just her? It seemed like other creatures here did not experience it as a dream and took things way too seriously.

She got to her feet and tested her wings. Yes, they could still carry her. She started flying around the room, cruising between the busy dwarves. None of them smiled. None of them talked. They just cooked with their heads down. This was unlike dwarves. These guys usually knew how to party.

Lixi had always liked dwarves. They were honest, straightforward, and had wonderfully long feasts. They treated fairies with proper respect, often even worship, which showed excellent judgment. And their sweets? Amazing. Buttery pastries, sugar-dusted cookies, cakes that melted on your tongue...

These silent, miserable dwarves felt wrong somehow.

The strange thing was that they were not cooking the normal dwarf food. They were cooking gnome cuisine. Why would they do that? Dwarf cuisine was very earthy—yams, potatoes, carrots, and lots of booze. Gnome cuisine was very oily—fatty meat, greasy pastries, and lots of fried food. While Lixi loved cupcakes, she definitely preferred dwarf food because it smelled much better.

She continued to zip between them, and then she saw greasy-looking gnomes walking around giving orders with small sticks in their hands.

"Faster!" one barked.

"More salt!" another shrieked.

Dwarves twice as tall as the gnomes and twice as wide were bowing and serving the gnomes all around. The dwarves smelled of fear, but the gnomes smelled of arrogance and unwashed clothes.

Gnomes. She wrinkled her nose just thinking about them. Sneaky, arrogant creatures who thought being cunning was the same as being wise. They had hygiene issues too, always smelling like they'd forgotten what soap was for. Worse, they didn't respect fairies. Didn't worship them, didn't honor them, barely acknowledged they existed. That alone was enough to earn Lixi's contempt.

Nearby, a dwarf carried a gnome on his back. Another dwarf sobbed on the ground while a gnome child was kicking her.

Lixi shot forward, ready to slap that little bastard brat into next week, but the pull hit her mid-flight, spinning her around. Something important urgently tugged at her mind. A room full of metal, oil, and evil was up the corridor. She could smell it.

Time to be a hero again.

Being a fairy was an important role, especially being her.

A coronet flickered at the edge of her memory. Silver wings. Thousands of faces turned toward her, waiting. The image vanished before she could grasp it, but she sensed her destiny was close.

Lately, she had been having weird dreams, which she disdainfully called her "too-real-dreams." They were dreams of burning cities, of kids crying, and of kids dying. She did not like these dreams at all.

She made a mental note to revisit all these memories. *Ha! Mental note, my ass.* She wouldn't remember to put on her wings in the morning if they were not attached.

She moved on toward the bad smell. The corridor was unusually wide for dwarvish architecture. It was about twelve feet wide and had a very high ceiling. As she continued, the smell of machine oil became almost unbearable.

Big metal doors were at the end of the corridor. They were heavy, bolted, and locked. She passed through them easily.

The noise hit first—hammering, grinding metal on metal, and the hissing of steam. Then, smoke, thick and oily, overwhelmed her. The room was enormous and extremely busy. Thousands of gnomes worked on what looked like different metal parts of a giant human body. Some were assembling giant hands, each finger as thick as a dwarf's torso. Others were hammering the toes into metal legs that towered over the workers. Several gnomes were inspecting hundreds of melon-sized metal eyes, polishing the glass lenses until they gleamed.

The smoke and noise were really bad, but she was pulled by an even greater evil. Something terribly bad was beyond the next door. She took a shallow breath and powered through.

The next set of doors were made of pure titanium, a rare metal the dwarves never used, as they thought it was unholy and hard to craft. She tried to go through the door, went back, and frowned at the doors. They were not harder to go through—nothing in this world was really hard to go through—but they were *endless*. Darkness surrounded her, pressing in from all sides. It was as if she went through the door but did not reach the other side. Maybe they were just thicker than she thought they were?

She took another try. One foot, two feet, six feet, twelve feet of solid metal passing through her body.

Lixi finally passed through and took a big breath in. The air was foul.

She scanned the room, and her eyes widened. A vast space stretched before her, row after row after row. Lixi flew higher, trying to see the rear of the room, but she could not.

A sixteen-foot ceiling stretched above her, lights spread across every few feet. The floor was filled end to end with giant twelve-foot-high metal human-like robots, all armed with giant swords and giant hammers. Silent. Motionless. They all reeked of pure evil, and they all had their shiny red eyes open, glowing in the dim light.

For a heartbeat, nothing moved. Then, as one, every head turned with a mechanical click. A sound like a thousand missiles locking on target filled the air. Every red eye shifted onto her position. Thousands of them.

All focused on her.

"Fuck my life," she muttered.

CHAPTER
SIXTEEN

This is complete and utter torture.

The camera flashes burned his eyes. Every two seconds, there was another burst of white light. The noise made it impossible to think clearly. Forty-something reporters were all shouting questions before he could finish answering the previous one.

James stood at the podium in the White House press room, the heat from the camera lights making his collar stick to his neck.

Next to him was the press secretary, smiling and cheerful as always. She'd touched his shoulder before they'd walked out and told him she was there to support him with everything he needed.

Helper? More like an executioner.

The president had been adamant that this was part of James's role now, putting him front and center to deal with everything that was happening across the country. It had taken James a long week of work to figure out he was basically the scapegoat for the entire administration. Everyone ran away from the mounting mess. Everyone except James.

The president's voice rang in his head from his "inauguration" meeting. "Do any of you want to be foolish enough to commit the political suicide of leading this war? Speak now, or shut up and let him run this shit show without objections!"

Well, at least the president had been honest. He had warned everyone in the room that it was a suicide mission and a fucked-up task. Then, the commander-in-chief had given it to James, who had happily taken it, not realizing he was being fooled in plain sight.

Did I really think he would empower someone outside the administration without a good reason?

"Mr. Secretary of Unnatural Phenomena," a young blonde reporter from CNN called. She was mid-twenties, probably fresh out of journalism school and hungry to make a name for herself. "Does this administration still stand behind and intend to continue to implement the Magic Protection Act?"

The shouting stopped. Even the camera shutters went quiet.

James blinked several times, a droplet of sweat running down his nose. "The Magic Protection Act was signed by the president and upheld in court last week."

He paused. The act itself had passed pretty easily. Most people were afraid, and frightened people like decisive acts.

The human rights organizations had been able to have their day in court, objecting to excluding humans with magical abilities from any law protecting the rights of humans, but the fact that a judge's head had been blown off by a convict with magical abilities the week before had made the case a slam dunk for the government.

"The law declares people with magical powers as wizards and therefore excluded from the legal definition of humans and the laws that defend them," James answered.

"Dumb it down," the press secretary next to him whispered angrily. "Make it shorter."

"The law is designed to protect our law-abiding citizens from unnatural forces," James added, remembering to check the key points he had to hit in the press briefing note in front of him.

The press secretary nodded and pointed at another journalist, but the blonde continued her line of questions.

"But, sir, your initial projections, which the administration communicated, that only point one to one percent of the population will have magical powers were wildly off. Almost fifteen percent of the examined population in the US have tested positive for magical powers. We have magic kids in every classroom, coworkers with magic in every office, every police department, in every golf club. Do you still think this is the right thing to do?"

James's eyes twitched. She was right. The numbers were staggering. These wizards were collected by the new well-funded task force, which James had made sure was only composed of people with no ties to any magical person. Camps had been created in the outskirts of cities and then in more remote areas to verify, process, and detain all of these human-like creatures. They were well taken care of, but the vast numbers made the job increasingly impossible. The reports used terms like "capacity issues" and "elevated tensions," euphemisms for overcrowding and riots.

"Yes, we are confident we can manage the situation. We urge the American people to stay calm." That was another talking point in his brief.

The population was not calm, though. Riots had started in big cities, instigated by both sides of the political spectrum. On one side, wizards and their supporters protested that they did not have to be detained, claiming they were peaceful citizens.

On the other side, thousands of people protested to get these wizards out of their cities and to protect humans from the dangers of unnatural power. Every major city now had protests. Some had turned violent.

"Thank you, Jane!" The press secretary's tone made it clear there would be no follow-up questions.

Don Bell, one of the more questionable journalists allowed into the White House, seized the opportunity to speak. "Mr. Secretary, reports claim that these magical traits are contagious. Can you comment on that?"

"That is completely untrue! Stop spreading this rumor. We ask you all to let us do our job and not take things into your own hands," James interjected, his voice agitated.

This was not the first time this rumor had been raised, especially on social media. Many companies fired all wizards, and many others banned them from their establishment and refused to serve them. The report had been debunked, but that was too late. Wizards were now "others," "not human," and "probably contagious."

Fear was becoming very dangerous. Fear created violence. Many states started making any simple use of magic illegal, and there were rising cases of police shooting people walking at night with flashlights.

Another problem was that people were panicking. Many killed wizards just because it was not illegal. Some killed any person they did not like because they claimed they were wizards. There was a definitive test to see if a person was a wizard or a normal human, but people did not want to wait the two days for the results. Testing labs were already overwhelmed, and response time for the blood tests now took weeks rather than days.

"Are you sure about that? Seems like the magical humans

are getting out of control," a conservative reporter prompted from the front row.

The easy questions were over.

Driven by fear or greed, many wizards abused their powers or just used them to get what they wanted. Calls about fireballs, heat waves, and laser-like rays were becoming common to all local law enforcement. It seemed that most of these wizards had the ability to generate harmful energy like fire that could harm others.

Another phenomenon was "fire gangs." They started in Los Angeles but had rapidly become popular in many inner cities. Last week, in Chicago, a single wizard had taken out an entire SWAT team before they could breach the door. Drug cartels and crime syndicates were fast to realize the powers of wizards and enlisted them, adding them to their forces. The fight on crime had become harder and much more violent. Most wizards did not want to join the cartels. They just did not have any other option after being fired and banned from any business establishment.

It was a shit show.

"We are—" James started to comment.

The conservative reporter did not wait for an answer, instead moving straight to the question his audience cared about the most. "How are the American people paying for all of this? Are we going to see more taxes levied?"

The room fell quiet again.

James was unprepared for the question. He looked at the press secretary. She shook her head. Was she telling him not to answer? Why not? It was brilliant.

"It's very simple," he said plainly. "Wizards are not humans, so we confiscate their bank accounts and use that money to fund the war on magic."

It had been his idea to fund the war that way, and he was

proud of it. Elegant solution. But was it also a good idea to tell everyone about it?

The press secretary's wild eyes locked on him. She was mouthing "no" with exaggerated movements in what felt like slow motion.

The podium suddenly felt unsteady under his hands. *Oh, shit, what have I done?*

The room held silent for one perfect second. Then, it detonated with screams of questions and flashes striking like lightning. James felt like he had stepped on a landmine.

The press secretary shouted over the mic that the interview was over and shoved James behind the stage to a back room. Her grip on his elbow was hard enough to bruise.

The door clicked shut behind them.

Her smile dropped. "You are such an idiot!" The sweetness was gone from her voice, replaced with something raw and sharp. "You just dropped the biggest political bomb on this administration. The government confiscating bank accounts? Are you fucking mad? This is political suicide."

"But it's the truth, and it is effective," James said, confused.

"Fuck the truth, fuck effective, and fuck you!" She stepped into his space, her pointed finger almost touching his chin. Then she spun and left, slamming the door hard enough to rattle the frame.

He was alone, his ears still ringing.

Was humanity even worth this? It was moments like these when his conviction for his mission was truly tested.

But this was his life now—daily briefings with the press, daily requests for clarifications from every branch of the government, the public trust in the government at an all-time low. James was the poster child of the biggest low point of humanity since the black plague.

And these were just the human wizard problems. Lately,

there were reports of halflings and werewolves in the forest areas in the northern US, from Seattle to upstate New York. In Canada, there were reports of vampires, but James highly doubted these.

He walked slowly to his office. Should he have said "asset reallocation" or maybe "funding displacement" instead? Any euphemism would have been better than "confiscate."

He shook his head. There were more important things on his mind. The freaking elves were still evasive. They apparently continued to add defense mechanisms that made all electronic and human surveillance nearly impossible to implement. Their location was a blind spot to all satellites. They made guided projectiles change their course and unguided projectiles miss their mark. Any human who tried to get within fifteen miles got sick and needed hospitalization. His team had theories—force fields or psychic interference—but none of it helped.

James was still haunted by what he had read in the book of Kador about the Catalysts, the wizards that would end humanity. He was absolutely sure the elves were involved.

"They are the source of it all," he had told his team again and again. "If we do not stop them, it is going to get a lot worse."

He neared his office and saw his executive assistant heading toward him.

"Tera Brown, the Kildare science attaché, is in your office. She says it is urgent," his executive assistant said.

"Thank you, Timon," James mumbled. He marched into his office.

"Secretary of Unnatural Phenomena, sir," Miss Brown said. She was tall, in her mid-thirties, and wore a lab coat. Kildare science division? That meant she was smart enough to be useful and professional enough to follow orders. She sounded frightened.

"Call me James," he said in a tired voice, trying to calm her down.

"Yes, James," she said.

"Come on, I don't have all day. What's so important?" He gestured to the guest seat and took a seat behind his desk.

She deposited herself in the spot he indicated, her back rigid. Something had her both nervous and excited. Good news, then.

"We found a way to get to the elvish village," she blurted.

"Is that so?" This was the first good news James had heard all day.

"We think that the elvish magic, umm, unnatural power extends to the air but not underground. We do not know if that is a limitation of that power or an oversight, but we were able to get to nine miles away from their stronghold without any sickness, by digging underground."

James genuinely smiled. It felt strange. He hadn't smiled like that in a long while.

"How long before we can get under their stronghold?" he asked.

"We estimate six months for a tunnel that will be able to support the transportation of heavy machinery and equipment," she said.

"We can't have that, Miss Brown. We have weeks, not months. We are on the brink of human annihilation. We cannot wait for heavy machinery." James stood up and looked down on the woman. "What is the fastest you can do it?"

"Two weeks, but that will gravely endanger our troops and put the entire operation at risk, James, sir," she said, timid again.

"Two weeks is barely fast enough. I want it done in less time. People who join the Army know the stakes. If we wait, the risk for humanity is much larger. The US troops will handle it."

James tried to keep his voice calm. There was no need to frighten her more.

She chewed her bottom lip.

He added, "Can you make it in ten days? If we do it at all costs?" He looked her straight in the eyes, holding her gaze.

"Yes, sir, we will get it done." She stood to leave. The fear was gone. Only determination remained.

God bless the effectiveness of his people in Kildare.

Yes, humanity is still worth it.

CHAPTER
SEVENTEEN

Thump, pain.

Thump, pain.

Am I dead? No, it's too painful for this to be death.

Brenda was swimming in black sand. She wasn't sure why or how she had gotten there. The sand scraped her back raw and clung to her skin, each grain biting like glass. It reeked of sweat and burnt oil. She tried to swim out of the sand, but it was endless. Everything around her was black.

Thump, pain.

At regular intervals came the thumping sound, then the back of her head would throb. Her body hurt as if someone was striking her back, shoulders, neck, and head with a baseball bat. Each impact sent white-hot spikes through her skull, and she tried to swim away from them.

Where was she? Where was Valor? Where was...what was the dwarf prince's name? Odel! That was right! Was he in this dark place too?

Thump, pain. Thump, pain. Thump, pain. Thump, pain.

This was unbearable. She opened her mouth to scream, but

her mouth was now too full of sand, sticking to her teeth and making it hard to breathe.

She heard harsh voices.

"Bring the cold water," she thought they said.

The sand was in her ears too now, making sounds muffled. She was losing her focus. The sand was getting in her eyes. She blinked and blinked again. A giant creature walked toward her, a spider or a scorpion holding something in its hands. She didn't remember scorpions having hands, but spiders' front legs could be called hands, and she'd seen nature films where spiders were quite dexterous.

The ice water hit her like a pile of bricks. Every nerve screamed. Her body seized, muscles clenching against the cold. She gasped, but the ice water flooded her mouth, freezing her lungs. She thrashed, jerking her hands and legs, trying to spit it out. Her eyes flew open. Her vision blurred and was limited. There was a high ceiling above with gold decorations on it, visible through her tears and watered-down blood, showing dwarves working, digging, crafting metal, cooking, and even fondling.

She turned her head sideways. Blood trailed across a white carpet, a long smear leading down a wide corridor. The corridor sloped toward her with stairs every few steps. The blood path started at the top and ended where she lay.

"Holy shit!" Her back throbbed where the carpet had scraped her raw. "That's my blood."

The thumps. Her head. The stairs. Someone had dragged her the entire length of the corridor, her skull bouncing off every step. No wonder everything hurt. The carpet had probably saved her from brain injury. Probably. She hoped.

Adrenaline washed through her body, and she managed to wail "Vaalluuu" and turn her head to the other side. Where was Valor? What had they done to him? Was he okay? Tears welled up again, blurring everything. She tried to blink a few times to clear her vision.

Beside her, a broken face stared back, eyes closed, broken nose, deep cuts on forehead and chin. Barely recognizable. Odel? The poor dwarf.

A few seconds later, a bucket of ice water splashed the dwarf. He convulsed, spitting water mixed with blood, and screamed. He opened one good eye. The other one was swollen shut and looked at her in terror.

Where was Valor? She wanted to scream for the dwarf to move aside. Odel's face was so close, filling her entire vision. She lifted her head. Pain exploded, and the world spun. She couldn't see behind him.

Another bucket of water hit the floor nearby, and she finally heard Valor. Valor was screaming, in what sounded like a combination of pain and confusion.

She called "vaaaggueerru" to him.

Odel tilted his head, his one good eye struggling to focus on her, the dwarf was clearly still dazed and not able to understand her. He was trying to look around but was facing sideways toward her, so his vision was completely blocked by her.

"Stand up!" It was a mean voice, a metal voice, an artificial-sounding voice. It sounded like it came from a broken speaker high above them.

Good luck with that, Brenda thought. She was pretty confident that she wouldn't be able to sit, let alone stand.

"Synthetics, make them stand," the metal voice said.

Metal fingers dug into Brenda's arms. Something harsh and cold pulled her up. The grip was unyielding and mechanical. She was like a doll strung up by hard strings. The thing holding her buzzed faintly, like an idling engine. She twisted to look back. Her neck burned, her vision dimming at the edges. She locked her eyes forward, blinking hard to clear them. Next to her, from the corner of her eye, Odel and Valor were held by two large dark figures.

Strong lights slammed on, their hum filling the vast space, forcing her gaze to an elevated platform. The vast room swallowed sound, making everything feel distant and hollow. A single small figure sat on a seat on the platform, the throne clearly not designed for someone so tiny. He had a crown with many large diamonds and rubies, and he wore a malicious smirk.

Well below the royal throne, on two plain wooden chairs, sat two heavy-built dwarves. Both wore wooden crowns that looked broken, and both wore tattered clothes. Their hands were tied to the chair arms, and their mouths were gagged. They both perfectly resembled Odel. These had to be Odel's parents, the king and queen of the dwarves.

"My name is King Kirchuk the Vicious," the small figure on the royal seat said. "You are summoned here to be judged by my royal self. Consider yourself honored. I will judge you, find you guilty, and execute you myself." He was speaking into an odd-looking microphone attached to the chair.

The small, ugly figure of the gnome king was perfectly lit in the large dark room. The light had no visible source. Everything about him screamed wealth and bad taste. His teeth were yellow but sparkled with embedded diamonds. His hair hung thin and greasy, slicked back with too much oil. His clothes were spotless, woven in silver and gold. Expensive. Ridiculous on him. The sword at his side was radiating blue light and clearly magical but far too large for him. The tip scraped the floor. He was the most unimpressive creature in the most impressive gear she'd ever seen. He looked like a large rat wearing a crown.

"Valor, son of Valor," the figure called into the microphone in a voice that resembled a bored TSA agent, "you are hereby accused of mass murder of tens of thousands of gnomes by refusing shelter and help during the big plague. How do you plead?"

Valor's eyes were bloodshot, and a large, serious gash went across his face from the left side of his forehead through his broken nose to his chin. His left shoulder rested at an unnatural angle. He spat blood before he tried to answer. Finally, he managed. "The elves do not recognize the gnome court," he said. His voice broke despite his effort to hold his head high.

"Bailiff, hit him at damage level five," the gnome king instructed in a bored voice.

A small gnome with a big iron rod circled behind Valor. Valor ducked just as the rod came down, but it still caught him on his neck and the back of his shoulder. The rod connected with a sharp crack. Valor screamed, high-pitched and agonized, and fresh blood poured from a new, deep gash on his shoulder. Brenda couldn't breathe. Valor's broken figure blurred before her.

"You bastards!" Odel screamed. "You fuckin' bastards!"

"Bailiff, gag him. Nose and mouth for the traitor," the king said in an annoyed tone to the mic.

The gnome with the rod moved behind Odel and wrapped a wide rubber band across the dwarf's nose and mouth. Odel fought, his head jerking side to side, but the band locked on. His face flushed red then deeper still, his veins standing out on his forehead.

"The elves do not recognize the gnome court!" Valor screamed.

"Bailiff, hit the elf at damage level seven," the gnome king said slowly, grinning widely at the bleeding elf and the dwarf fighting for his life.

Odel's parents screamed, their cries muffled by their own gags.

The gnome with the rod went back to Valor and with a businesslike manner hit him. Valor pulled himself down again. Why would he do that? Valor was much, much taller than the gnome, and these attempts to duck were just making it worse by exposing his neck and face to the iron rod. This time, there was the sound of broken bones.

The second the rod hit, Valor screamed again. "The elves do not recognize the gnome court! You are evil scum and will never see any grace from the high elvish!"

Why is Valor doing that? Is he trying to get himself killed?

"Bailiff, hit him at damage level ten!" the king screamed into the microphone.

Brenda's ears burned from the pain of the metal sound.

The gnome hit again in full force. Valor pulled himself down again. This time, there was definitely a sound of broken bones but also broken metal.

Brenda's jaw went slack. The collar around Valor's neck was now shattered. That was why he had kept ducking. He'd been trying to get the gnome to break the necklace preventing him from using magic. Sneaky bastard. Pieces of the Necklace of Brathloom were scattered across the floor.

Valor dropped to the ground. Everything stopped. Blue light bloomed from his body, cold and brilliant.

The glowing elf screamed. The sound echoed through the vast chamber, promising violence and revenge. "Son of a—"

CHAPTER
EIGHTEEN

Tanya sat at her desk in a small office at a shared workspace in Toronto. It was past midnight. The building was quiet except for the hum of the projector and muffled bass from a bar a few floors down. The office smelled like stale coffee and cleaning detergent. She leaned back, watching the presentation.

"I present to you: Nyos!" Yan Chew announced with an overdramatic gesture.

He was a new member of her den. Her den. Goosebumps prickled her skin. Boris had a den. Now she had a den. The words felt foreign and powerful in her mind. It was like she was wearing someone else's crown and discovering it fit.

Yan was the first member of her den. She'd burned through ten hours of business audiobooks in the past week, cranked to triple speed. Her vampire hearing made the sped-up voices sound like bats talking. It was weirdly pleasant. *From Startup to Empire* taught her that before you hire executives, you need a sexy product. That was the goal of this meeting.

"The Nyos..." she said hesitantly.

"Drop the 'The.' Just Nyos. It's cleaner." Yan gestured with his hand as if writing the word Nyos in the air.

"Nyos..." She tasted the word in her mouth.

"Yes! Exactly!" Yan smiled, revealing a mouth full of sharp, pure-white teeth. He was dressed in all black—a silk shirt and pants with a dark, flowery scarf around his neck.

Tanya had never met anyone dressed so fashionably. A few days ago, this man had run the top branding firm in Canada. Now he sat in her rented office, desperate to impress her. Yan was exactly the kind of polished, professional asset she needed. Best of all, he was utterly hers.

"Vampires are so yesterday's trend," Yan continued. "Yes, you can still sell passionate vampire romance stories, but nobody with class wants to join that club in earnest. They want finesse. They want to be part of something new. To belong. Nyos."

Yan pressed the small black controller in his hand. The presentation changed from shiny silver letters spelling NYOS across the screen to a pie chart.

"We ran a quick online survey, and Nyos tested ninety-seven percent positive with both males and females aged twenty to thirty-five."

A slow smile spread across Tanya's face. With numbers like that, recruitment would be easy.

At the beginning of this week, she had met Yan at a conference she sneaked into. He had been presenting his marketing strategy for the top cigarette company in Canada. She studied him. The wounds on his neck were still visible. Now he was her head of branding.

Yan clicked the controller again. The title "Core Values" appeared at the top of the slide. Tanya's lips curled upward. Core values. That was where the real marketing magic started. This was going to be good.

"Let's start with what really matters." Yan's voice sharpened, taking on the rhythm of a rehearsed pitch. The projector cast harsh white light across his face, making his teeth gleam.

Click.

The words "Out with the Old" appeared as the first bullet point.

"Being human is to be old, to be boring, to die. Being Nyo means reinventing yourself. To be cool. To be glamorous. To be a new and better human. To live forever." Yan's voice rose, each word hitting harder than the last. He gestured from his head down to his torso, like a game show host presenting a prize.

Click.

The words "Caring About What Matters" appeared as the next bullet point.

"To be human is to destroy the world and its resources. To be Nyo is to fight for what is right! We operate at night to save electricity. We feed on humans to save the animals. We turn other humans to grow our cause." Red light flickered in Yan's pupils, spreading outward until both irises glowed.

Click.

The words "Revolution by Evolution" appeared as the next bullet point.

"To be human is to be outdated, to be part of the past. We are the next step in humanity's evolution. We are stronger, faster, smarter, sexier, cooler. We are the future of humanity. A better future."

Tanya found herself leaning forward, caught up in the rhythm of his delivery.

Click.

The word "Belonging" appeared as the next bullet point.

"To be human is to be alone and to suffer from loneliness. Being a Nyo means that you are part of a movement, of a family. You are good. You are just. You can do anything in the name of the Nyos and still be virtuous." Yan raised his hands, sounding like a preacher on a religious TV channel.

Tanya clapped enthusiastically. The pitch was as brilliant as it was predatory. It turned murder into environmentalism, turning humans into recruits. Part of her was horrified at how much she wanted to believe it herself. After so many years of being prey, it was refreshing to be on the predator side.

"Thank you, Tanya." Yan fell backward into his chair with a theatrical collapse, his arms spread wide like an actor taking a bow.

"Beautiful," Tanya said, "but will it work?"

"Tanya, darling! If there's one thing I know how to do, other than being great in bed, it's user acquisition. You will be the hottest brand in Canada." His eyes had a glazed, unfocused quality, like he'd had three drinks too many. "Potentially the hottest trend in the world," he added, taking out a cigarette and lighting it up.

The flame brightened the room for an instant. Tanya's vampire senses caught every note—the sulfur from the match, the first burn of paper, the tobacco underneath. The familiarity of "darling" should have annoyed her, but coming from Yan, it sounded more like a sales pitch.

Tanya's chest warmed. As a child, other than for sexual exploitation, she had never felt wanted. She was never cool, never inside society's circle. She'd spent years invisible, disposable. Now she was a vampire running a recruitment campaign for her den, and finally—*finally*—she belonged. Her den was going to be the coolest thing in the entire world. She would be the center of the circle.

She leaned forward. "When do we launch?"

CHAPTER
NINETEEN

James's pen tapped against his office desk. *Tap. Tap. Tap.* The last two sentences stared back at him from the screen. He'd been at this since six in the morning. The prophecy refused to yield its secrets.

Catalysts of fire, water, air, and earth will come. They'll cast the last spell to end the time of man.

Kador had an incredible talent to predict the future. It was James's job to act accordingly and save humanity. He had to fight magic from coming back with all his might, and right now, it was an uphill battle.

No good things came easily.

He stood to leave for the morning briefing with the president when he noticed a strange email with the subject line "Urgent: Major Risk to Pandora."

That was the code name for his office in the White House, and the email was from one of his people, a Kildare loyalist in the NSA leadership.

He read it.

Hello, Secretary James,

Please be advised that Project Pandora is at high risk. In this morning's briefing of the NSA leadership, we have been instructed by the head of the NSA to create an immediate contingency plan for "pivoting toward embracing the positive change humanity is undergoing and prepare for a peaceful resolution of the situation we are in."

Rumors are that similar messages came from other ministries and other government offices.

Best regards,

Jordan Silva

JAMES'S JAW TIGHTENED. His fingers remained frozen on the mouse. The email sat there, each line worse than the last. Honestly, he'd expected this. Just not today.

A few very powerful and rich people had started developing magical powers. This left the president with a difficult choice—forfeit the funding coming from these donations and continue with the current plan, or pivot to a more accepting and accommodating direction toward "unnatural powers." James knew that money was stronger than any goodwill toward the future of humanity.

In addition to the wealthy individuals and their lobbyists, there was public outcry against the laws passed in some states banning wizards from work or health services. The administration was pressured by both the left, who believed that wizards were humans, and the right, who wanted economic stability, for them to make things right, and resume normalcy. The polls showed the support for the president was at an all-time low.

James made his way from his small office in the White House to the presidential morning briefing. The war on magic had been the top story of the press for the last month, and the president demanded daily reports.

Today, the president was preoccupied with his phone during the entire meeting. The briefing focused on reports of hunger strikes across the US in solidarity with the wizards. The reports indicated that, in many states, wizards were not allowed into establishments and were going hungry.

After the report ended, the president stood, tucked his phone in his pocket, and walked out. He didn't glance at James. Didn't nod. Didn't acknowledge his existence. That had never happened before.

On James's way back to his office, the president's chief of staff, Janet Holmes, stopped him in the corridor. Janet was an icy bitch and had always behaved as though she hated him. James recalled the report that showed the chief of staff's boyfriend was a wizard who'd been refused service in a hospital after a car accident and had passed away shortly after. People had the irrational tendency to take things personally and lose sight of the larger perspective.

"Hi, James. I just talked with the president. You're to excuse yourself from tonight's summit." Janet smiled. Her eyes didn't.

The summit had been planned for weeks. *His* summit. *His* keynote address. Industry leaders, government officials, press... The goal was to win the hearts and minds of this audience to support the War on Magic. This didn't make sense.

"What?" James bit out.

Janet said nothing.

"What do you mean?" James stammered. "I'm the keynote speaker! I demand to speak to the president." He started to go back to the Oval Office.

She grabbed his arm. "I was told to have security escort you out of the White House if you make a scene." Janet's voice was calm and cold, and she looked straight into his eyes, her face close to his. "James, please make a scene. Make my day."

Am I getting fired?

James turned on his heel and walked back down the corridor. Every intern and staffer in the hallway suddenly had somewhere else to be.

His office door clicked shut behind him. He stood with his back against it for ten seconds before moving to his desk.

The day dragged on. James sent an email to Scott, the head of the NSA. No reply. He sent another to the Deputy Director of Homeland Security. No reply. He refreshed his inbox. Nothing. He opened his sent folder. Fifteen emails sent. Zero responses.

His phone buzzed constantly as texts from his inner circle flooded in. "What's going on? We've been locked out of the summit prep room." "My access badge won't work on the third floor anymore." "Did something happen? Nobody's answering my calls."

James stared at the messages. He had no answers to give them. The speculations were flying, and people were agitated, but he had nothing to tell them.

The pattern was clear. Active conversations had gone cold. Phone calls went to voicemail. He was being systematically isolated.

James opened a blank document and started typing plans for what they would do without government support, contingencies, and alternatives. Making effective plans in uncertain times was always something James excelled at. They had to be successful with or without the US administration. He was as determined as ever.

The day was nearing its end when James turned on the TV in his office, poured himself a glass of whiskey, and watched the coverage of the summit. His summit! His head tilted back against his chair, and his eyes closed slowly. The reporter's voice droned on. Smoke filled his vision. No, that was the dream. He jerked awake. The TV showed a shot of the White House. His eyes closed again. Cities burning. The prophecy in letters of fire. A voice screaming. From the dream? From the TV?

Hands grabbed his arms. James's eyes shot open. He was moving, being pulled. His chair tipped backward.

"Sir, we need to move now!"

The voice was right in his ear. Two agents, one on each arm. His feet scraped the floor as they hauled him up.

"What is happening?" he demanded.

Their pull was so violent, and their grip was iron. He'd never been treated like this in his life. They were running down the corridor at breakneck speed despite his efforts to stop them.

"Sir," the Secret Service agent screamed, holding his left arm, "you are being evacuated to the presidential bunker. There has been an attack on multiple government representatives. Please stop resisting and come with us."

James stopped fighting.

At the end of the corridor, a heavy steel door opened. They pushed him through. The bunker was bright, clinical, and cold.

A junior press officer and several mid-level Army officers were already inside. Three big TVs on the wall broadcasted news from the top channels. Every screen showed Washington burning. "Attack on Washington" was the caption that caught James's eye.

The footage alternated between a few repeating clips—the summit building in flames with fire department trucks rolling in, a helicopter view of Washington showing multiple sources of fires across the city, and what appeared to be a live standoff in front of the White House.

"Secretary James Webber! Thank God you are here!" The press officer's voice shook. "There has been a terrible attack. Did you see the news?"

"No," James said dryly. "What's happened?"

Relief washed across the press officer's face. He looked like he was still in college, not nearly old enough for a position of power.

"There have been attacks on multiple government offices. The Top of the Hill Conference Center was completely demolished. Most ministry buildings are under attack from what appears to be a very organized group of wizards." The press officer's left eye twitched as he said the word "wizards."

"There are several police reports of houses across the city being burned to ashes in a matter of minutes," the officer added.

An Army officer joined their conversation. She was plain-looking and taller than the press officer, almost as tall as James. "Secretary Webber, I am Lieutenant Marie Ortega, Intelligence." She shook his hand with a firm grip.

"Ortega," James said, "what can you add?"

"They are correlating the attacks, and they seem to be targeting every top branch of the government. We think most Supreme Court judges and Cabinet secretaries were hit in this strike. The reports from the summit are catastrophic, sir. We do not think anyone survived." She released his hand. Her face showed nothing. Not fear, not shock, not grief.

"Am I the designated survivor?" James asked.

"No, sir." The press officer swallowed hard. His face had gone pale. "As far as I know, you were supposed to be relieved of duty tonight. I was preparing the press release when all of this happened."

"Oh." It was all James could think of saying.

"Sir," Ortega said. Her voice was steady, but James heard uncertainty underneath. "The designated survivor, the secretary of agriculture, was on his way here. His armed limo was hit on the way. We have reports he did not make it."

James took a deep breath. His hands grabbed his face, his fingers digging into his temples. *What a shit show.*

He turned back to the TVs. The broadcast was from a news

chopper focusing on the yard in front of the White House. The screen showed a woman gripping an officer with one hand, the other hand glowing with a yellow-red fireball.

"What is happening in front of the White House?" James asked.

"An unidentified woman took a police officer hostage, sir," Ortega said. "The Secret Service negotiator is trying to control the situation. They are seeking the White House administration's approval in order to take action in front of the news media."

She looked at him quietly. What was she expecting him to say? He didn't understand. The silence continued for a few more seconds.

"Sir," she finally said, "as far as we know, you are the only survivor of the entire top executive branch."

Oh. James tilted his head. It finally hit him. *The White House administration...is me now.*

He moved closer to the TV screen that shot the incident from a better angle. The woman turned toward the camera. James recognized that face immediately. Rosy Underwood. The fucking bitch who had almost killed him when she blew up his government facility. She was speaking. A video appeared to be captured from a smartphone camera and streamed on a few social platforms.

The entire world was watching fucking Rosy Underwood.

"Turn the sound up," James said, and the press officer complied.

"This was a mistake!" Tears covered Rosy's cheeks. Her mouth pulled down in a deep frown. "We want our lives back! We are humans too! We deserve rights! We deserve health! We deserve to live. We are hungry!"

"Release the officer, and we can talk." The negotiator's voice came through, muffled and distant. "It's all going to be okay."

"Shoot to kill," James said in a flat voice, turning to Lieutenant Ortega. "Relay that message to the Secret Service officer in charge."

"But, sir," the press officer said, "there are hundreds streaming this. We can't just kill her like that."

James ignored him completely. He looked at Ortega. "Do I need to repeat myself, Lieutenant?"

"No, sir," Ortega said. She picked up the phone.

James turned back to the screen. A moment later, a shot was heard. The camera shook and went out of focus. When it stabilized again, Rosy Underwood had a hole in the middle of her chest, blood oozing down her dirty blue shirt.

Rosy looked down at her chest in shock then said, "Shit," before she blew the officer's head off with her fireball. His body hadn't yet hit the ground when two more large fireballs left her hands, evaporating the negotiator and hitting the White House.

The camera destabilized again as the person holding it ran away from the scene. The stream switched to a news chopper's view. The tiny figure was shooting fireballs all across the White House.

James could feel the impact in the bunker. It was slight but noticeable.

"Take her out!" he screamed at Ortega. "Shoot her, burn her, blow her up. I do not care. I want her fucking dead!"

Ortega said a few things on her phone.

The chopper camera showed threads of light converging from the sky and the White House roof. Multiple weapons, all calibers, all firing at once. Rosy's figure disappeared. What remained was a pool of blood and scattered pieces. For a second, it all looked very calm, especially because the screams were not picked up by the chopper camera.

Good riddance.

James walked back from the screen and studied the entire

wall of news coverage. One TV screen in the center of the wall showed his photo. Underneath was the title "Secretary James Webber reportedly the sole top-ranking survivor of the executive branch of the government." Soon, all of the screens showed his face on the media wall.

James smiled. Sometimes good things did come easily. This was panning out to be a very good day.

CHAPTER TWENTY

"...A bitch!"

Brenda's lips twitched into a smile despite everything. Valor swearing. She kinda liked it.

Valor's hands moved in patterns. Light blazed from his fingertips, and the air crackled with magic. Then words filled her vision, appearing one after another in rapid fire.

Valor's hand shot to his forehead. "Haste Self" appeared in her vision. Suddenly, he moved in double-time, his body blurring at the edges like a film played too fast.

His hand touched his chest. "Critical Heal." Blue light exploded across his body, bright enough to make her squint. Brenda watched the gash on his forehead knit itself closed, skin flowing together like water. His broken shoulder snapped back into place with an audible pop that made her wince. Bruises faded from purple to yellow to nothing in seconds. Blood still soaked his clothes, but underneath, his skin was whole.

The gnome king's scream tore through the hall, dark spit covering his lips.

Odel thrashed against his restraints, face going from red to purple to blue. His eyes bulged, his veins standing out on his neck as his body fought for air it couldn't get.

The bailiff stood frozen over Valor, the iron rod still raised, his face caught between surprise and confusion.

Valor's eyes locked on Odel. His finger pointed at the dwarf's face. Blue light shot out and hit the gag. "Teleport Object, Partial Fail." The words appeared in her vision as Valor grunted in pain, clutching his hand to his chest.

Brenda's eyes snapped to Odel. Half the gag lay on the ground. The other half had simply vanished, leaving a clean edge where it had been severed. Odel gasped, sucking in air.

Valor pointed at the dwarf again, and blue light flashed around Odel's body. "Major Heal" flashed in Brenda's vision. Odel's open wounds started to close rapidly, and his skin turned from purple to his normal brown.

Valor finally looked at her. His eyes were blue, hard, and cool in a way that made her fear him a little. He was not the young elf she knew. This was a cold and hard elvish prince.

He pointed at her. "De-Spell Magical Object." The Necklace of Brathloom around her neck fell apart, its beads scattering on the ground.

"Minor Heal." All the pain in her body went away in a split second. Her mind felt clear for the first time since she had been dragged into the mountain. Did the healing magic clear the drug's effect?

Valor dropped into a fencing stance and whispered words Brenda couldn't hear.

"Summon Sword." The spell name appeared in her vision. The last time he'd tried this, with the zombies, it had failed. Would it work now?

Golden light coalesced in Valor's hands, solidifying into a blade. The sword was beautiful, royal, the polished metal reflecting the light in the hall. His fingers closed around the grip.

It worked!

Valor moved fast as lightning. One moment, he was standing. The next moment, his sword was buried in the bailiff's chest. The blade punched through the gnome's back, black blood dripping from the golden metal.

Brenda's breath stopped in her throat. She'd never seen Valor being violent. Not like this.

The bailiff's eyes went wide, his mouth opening in silent surprise. Valor pulled the sword free, and the gnome crumpled. People died here. This wasn't a game.

But there was no time to process. Valor grabbed the heavy rod the bailiff had been holding, snatching it from the air before it hit the ground. He threw it to Odel, who was already on his feet. The dwarf caught it effortlessly, spinning the massive weapon in a way that looked to Brenda very heroic.

We might get out of this alive.

Brenda glanced behind Valor, and her optimism died.

The thing towered twelve feet tall, all metal and grease. Red eyes glowed in a face that was almost human but wrong in every way. Bulky limbs hung at its sides, each one thick enough to crush bone. Dark grease dripped from its joints.

"Synthetics! Kill the prisoners!" The gnome king's scream echoed through the hall.

Movement flickered in her peripheral vision. Brenda spun. A greasy giant robot stood behind her. She twisted to look at Odel. A third lurked behind him.

They were surrounded.

Valor pointed at her and Odel, then touched his own mouth. "Private Conversation."

Valor's voice boomed inside her head. "Get ready."

Brenda gasped. It was like someone had opened a door in

her mind. She could feel them there, Valor and Odel, their presence sitting in her consciousness like houseguests. Valor felt cool and calm. Odel felt solid like stone. It was intimate in a way that made her uncomfortable and whole all at once.

"Brenda." Valor's telepathic voice cut through her awe. "Fireballs. Hit the synthetics as hard as you can. Odel, free your parents. We need their help. Everyone, stay out of the synthetics' reach. I'll hold them off."

"My parents!" Odel's mental voice cracked with emotion. "Yes. Yes, I'll get them."

Brenda smiled. Time to fireball some synthetics' asses.

"*Valashi!*" her voice boomed.

Heat gathered in Brenda's palms, building until her fingertips glowed orange. She thrust her hands forward, and three fireballs erupted from her hands, one after another. They flew straight, trailing flame, and slammed into the synthetics' chests. Fire bloomed across greasy metal. The synthetics staggered back a step. Grease ignited, sending up black smoke.

But when the flames cleared, the metal underneath looked undamaged. They weren't even slowed down. Their hands turned into a collection of knives and needles which they swung toward her and Valor.

Brenda threw another fireball. The magic gathered in her palms then stopped like hitting a wall. Without any apparent reason it reversed, slamming back into her hands with the force of a hammer blow. Pain exploded through her palms and shot up her arms. Her skull felt like it was splitting open from the inside.

She gasped and pulled her hands against her chest, her fingers trembling. The magic had backfired! That had never happened before.

Valor never stopped moving or casting.

"Armor Skin." His body shimmered, his skin taking the gray shade of stone.

"Lightning Speed." He became a blur until he gave a grunt of pain. One spell failed.

"Rapid Rust." Brown spread across the synthetic's arm.

"Enhanced Sword." His blade blazed brighter and then faded. He gave another grunt. Another failure.

"Lightning Sword." Electricity crackled down the golden blade.

Valor's sword smashed into the synthetic's arm, breaking off knives and needles, but the synthetic was faster. Its other arm lashed out, its claws raking across Valor's chest.

Blood. So much blood. It soaked through his shirt in seconds.

No. No no no.

Brenda's hands were up and glowing before her brain caught up. "Heal!" The spell came from somewhere deep, instinctive, and desperate.

Blue light washed over Valor. His wounds closed, flesh knitting itself together at unnatural speed. He glanced back at her for a split second, surprise in his eyes, then turned back to the fight.

She had healed him.

Awesome.

Valor brought his sword down on the robot's attacking hand and took it clean off at the bulky metal elbow joint. The arm fell off with a loud metal sound, but the synthetic took the opportunity to hit Valor's back with its other arm. Valor grunted in pain, and Brenda cast another healing spell.

Exhaustion crashed over Brenda like a wave. Too many spells. Too fast. She'd felt this before, the weakness that came before passing out.

Something slammed into her shoulder from behind.

The world exploded in pain. Her shoulder burst into white-hot agony so intense she couldn't think, couldn't breathe, couldn't scream. That blow could have hit her head. Some distant part of her brain was grateful it hadn't, but that thought was tiny, drowned in the ocean of pain.

The world spun. She was falling.

Brenda caught a glimpse of the synthetic behind her, its arm covered in knives and needles, pulling back for another strike.

"Heal." The word came out on instinct, a gasp more than a spell.

Blue light flickered across her shoulder. The aching dulled from unbearable to merely terrible. Her arm was still screaming, still useless, but she was conscious and alive.

The synthetic stood over her. For a moment, it didn't see her, its head swiveling slowly like it couldn't track targets on the ground. Then its red eyes locked on her.

Brenda tried to move, but her body wouldn't respond. The exhaustion, the pain, the blood loss...

She was done.

The synthetic's arms raised high, needles glinting.

This was it. This was how she would die.

Metal screamed.

The synthetic's head caved inward like a crushed can. A hammer, massive and shining, had struck it from behind with the force of a freight train. The robot toppled forward. As it fell, one needle on its left hand caught Brenda's thigh, tearing through fabric and skin.

Fresh pain exploded. She gasped, too tired to scream.

Behind the falling synthetic stood a dwarf. Not Odel. This one was larger and older with a gray, braided beard. He held the massive war hammer like it weighed nothing. Odel's father, clearly.

Brenda struggled to her feet, keeping weight off her shredded leg. Through the pain and exhaustion, she saw the tide had turned. Three dwarves surrounded one synthetic. Odel and his parents moved like they'd fought together for centuries, their hammers rising and falling in practiced rhythm. The synthetics tried to defend themselves, but three war hammers were too much. Metal dented, then cracked, then caved.

Valor dueled the last synthetic, his sword a blur of lightning and steel. Each strike targeted joints and other weak points. The synthetic's arms fell away. Its legs buckled. Then it went down.

Brenda pointed shaking hands at Valor and the dwarves. "Heal. Heal." Blue light washed over them, closing wounds, restoring strength with her last reserves of magic.

The final synthetic tried to rise. Odel's father brought his hammer down on its head. The red eyes flickered and died.

Silence fell over the throne room except for their ragged breathing. The synthetics lay in pieces. They'd won.

Valor lowered his sword and swayed on his feet. The dwarves leaned on their hammers, their chests heaving.

"You fools."

The gnome king's voice, dripping with malice, came from behind them.

Everyone spun. The king sat on his throne, completely unharmed, a smile splitting his face. "You think that was all of them? You think three synthetics was my army?" He laughed, the sound echoing off stone walls. "I have hundreds of thousands of them. You've seen nothing. The world will burn under my mechanical soldiers. Every kingdom, every city, every pitiful living creature will kneel or die."

His hand rose slowly, theatrically. He placed it over a large red button set into the throne's armrest.

"I love this part," the gnome king said dramatically.

He waited another second and pressed the button.
A deafening siren filled the hall.
They hadn't won at all.

CHAPTER TWENTY-ONE

"Oh, snap!" Lixi said.

She heard sirens. Had she tripped some defensive magic rune?

All the robot eyes turned bright red, and a siren echoed in the distance. The heavy metal door behind her started opening, revealing layers upon layers of different metals. Walls shifted and moved, and a huge corridor opened up behind her leading upwards.

In front of her, the robot army was starting to move toward her, up the corridor. These things stood twelve feet tall, greasy steel plates for skin, hydraulic joints hissing with each step. One of the robots raised its metal arm. A metal rod tipped with wire extended from the robot's arm. The robot zapped Lixi as she was turning to look at the corridor behind her. It nailed it straight on her ass.

Lixi almost fell to the ground. That hurt worse than a wasp sting! She bared her teeth at the greasy metal thing. Sparks of green magic danced between her clenched fists.

Ice spears shot from her palms, piercing through metal

chests. Wind cyclones lifted some robots and smashed them into walls with a satisfying crunch. Fireballs exploded against robot heads, melting their glowing red eyes into slag. Several robots crumpled, metal screeching. Others sparked, their arms twitching uselessly.

But there were too many of them. She was able to destroy about two hundred, but there were many thousands of them.

Another robot next to her raised its rod-like arm, and Lixi decided to do what royalty had been doing since the start of history in the face of danger—she ran away to save her ass.

The corridor was large enough for her to fly faster than the robots despite the fact that her wings and butt hurt like hell. The robots were fast as well and coordinated enough to move very rapidly together after her in the corridor. She was able to keep the distance but not grow it significantly.

Her wings burned. Each beat felt like knives in her shoulder blades.

Behind her, the coordinated thunder of metal feet never stopped, never slowed.

She counted wingbeats to keep herself focused. Five hundred. A thousand. The corridor stretched endlessly ahead.

After a long while, the corridor opened into a great hall. The cavern stretched five stories high, carved pillars holding up the distant ceiling. It looked like a typical royal dwarf reception hall. Lixi often wondered if the dwarves were compensating for their height. She wrinkled her nose. Dwarf halls never used to smell like unwashed socks and machine oil.

Then she saw her friends! There was Brenda, who she really liked, and her wonderful Valor! How did they get here? Were they here for the cupcakes? They didn't look hungry, but more... frightened. Brenda's face had drained of color. Valor stood frozen, his fingers white-knuckled on his sword hilt.

Oh, shit. They were not looking at her at all. They were seeing the crazy robots behind her!

"This is bad! This is really, really bad!" Lixi could easily save herself, but saving her friends required dealing with the freakin' robots.

Fine. Time to work.

She twisted in the air, flying backward, and thrust both hands forward. "Oxidus!"

The spell hit the front line. Metal corroded instantly, robots collapsing into piles of rust-eaten scrap. Ten down.

"Meltus!"

The next wave melted, steel dripping like water. Another eight gone.

"Dustarus!"

More crumbled to dust, atomizing in gray clouds.

But for every robot she destroyed, three more stomped forward. The corridor was packed with them, wall to wall, a seemingly endless army of greasy steel. Her spells barely made a dent. It was like trying to empty the ocean with a teaspoon.

At the speed she was flying and the robots after her, she had about fifteen more seconds before the first wave of robots reached her friends. This was all the time she had, and there wasn't any magic she could think of that she, by herself, could cast to solve this.

Then it hit her. She was not alone.

She tapped immediately into Valor's powers. Water crashed into her, cold and fresh like a mountain stream. Next, she reached out and offered her bond to Brenda. To her surprise, the young human immediately understood the mental request and accepted it. Fire flooded through Lixi's veins, warm and fierce. She already had air from her own fairy nature, but for the magic she was planning, she still needed earth.

She quickly sent a mental thought to Valor. *"Is the dwarf next to you a friend?"*

"Yes, I trust him with my life," Valor replied instantly.

Nice. The elf could make decisions fast when it mattered.

Lixi tried to bond with the dwarf, and he looked around like someone tapped him on the shoulder. She tried again and again, but the silly young dwarf did not get the hint. She had seven more seconds.

Valor must have felt all that because he softly tapped the dwarf on the head. "Open your heart and say 'Yes' in your mind."

The dwarf scratched his beard, frowning at the empty air around his head, but he did as he was told. Earth slammed into her, solid and ancient as mountains.

Now Lixi had all the elements of magic at her disposal. She was all-powerful. Well, even more all-powerful than usual.

She turned around and cast Portal to Another World between them and the robots. The portal ripped open between her and the army, a shimmering oval twenty feet tall and wide. Through it, she could see rivers of molten rock flowing through a hellscape of black stone and red sky. Heat blasted through, making the air ripple.

Simultaneously, she cast an illusion spell. The robots would keep seeing her friends instead of the lava world they were running toward.

As a kid, Lixi used to cast Portal to Another World just to peek at other places, sometimes even hopping through for quick visits outside the fairy world. The Lava World had been one of her least favorite destinations. Not a single cupcake. Just fire and death and the smell of burning rock.

Back home, this spell had been easy. A child's game. Here, though? Even with the powers she borrowed from her friends, her hands shook with the effort and sweat poured down her face. The portal wavered, the edges rippling like water. She gritted her teeth and poured more power into it. Her vision tunneled, darkness creeping from all sides, but she held it steady.

It was extremely hard to maintain such a powerful spell at such a wide area for such a long time, especially with the weird problems magic had had in the last six hundred years, but Lixi was that kind of awesome fairy.

Need thousands of robots to see something that wasn't there?

Keep them marching forward into lava instead of stopping?

Lixi got you covered!

In the next five minutes, the silly bad robots dashed straight into a hellish pit of lava. Lixi heard screams in gnomish, then the ring of steel on steel and Valor's voice chanting a spell. Her friends were fighting for their lives, but she had to focus on maintaining her spell.

When the last robot went through the wall, Lixi closed the portal and stopped the illusion. Immediately, her wings gave out mid-flutter. The floor rushed up. She tried to slow herself, but her arms wouldn't respond. Stone slammed into her shoulder, then her hip, then her face. She tasted rock.

She couldn't feel her fingertips. Her wings folded against her back, too heavy to move. The ceiling spun above her. Or was she spinning? Stone pressed cold against her cheek. Giant boots stomped near her head. Brenda's boots, scuffed leather. Valor's boots, elven soft-sole.

It was a strange angle to look at her friends from the ground gazing up. Brenda had more hair on her legs than Valor.

The fight was over. Valor was holding the gnome king by the throat with one hand, raising him up in the air. Blood dripped from a cut on the elf's arm. Valor's jaw was set, his eyes cold as winter. The gnome king was crying, begging for his life, raising his hands above his head. Lixi knew gnomes would sell both their fathers and several of their mothers to get a good deal, let alone save their lives.

"Please let me go, I have five kids and two wives!" Warmth spread through the room, soft and cloying like honey. The gnome king was casting a strong and effective natural empathy spell.

Pity rose in Lixi's chest. Poor little creature. So small, so scared...

No.

She shoved the foreign emotion away. She'd felt gnome manipulation before. This king was as pitiful as a cobra. But it was definitely affecting everyone in the room. Tears welled in Brenda's eyes as she watched the small creature plead. Odel's face softened, pity in his eyes.

But Valor resisted the spell. Using their shared link, he cast his own powerful spell. He looked into the king's eyes and said, "Evil to Ash."

The king evaporated into a pile of gray ash that smelled like sulfur and an evening after eating too much bean stew. Valor opened his hand, and the ash scattered, drifting to the stone floor.

Brenda threw up in the corner.

CHAPTER TWENTY-TWO

The red light on the camera blinked on. James felt the heat from the studio lights and saw his reflection in the black lens staring back at him. Behind the camera, three technicians watched in silence. The teleprompter began scrolling. He took one calming breath, kept his expression grave, and controlled his breathing to steady his voice. The performance had to be perfect. The junior press officer had drilled into him that he needed to sound like a father breaking bad news and look like a man bearing an impossible burden.

"My fellow Americans," James said to the camera. "We have suffered one of the greatest losses in the history of our nation, one that will remain in the history and collective memory of our country for all time. Today, at eight p.m. Eastern time, a vicious attack took place in Washington. Our president, vice president, all members of Congress, all members of the Supreme Court, and countless leaders in the US government were murdered in a horrible terrorist attack by a group of unnatural power wielders. These evil wizards have attacked our country at its core, intending to overthrow the government."

James paused. Five seconds, the press officer had said. Let the news land. The term "evil wizard" was an addition made by the junior press officer. James still could not remember the press officer's name, but the phrase was perfect. Childish, almost.

That was the point. "Evil wizard" sounded like a fairy tale villain. It made the enemy something simple to hate and easy to fear. Killing an "evil wizard" was a good thing to do. Four syllables of pure propaganda.

James watched the camera lens, imagining millions of faces going slack with shock. He counted silently. The studio stayed quiet around him. The technicians didn't move.

After five seconds passed, he continued.

"But we are strong! We are resilient! We have a succession plan, and we shall not perish or go quietly into the night!" James delivered the line exactly as rehearsed, his voice rising with carefully measured emotion and passion. "My name is James Webber. I served as the secretary leading the effort against unnatural powers. As the next in succession, I am now the acting President of the United States of America."

On the monitor to his left, a red stripe appeared at the bottom of the screen—Secretary James Webber was sworn in to become the 49th President of the United States of America.

Good! Right on time.

Three hundred million Americans and countless people around the world were learning he was in control. He'd activated the wartime broadcasting directive an hour ago. Every channel on every network was forced to carry his speech uninterrupted. No talking heads to spin his message. Just him speaking directly to the American people.

"With the help of the armed forces, the Capitol police have managed to eradicate the danger. We have retaliated and, as far as we know, destroyed every evil wizard within the greater city limits. If you are a non-hostile wizard, you are ordered to leave the city within the next five hours or be considered armed and dangerous. We will not hesitate to protect our city and our citizens. We are in times of war, and magical creatures of all kinds are considered dangerous. In the coming hours, I will form a temporary cabinet of the remaining leaders of the government. We are working hard to reestablish the branches of the government and working with the military to take decisive actions against this attack on our sovereignty."

Remaining leaders of the government. What a joke. Within twenty-four hours, every cabinet position would belong to someone from Kildare. His people. The ones who'd been preparing for this moment, who knew the real plan. No more bureaucrats worried about polls and public opinion. Just efficient, loyal operators who understood that extreme threats required extreme solutions.

And now came the stick. Finally. James felt the weight lift from his shoulders. No more committees, no more oversight, no more limitations, no more politics. Just power to do the right thing immediately.

"In order to protect the government and you, the citizens, we are extending the Protection Against Unnatural Powers Act. Every person with unnatural powers should be considered a national risk to our country, as well as a personal risk to you and to your loved ones. We have designated Los Angeles as a gathering city for all law-abiding wizards. Every person with unnatural powers is ordered by the new act extension to relocate to Los Angeles. We will provide buses and train tickets to those who cooperate. Those who comply will be protected, housed, and provided for in designated safe zones." He fixed his gaze on the camera, his jaw set. "I call upon all wizards: I urge you to stop attacking innocent citizens and government officials. We will not harm you if you comply immediately with our transfer order. If you are not a wizard, please evacuate Los Angeles as soon as you can."

This part of the plan had been Marie Ortega's idea. She'd pointed out that LA already had the largest population of people with unnatural powers, and the magically enhanced drug wars of the last few weeks had driven out most of the non-magical civilians. She suggested it would be simpler for the Army to control and deal with a highly concentrated hostile population when there were no innocents left to worry about.

James had already decided she would make an excellent Secretary of Defense. Anyone who could be so cold and effective deserved a position in his cabinet.

"Anyone with unnatural powers found outside of Los Angeles after eleven PM Eastern time this Friday will be considered an active terrorist and will be dealt with appropriately." He looked directly into the camera, his expression cold. "Anyone aiding a person with unnatural powers after the next forty-eight hours has passed will also be considered an active terrorist and will be dealt with appropriately." He nodded, face grim.

"Let me be clear—hiding, feeding, housing, and transacting in any way with any wizard will be considered a wartime crime and will be severely punished. We will not tolerate treason within the borders of the United States of America. Humans helping wizards will be considered enemies of the State. If you encounter a wizard, please call the authorities or dial 911. If you see something, say something. We must remain vigilant for our safety and for our country."

End the shit sandwich with a little bit of hope. The formula never failed—terror, then comfort. Beat them down, then offer a hand. They would be so grateful for the hope that they wouldn't question the rest.

"Your government is committed to protecting you. Our military is strong and committed to protecting you, and your police and emergency forces are on the highest alert. We will overcome this great tragedy. We will survive this horrible attack. Our allies are coming to our aid, and we will continue to keep a watchful eye on our enemies."

And now to close the deal. The closing line was always the most important. James added some warmth to his voice and softened his gaze at the camera lens. *Give them something to feel good about. Make them part of something bigger.*

"God bless you. God bless all who lost their lives today, their families, their friends—and God bless America."

James Webber, the 49th President of the United States of America, faded from the screen, and the US flag appeared on the teleprompter. The red light blinked off.

James allowed himself a small, private smile. Perfect. The speech would play on every channel for the next hour. By morning, the buses to Los Angeles would be full.

He stepped away from the camera.

Done. He had a war to win and a country to run.

CHAPTER TWENTY-THREE

"Press the unmute button, Boris!" Tanya repeated.

Tanya's shoulders shook with loving laughter as she watched Boris navigate his side of the video call. The ancient vampire really did not know his way around technology. His face was too close to the camera one moment, too far the next, like he couldn't figure out the right distance. For once, she was the one teaching him. She'd been born into a world with technology and felt comfortable using it.

Boris finally found the unmute button. "Yes, found it! How are you doing, Tanyushka?" he asked in a loud voice, as if he needed to speak up to carry his voice over the ocean.

Tanya had been anticipating this call. So much had happened in the month since they'd last spoken, so many things to share. Making Boris proud mattered more than she liked to admit, even to herself. She felt that flutter in her chest again, the desire to show him everything she'd accomplished.

"Doing well, Boris. We are already five hundred strong." She kept her voice casual, leaning back in her chair with studied nonchalance, even as immense pride expanded in her chest.

His eyes, looking, of course, in the wrong direction, widened slowly. He blinked twice, as if checking he'd heard correctly.

"Wonderful, Tanyushka! How did you manage to get so many vampires turned so fast?" He leaned forward, his eyes bright with genuine delight, and Tanya felt the unfamiliar flush of being seen, truly seen, as capable.

"With technology, Boris," she said. "We created an ad campaign for a set of night events across the city. We are now branching out to five other cities across Canada. I also acquired a marketing team."

She had hired the best agency money could buy. Then, she'd made them an offer they literally couldn't refuse. Turns out, marketing vampirism was easier when your marketing team actually were vampires.

"Together, we rebranded ourselves to Nyos," she continued. "We are the Nyo community, an exclusive club whose members are the next generation of humanity."

"Nyo community?" Boris repeated the phrase slowly, like he was testing its weight. His face scrunched, the way it always did when confronted with modern terminology that had no equivalent in the old languages he still thought in.

"Vampires have a bad reputation and did not test well in our surveys," Tanya continued.

Boris's eyes widened in surprise. "What do you mean, you're not vampires anymore? You are a vampire queen!"

"Yes, Boris, but humans these days do not appreciate the truth. They want lies to keep them comfortable in their lives and to feel safe and fulfilled," Tanya explained. "Nyo-clubs are by invitation only. We have tens of thousands of applications from all over the world. Fifty thousand applications last month alone and climbing. Nyos are stronger than ordinary humans, they live much longer, and they work at night to protect the environment."

"How does working at night protect the environment?" Boris asked, confused.

Initially, she wondered the same, but her marketing team had shown her the survey data, the focus group responses, and the social media engagement metrics. None of it had to *be* true. It just had to *feel* true, and apparently "protecting the environment" felt very true to people who wanted to feel good about themselves.

"It does not matter. One of the marketing researchers found that it's a compelling value proposition, so we added it, and it works!" A proud smile crossed her face when she mentioned her team, the kind she couldn't fake even if she had tried. "We have gotten a budget from three environmental non-profits because of this strategy."

"And what are zombies then? Special non-living?" Boris asked with a grin.

"You are starting to get it!" Tanya said with a smile. "Well, first, we do not really need a lot of zombies. We use them mainly as gatekeepers in our clubs. We choose only fresh, visually unharmed, and aesthetically pleasing bodies to create our 'Nyo-secondaries.' We make sure to cycle them out once they start to rot. We pick them carefully, so they last longest and have more brain capacity."

"Recycling zombies," Boris murmured, nodding slowly.

He had the look of a parent watching their child explain a school project about something completely outside his expertise—supportive, proud, and utterly lost—but that was fine. Tanya knew he didn't need to understand the details to trust that she knew what she was doing.

"How are you dealing with all the madness happening in the US? Such a violent nation, hunting their own wizards." Disdain dripped from every syllable. Boris shook his head slowly.

Tanya nodded. "We are taking advantage of that. Nyos are

the next evolution of humans. They are not wizards. They are the positive force that is created by humans working together to improve themselves."

Besides, nothing created better cover than chaos. While humans fought each other over magic, she was building something they wouldn't notice until it was too late.

"We are humanity's answer to unnatural forces. We are the truly natural forces," she said, stating the practiced marketing slogan.

He stared at her in silence. She looked at him, equally quiet. Neither of them moved for a long moment, the ridiculous pitch hanging between them for a long second.

"Truly natural forces." She'd actually said that with a straight face. About vampires. She bit the inside of her cheek.

Finally, Boris's eyes crinkled at the corners. Tanya felt a smile tugging her lips. Then they both broke, laughter spilling out simultaneously. It felt good to laugh with someone who understood exactly how insane all of this was and how perfectly, brilliantly, it would work anyway.

"Tanya, you are a genius! I want you to start your own sub dens after you finish with North America. Maybe a South American sub-den?" he asked.

Warmth flooded through her chest. Boris believed in her enough to offer this. He trusted her methods enough to let her expand beyond his direct oversight. She wanted to say yes immediately. She wanted to start planning tonight.

But she also knew better.

"Boris! That is a huge honor! However, I am not ready yet. I have just started this den."

Truth be told, she was already thinking about it. Chapter would be a much better name than den.

"Nonsense!" Boris shouted, leaning too close to the screen. His face filled her entire monitor, his nose almost pressed against his camera. She bit back another smile. "The elves are weak and few. The humans are fighting amongst themselves. You are doing so well. I want you to establish a strong base in Canada and start to branch out to the US within the next ten years."

"Boris, in ten years, I can conquer the entire world for you. These new times are fast." She met the camera straight on. "A whole country is easier to turn now than a single village was six hundred years ago." Not a hint of doubt touched her voice.

"Very well. If you can do it faster, do it. We are taking our time here in Europe. The humans here are confused and frightened by the American brutality toward wizards. The European Union is trying to pass wizards-protection regulations that will allocate funds for creating future legislation across the union." Boris's voice became slow, and he waved his hand in slow motion. "Everything in this EU is taking forever, and that is the way I like it."

She admired his patience, although she did not share it. She enjoyed going at her own fast pace.

"I do not think the new US President is going to let the European Union sign any protection laws. After the attack on Washington, the Americans are fighting strongly against any wizard claims to human law. They will face legal hell if wizards are protected in any way around the world. They might not block the European Union from being a sanctuary for wizards, but they will block any attempt to protect them internationally," Tanya said.

"Yes, Tanyushka, you understand these things better than I do." Boris waved one hand in a slow, dismissive gesture, and he leaned back against his chair. "You are doing well, Tanya. Just do not go too fast for your own good."

"Of course not, Boris. I will take it slower from now on," Tanya said.

They exchanged goodbyes, Boris fumbling with the end-call button for several seconds before his video feed finally went black.

The moment his face disappeared from her screen, Tanya's careful, modest expression melted away. She leaned back in her chair, a wide smile crossing her lips. Slower. Right.

Vampires, just like humans, sometimes needed an embellished truth.

CHAPTER TWENTY-FOUR

"Unicorn! The answer is unicorn!" Lixi said. She folded her wings and sat on the edge of a high rock. "Unicorn is the answer!"

They all turned to stare at her. Brenda's eyebrows shot up. Odel's mouth opened slightly, and Valor blinked twice. Was time working backward again?

The mountain chamber was quiet now, the distant echo of dwarf celebrations had finally faded. Torchlight flickered against stone walls.

They all sat in a circle. Brenda wore a festive red dwarvish dress that looked too short for her comfort since she kept tugging at the hem. Odel was in his royal clothes of leather and iron with battle-scarred hands resting on his knees, and Valor wearing his spotless light blue elvish attire that somehow never got dirty. Lixi, of course, had created the most festive magical royal gown she could think of, because why the hell not? It sparkled in green and white and was absolutely fabulous.

They had been partying for the last month in the true dwarvish spirit of taking your time when it came to celebrations. With the gnomes banished from the mountain forever and the dwarves taking over again, the first order of business was, of course, drinking and celebrating dwarf-style. Stone mugs the size of a medium boulder. Barrel after barrel of something that tasted like honey and fire.

Two weeks into the celebrations, they almost had a political catastrophe. Lixi, Valor, and Brenda were finishing a long night of drinking and dwarvish poetry reading. Brenda tapped her fingers on the table and yawned. She leaned toward Valor. "Can we maybe hurry Odel along a bit? We've been celebrating for two weeks straight."

Valor's eyes went wide. Lixi actually gasped.

"Brenda," Valor said, his voice dropping to a horrified whisper. "You can't rush a dwarf. That's incredibly rude."

"Offensive," Lixi added, shaking her head. "Like, really offensive."

Brenda sank lower in her seat. "Sorry. I didn't know."

"Well, now you do," Lixi said. "Never suggest hurrying a dwarf. Ever."

They never spoke of that indiscretion again.

For days the mountain halls shook with dwarf victory songs until Lixi's teeth rattled. She'd enjoyed seeing Brenda dance with Valor, her short dress twirling as he had spun her around, and even seeing Odel smile from time to time, his scarred face softening with each toast. The party itself was, of course, legendary.

Valor cleared his throat after Lixi's interruption. He straightened his shoulders, clearly trying for a formal posture and landing somewhere near stiff. "As I was saying, I gathered you all to ask you to help me with my quest, a quest that needs all of us, a quest to bring back magic to the world in full force. If there is anything the last battle has proven, it is that we must have strong and stable magic to battle evil," he said in a somber voice.

Lixi jumped to Brenda's shoulder and loudly whispered in her ear, "Why is he so serious? I have no idea what he is talking about, but it already sounds fishy."

Brenda could not hide her smile. "Give him a break, Lixi. This is the first time he is leading a team quest. I think he's a little anxious."

Valor gave them both a look. "You know I can hear you," he said quietly.

Lixi jumped back to her rock and tried to avoid Valor's glare.

Valor continued, and she felt his gaze on her. She had consumed too much sugar in the last two days. Those damn dwarves with their delicious cupcakes and cakes. She felt her tail wiggle from the sugar rush, and she didn't even have a tail! It was always so hard to concentrate after eating too many of those slices of heaven.

"As you know, for a level ten magic, you need wizards from all elements. We need fire, water, air, and earth. We have these in this room," he said, gesturing to his friends.

Something bothered Lixi about what Valor said, something she could not remember. It buzzed at the back of her head like an annoying butterfly. Truth be told, she'd never met a butterfly that wasn't a complete jackass. Always fluttering around like they owned the damn place. Her mind wandered to catching butterflies and showing them who's boss. She hummed to herself.

"Lixi!"

It was Brenda calling her. Her voice was like a schoolgirl nudging another schoolgirl to pay attention to the teacher. In her previous mission with Jin, Lixi heard a lot of that.

Lixi focused again on the present. Valor's eyes locked on to her.

"Do you, Lixi of the Fairy, agree to join the quest to bring back magic? To tirelessly and delicately work, fight, and use your magic to complete the quest? To follow me, Valor of the Elves, as the leader of the quest, and to protect and aid your quest's band as if they were your brothers?"

Having completed, and even led, endless quests in her life, Lixi knew the binding effect of the quest magic. She knew her answer would protect her but also force her onto a certain path of destiny. She had not joined a team quest in at least five hundred years.

They were all staring at her expectantly. The fresh glow of quest magic shimmered faintly around Brenda's wrists, around Odel's chest, around Valor's hands. She was the last to be asked to join. All the rest had already agreed and were bound to the magic.

Which meant Valor asked her last. Smart kid. He knew she was, by far, the most powerful wizard in this room, and custom dictated she join last so her power wouldn't pressure the others into saying yes.

"I do," she said.

The magic hit her immediately. Warmth bloomed in her chest and raced outward through her limbs and her wings, tingling at every fingertip. She could feel the others now, all three of them, like phantom heartbeats syncing with her own. It was so much like the temporary bond they'd struck during the battle, but unlike the battle, this quest bond would last much longer.

Brenda's magic pulsed bright and uncertain. Odel's felt solid as mountain stone. Valor's thrummed with nervous energy. Threads she couldn't see but definitely felt linked them all, binding them together. A band of wizards. Her band.

Using the new bond, Lixi could now get a better insight into her band members' motivations for joining the quest. Brenda was enjoying magic even more than Lixi enjoyed sugar. For Brenda, this was a fun and wild no-brainer. Odel felt deeply grateful to Valor and indebted to him and would do whatever the elf asked. He also wanted to explore the outer world after spending his entire life under the mountains. The fight with the gnome king made Valor realize that the only way to protect his loved ones was with strong magic. Lixi had seen the realization grow within him since the fight. Seeing his friends hurt had broken his heart, and saving them with his magic had mended it back together. And Lixi? Her motivation was always YOLO. Being immortal meant you had an extremely high risk tolerance and a "fuck it, let's give it a try" attitude.

Valor looked relieved, his shoulders finally dropping from where they'd been hunched up near his ears. Poor kid. He did not know how hard this was going to be and how high the cost. How did she know that? Was she remembering the future again?

"Okay, this should be pretty easy and painless," Valor said cheerfully, as if hearing her thoughts.

Valor opened his side stash and removed a small, golden scroll. The casing glowed painfully in Lixi's eyes, making them water. Static electricity made her hair stand on end. That was a powerful scroll. She had only seen a few like it in her lifetime.

"This is a scroll my father located and summoned a few weeks ago, using the magic power of the most powerful elvish wizards." He held it up. The sheathing glinted in the torchlight. "It is a spell at the highest level of power, level ten. It requires the power of all the major elements of magic. It will restore magic to its full and original power in the world."

He instructed them to sit in a circle and put their hands forward, channeling their power into the center. Lixi settled in a spot beside Brenda.

Valor placed the scroll on the stone floor between them with reverent care and smoothed the edges flat. He took a breath, then started chanting.

A stream of light emerged from Valor's hands and touched Brenda's hands first, then arced to Odel and finally to Lixi. Where it touched her skin, it was warm and ticklish and smelled of cinnamon.

Light emanated from all their hands, each in a different color—yellow from Brenda, brown from Odel, white from Lixi, and blue from Valor. The illuminated strands merged and collided into a whirlpool of colors and light, a tornado of power swirling faster and faster. Lixi's wings tickled and shivered. This was a powerful spell.

Valor continued chanting, and the words appeared in Lixi's mind. She started chanting them with all the rest. Their voices wove together, even Odel's low rumble finding harmony with their higher tones. The lights and the swirls blazed faster and brighter.

And then, it was gone. Not in a fantastic, wonderful way, but in a nauseating horrible way of a failed spell. The whirlpool stuttered and collapsed inward, and a wave of sickening foul energy burst from the scroll outward. It passed through them, cold and wrong, rippling out into the world beyond. The cinnamon smell turned sour and bitter. Lixi dropped to the floor like a zapped mosquito, her wings cramping, her ears ringing. Odel vomited to the side, and Brenda fell to her knees in a painful grunt.

Only Valor stood there, holding his hands forward, pale and trembling, his eyes wide and unblinking.

"It didn't work," he said softly.

Lixi picked herself off the ground and flew to the scroll lying on the stone floor. She touched it with careful hands. Weird. It did not burn like most scrolls once they failed. When her eyes landed on the scroll's words, she understood immediately what happened. The spell scope was too broad, the power requirements too high. *Oh, shit.*

"Valor, where did your father summon this scroll from?" she asked.

Valor stared at nothing, his jaw slack, like his brain was still trying to catch up with what just happened. "He did not tell me. He just said that it will bring magic back to this world in full force."

"Full force for sure. This is not a level ten magic. This scroll is way above that," Lixi said dryly.

"What do you mean? There is no higher level. Level ten is the highest level of magic in the world." he said.

"This world," Lixi corrected him.

"What?" Valor asked.

"This world, not the world where this scroll originated from. Your father got his hands on world-altering magic. This magic will transition this world from magical-enabled to magical-centered. That is definitely a higher-than-ten level scroll." Her voice dropped, all humor gone. The glow of the scroll shone on her face. "This is an awesome scroll of magic."

A small voice in her head spoke of a déjà vu. This moment, this scroll, felt horribly familiar, terribly wrong, and powerfully right. A shiver ran down her spine. *Did this already happen to me?* Time was such a weird thing.

"Then why did it fail? We have all the elements of power here in this room. We meet the requirements," Valor said.

Come on, pretty boy, use that elvish brain, she thought.

"You are meeting the requirement of a level ten scroll. You are missing one key requirement for this scroll," Lixi explained.

"What is it?" he asked.

They all looked at her. Had time moved sideways again?

"Unicorn! The answer is unicorn!" Lixi said.

CHAPTER TWENTY-FIVE

James woke with his cheek against the bathroom tile of his private, presidential lavatory, the chemical sting of disinfectant mixing with the sour stench of vomit. His vomit. He could see it splattered across the toilet, the floor, and the wall in front of him. His stomach lurched again but came up empty.

The fluorescent lights pulsed and swam above him. He squeezed his eyes shut. His shirt was plastered to his skin with sweat, cold now, making him shiver despite the stuffy air. Every breath tasted wrong, metallic and acidic.

Three deep breaths. In through his nose and out through his mouth.

The bathroom gradually stopped spinning. When he opened his eyes again, the tile stayed still.

What the hell had happened?

The last thing he remembered clearly was sitting down to do his business. Then, something had hit him. It was a wave of nausea so powerful it had felt like his insides were being ripped out through his throat. He'd barely made it off the toilet before collapsing. The nausea had overpowered him without warning. Total system failure. His body had simply...rebelled. For maybe ten seconds, it had felt like someone was trying to tear his soul out through his ribcage. Then nothing. Gone.

He had never gotten sick like this. He never got sick at all. This had been violent, instantaneous, inexplicable. It didn't make sense. His head still ached, and black dots drifted through his peripheral vision. He checked himself over. The vomit had missed his suit. Only his shoes needed attention. He grabbed paper towels from the dispenser and wiped them clean, methodical swipes until the leather gleamed again.

No need to waste time changing. He could go straight back to work. At least it had happened here, in private, where no one would see their new president on the bathroom floor.

"Time to go back to work," he said, his voice still shaky, echoing in the empty bathroom.

He had a lot of work in front of him. In the last forty-eight hours, James had used his bureaucratic superpower to rebuild the US government with his people. The Kildare Organization was full of talented, dedicated people who had taken the place of the lazy, stupid, and, most importantly, dead government officials. Over the next two weeks, they would form the most effective government this country had ever seen.

A month in, and it still felt surreal to cross that threshold. The desk, the flags, the seal on the carpet were all his now.

He strolled into the Oval Office, his Oval Office, and immediately knew something was wrong.

The atmosphere in the room was off. His people stood in a tight cluster near his desk. Marie had her phone out, her expression grim. The wall screens showed news feeds, red alert banners, and aerial shots of wreckage. These people didn't rattle. They were even-keeled and effective under pressure, but right now, they were agitated, and that took a lot.

Marie Ortega, his newly minted Secretary of Homeland Security, approached him. “Mr. President, we are getting very strange reports of people losing consciousness and getting very sick all across the country in the last few minutes.”

“How many reports?” James’s jaw tightened.

“We have at least fifteen airplane crashes, most of them light planes that were not on autopilot.” Marie glanced at her phone screen. “One commercial flight landed very badly. We’re still assessing casualties. More than a thousand severe car accidents have been reported. Hospitals across the entire nation are reporting an influx of patients.”

James moved to his desk and braced his hands on the edge. His knuckles went white. “A magical attack?”

“We’re assessing,” she answered, her eyes hard. “Could be magical. Could be something else.”

The blood drained from James’s face. His fingers pressed harder against the desk edge. If magical creatures were attacking them at this scale, it would be challenging for him to rebuild the government and be prepared to retaliate effectively. His entire plan was to concentrate the magical population in one area of the country and then find a good reason to nuke them to kingdom come.

This strike was coming too soon. Way too soon.

“The attacks seem really sporadic. This does not make any sense,” John Staten, one of his health officials, said. He pulled out his phone.

John was always cold and effective.

“Please bring me the hospital reports of selected people affected by this attack and make sure they also test for viruses, magical-traits blood tests, and toxins as well. Do not wait for comprehensive results. Give me the data as it comes in.” John spoke into the phone with the same tone he’d use to order coffee.

Marie stepped closer to the desk. "I suggest we drop a few bombs on wizard centers in LA. The wizards need to understand we have a strong will and vast retaliation capabilities."

James said nothing. Let them work through it. A good leader empowered his team to do the right things on their own.

"Good idea. Once we confirm it's really them behind this, we also have a few biological capabilities we can unleash on the wizard population in LA," John added, still on the phone. He covered the mouthpiece. "Give them a good eye-for-an-eye lesson. The optics would be perfect."

"Agreed," someone from the back of the room said. "Show strength now."

"We could accelerate the quarantine timeline," another voice offered. "Use this as justification for immediate roundups."

James listened to his people efficiently catalog and outline their options. This was good. This was what he needed—competent people who understood what had to be done and didn't flinch from doing it. After weeks in the previous government administration surrounded by weak-willed bureaucrats who agonized over every decision, this was refreshing.

The door to the Oval Office opened. John's secretary appeared in the doorway, out of breath. The room went quiet. She crossed to John quickly and handed him a single sheet of paper.

John read it. His eyes widened. Then, a smile spread across his face, slow and satisfied. "Gentlemen," he said, looking up. "I think we are in the clear."

James felt everyone's attention shift. The room stilled, all of them waiting.

"I just got results of fifteen patients in four different hospitals across the nation. A hundred percent of the patients tested positive for magical traits." John's smile widened. "I would estimate that all the people affected are wizards. All of them. Either they didn't know they had magical powers or were hiding them." John scanned the room. "This is wonderful."

The press secretary's eyes brightened. "This is great! Another reason to 'quarantine' all wizards. We can tell the press that they might have infectious diseases. We have been getting pushback at the state and regional levels. This will seal the deal."

"This will work to our advantage," John said. "We have been trying to get as much of the population tested as possible. Now we can get a list from the CDC of all the people who were sick. We basically had the biggest population test for magical powers we could ever have asked for."

"Oh, this is good!" Ortega was already typing on her phone. "I will direct the national guard to use that CDC list for quarantine notices. We will have all these wizards in LA within the next seven days."

"Make it so," James said. He kept his voice from cracking and held his shaking hands under the table.

The room erupted. Someone clapped. Someone else laughed. James heard voices overlapping, excited, energized. "Finally." "About time." "Perfect." People were smiling, confident and energized again. Wizards were finally getting what they deserved after the horrible attack on the Capitol. Now, justice would be served. It would be swift, efficient, and good for humanity.

A cold shiver crept up James's spine, and his stomach cramped, the same sensation from the bathroom but duller. Distant.

His grandmother's voice came to him suddenly, clear as if she were standing next to him, that harsh Eastern European rasp she'd never lost even after fifty years in America. "The graveyards are full of people who thought they were irreplaceable. Remember, everyone can be replaced."

She'd said that to him when he had been too young, too cocky, too certain of his own brilliance. He'd laughed it off then. Just morbid old-world pessimism.

He wasn't laughing now.

His hands were still shaking under the table. He stared at them and thought about the bathroom floor, the vomit, the sudden, violent attack that came from nowhere.

People were losing consciousness all across the nation. Getting sick. All of them tested positive for magical traits.

All of them.

The cramping in his stomach intensified. The room felt suddenly too hot, too bright. His collar was too tight.

My God. Why was I so sick in the bathroom?

Tell me it's only a coincidence.

CHAPTER TWENTY-SIX

Lixi felt all their eyes turn to her. She smiled back, her wings fluttering, still tingling from the failed spell. It was nice to be appreciated for being a useful member of the team.

Valor spoke first. "Lixi, why do we need a unicorn? I have never heard of a magic that requires unicorns." He gestured at the scroll between them.

Lixi wanted to say, "Well, that is because you haven't learned how to shave yet," but he was an elf, and that reference would have been lost on a race that never grew beards.

Instead, she spoke as slowly and as clearly as she could. "A unicorn's special trait is the ability to amplify magic. They can help wizards cast spells higher than their capabilities. Higher-level spells can have all sorts of requirements. In this case, unicorns are the only way we four could ever execute this spell."

"Why didn't my father tell me about it?" Valor wondered, half to himself.

"Good question. He should have known better. He was with me when..." Lixi stopped.

They all looked at her weirdly again.

Lixi had a distinct feeling she'd had this conversation before. Or was it in the future? Time was strange like that.

Valor tilted his head. "Do you know my father, Lixi?"

Lixi tilted her head as well, mirroring him while reaching back through the foggy centuries. Memories flooded her mind, confusing, fractured, and fragmented. The world spun around her. Fairies were not occupied with memories. The past and the future were silly concepts, like table-side manners. From time to time, memories and caring about the future did have some importance, and Lixi knew this was one of those important times.

"I did...many hundreds of years ago. He was young, and stupid, and came to my world with a human friend." Her voice dropped, weighted by centuries. "Your father was a powerful elf wizard, and his best friend was an almost equally powerful human wizard called Kador. They came to seek power and adventure in the fairy world, and that is what they found."

Lixi's eyes lost focus. Some of the memories did not come back to her, and she was totally okay with that. Some memories were better left in a deep dark box forever. That was her mental health strategy.

Valor's voice hardened. "Kador was not my father's friend! He was his student! Kador was the piece of shit who destroyed magic and brought all this mess on us. He killed all my brothers! He killed so many magical creatures." His voice went up with each statement. His words echoed off the stone walls.

Lixi's expression softened, her eyes crinkling at the corners. He was so young. Elves his age should be worried about collecting flowers for their girlfriends, not about some dark past.

"Valor, what grownups see and how kids interpret it is often different," she explained as patiently as she could. "You weren't even born when all of this happened. When they came to the fairy land, they were closer than brothers. They came to see us to ask us permission to roam the land."

"Wait, what?" Brenda interrupted. "Why would they ask you for permission? Are you police or a government official or something in your land?"

The answer was there, just out of reach.

"I do not remember," Lixi said. "I do not know why, but my memory is patchy and elusive in this world. I think it has something to do with the weak level of stable magic in this world. It feels like I am always tipsy or a little stoned. My memories and sound mind come and go. Sometimes I think I remember that I was someone important, but then for a few decades, it all seems like a dream." Her ears and wings dropped low, the usual glitter on her wings dimming. "That is why I enjoyed being a tooth fairy for so long. Kids do not care if you are forgetful. They accept you the way you are. Something happened to me...something broke my mind...and I do not know why." Her voice was very, very small.

The torch flames flickered in the stillness.

Valor wasn't about to let this go. "Lixi, focus. Why did my father not know how powerful this spell is?"

"Your father and Kador came back from the fairy land to this world with this powerful spell, which they could not cast. They also brought me to help them out. I do not know why, but I know I was bonded to both of them for a long while." A mischievous smile flashed through Lixi's face, gone as quickly as it came. She hoped they didn't notice it.

Brenda's pupils widened.

"This spell they brought back was complex and powerful," she continued. "It taught them a lot about the essence of magic and about its source of power, and through a process of studying it for hundreds of years, it made them the most powerful wizards in existence." Her wings fluttered with the memory.

"Many years later, after you were born, Valor, your father had a breakthrough. He figured out that powerful magic spells can be unlocked and cast when combining the powers of different species. He discovered the magical elements system and unlocked wonderful magic spells that combined the magic of the dwarves and the magic of elves and so on. It was the golden era of magic." Lixi's voice was soft and nostalgic. She could almost taste the joy she had experienced during that time.

"Kador was still obsessed with the scroll they both brought from the fairy land. He was sure it would unlock an even further advancement. He was possessed by dreams of villages burning, of mothers holding their burnt babies in the ashes of cities. He was sure he could prevent all of that from happening. At a certain point, he discovered that the spell required a unicorn to cast it. He begged your father to join him on a quest to unlock this spell, but your father was obsessed with something totally different."

Lixi saw the suffering in Valor's eyes. She wanted to comfort him, but the memories pulled at her.

"Your father found old maps that spoke of a vast land to the west of Britannia," Lixi continued. "The map talked about many other species that lived in that foreign land. Your father wanted to discover the other species and their potential new elemental magic. He was haunted by a dream of a future world with no plants, with no animals, with no nature and thought they could prevent this future with better understanding of the elements of magic. Your father thought that the scroll had given them all they needed even without casting it, and his mind was set on leaving the mainland and setting course for the new land of the west."

What came next was almost too painful to utter.

"I am not sure what happened next," she mumbled. "This is when I started becoming even more forgetful. The rift between them made me very, very sad. We were an amazingly powerful trio, but I could not keep us together. Kador told your father he was wasting his time seeking other lands and that all the power they needed was in this scroll. They had a horrible fight, and I do not remember how it ended. I think at a certain point we all agreed to find a unicorn and cast the magic, but it did not work, and I don't remember why. We failed. Their friendship was torn, and so was my heart and mind." Her wings and ears were low again. "They were my friends. I haven't heard from either of them in six hundred years," she said very flatly.

Six centuries of loneliness.

"That's a heartbreaking story." Brenda touched Lixi's hand with her finger. "I am sorry you had to go through that."

The warmth of Brenda's fingertip against her tiny hand felt nice. Lixi blinked rapidly, her wings trembling.

"This does not explain why my father wants me to cast this spell now or even how he got this scroll into his possession," Valor said.

"I don't know why he wants you to cast this scroll, Valor, but it would be easy for a wizard at your father's level to summon any object he has studied well, and there is no object in the world that your father studied more than this scroll," Lixi said.

"I need to talk to my parents," Valor said. "I cannot do it from here. I need to get out of the mountain so I can reach them with a Meeting of Minds or even a Message Spell."

"So we shall," Odel said in a resonant voice. He seldom spoke, but Lixi loved his deep, rich voice. It resonated off the stone walls like a drum. "Tell me, Honored Fairy," the dwarf addressed her after a deep bow, "where should we find a unicorn if we require one to complete our bonded quest?"

Lixi suspected her moments of clarity and recovered memories might be part of the Quest magic. This magic was binding them all together but also giving them the abilities to complete the quest itself.

Then Lixi hit her forehead with the palm of her hand. “I know a unicorn! His name is Bob. He’s an asshole, but he’ll probably help us.” Her mischievous tone was back in full force.

Brenda snorted. “Bob?”

CHAPTER TWENTY-SEVEN

The magical tsunami hit Tanya during their morning progress review meeting. The sensation knocked her out of her chair at the conference table. She and everyone who surrounded her lost their lunch.

It felt like someone had washed all the magic away from the room for a few seconds. Sound warped, stretching like a recording played too slow. In these few seconds, Tanya understood what it felt like to be drowning. She gasped for air, but filling her lungs did not help. Her essence was yanked away from her. It felt worse than death. Of course it did. She was already dead and quite enjoying it. The absence of magic was like losing her soul.

Tanya vomited again. All the vampires in the room clutched their stomachs, crying out or throwing up. A boy with a torn left hand and a broken neck had been standing in the corner and started to clean the floor. He had been young, maybe five years old, when he had been turned into a zombie. He moved slowly on his little feet.

Good help is so hard to find these days.

Was it the magical glitch from the elvish prince Boris had been worried about? Was it that lunatic in the White House? She pursed her lips and shook her head.

If Tanya had to bet, she would put her money on the elves. She had never met the elves, but it did not stop her from hating them. Where she came from, hating something you did not understand was a natural condition. Life was survival made possible by suspicion.

Magic was so fragile. They were all so impacted by it.

Her jaw tightened. She couldn't afford vulnerabilities.

She rose to her feet and returned to her spot at the meeting table. Some of the vampires, or should she say Nyos, were unconscious, in their seats or on the floor. Others were still trembling, wiping their mouths.

"Back to the table, please, Nyos." She steadied her voice, but the strain was there, audible.

Her second-in-command and her new lover, Joey, went back to stand in front of the big screen. "What was that, Tanyushka?" he asked, wiping vomit from the corners of his mouth.

She liked that he called her Tanyushka but not in public. It was more of a between-the-sheets kind of thing. She would talk to him about it next time they were between the sheets together.

"Someone or some*thing* fucked with magic. I felt it drain away for a few seconds." She could still feel the phantom void. "Nyos aren't just affected by magic, Joey. We're made of it. It's in our bones, our blood, everything." She studied the vampires around the table. Some still seemed shocked. "If magic breaks completely, we won't survive it. None of us will. We need to find out who's threatening our existence."

"What should we do?" Joey looked at her, waiting for direction. He had sharp cheekbones and broad shoulders, a perfect symmetry that made people stare. The question itself proved beauty and brains rarely came in the same package. Unfortunately, he usually needed her to connect the dots for him.

"I want a targeted campaign and possibly a personal seduction mission. Get me the top hundred greatest scientific human minds. I want them all Nyoed and working on figuring out what happened and how to protect us from this vulnerability," she said.

"We will get right to it, my queen," he said. He asked one of his aides to take note. His eyes widened for just a moment before he straightened. The casual intimacy dropped from his voice. His posture shifted, more formal now. Maybe he was smarter than she thought.

By now, all of the Nyos were back at the table. Side chats and anxious voices filled the large room. Worried glances. Hushed speculation about what had just happened. She didn't like weakness. Fear and uncertainty were good for humans, not for her people. It was time to shut it down.

"Silence, please! Let's continue with the presentation of the expansion plan. This is important!" she announced, and the room fell silent.

"Yes!" Joey said, bringing his attention back to the presentation. The screen flickered, then displayed a map of North America. Red dots marked their current positions. "Following our great success in Canada, we will be growing our organization in the US."

He pointed to different cities across the US and the Canadian border, centralized in Vermont and upstate New York.

"Unfortunately," he continued, "after a few successful campaigns, we've hit a major setback when Washington was hit by wizards. Our campaigns were banned by the social media networks, who are worried about government retaliation. Although we have no connection to magic, they are afraid that the US government will not look fondly on anything that deals with humans with powers."

The screen showed an email from the largest social network letting them know that their ad campaign had been suspended.

Tanya frowned, but she added nothing.

"In addition, we paid a large sum to smuggle our US-based new recruits into Canada. Our legal team assured us that the government mandate for anyone showing magical powers does not include us, but the US is in such panic that we didn't want to take the chance," Joey said.

Tanya nodded. The situation in the US had been a clusterfuck. All wizards had been forced to move to Los Angeles, but things were going slower than expected. Despite the forty-eight-hour mandate, many wizards had failed to reach LA before they had been butchered by police forces and panicked civilians. Human rights groups tried to appeal the federal mandate, but the court system was in chaos with all judges in the Supreme Court recently murdered, and several local judges around the US had been discovered to be wizards. There were reports of the National Guard and even the army fighting pockets of wizards in big urban cities.

Chaos meant opportunity, but only if one could survive it. Tanya didn't want to attract too much attention right now. She remembered her mother's stories about burning witches in the old days. Fearful humans were dangerous and violent creatures.

"Yes, we better ditch the US expansion plan for now. How about Mexico?" Tanya suggested.

"They are afraid of the US. I think most countries are. Canada is an exception, as we have several Nyos in top positions in the government. Our recommendation is to expand vertically here in Canada, grow our base, and wait it out. We believe that humans will resolve the conflict with the wizards in the next six months, and we can try again," Joey said. He shifted his weight, as if ready to be schooled by her for not being bold enough.

She took a deep breath. Boris's advice echoed in her mind. *"Do not go too fast for your own good."* Patience. They had eternity.

She smiled and scanned the room. Her fingers drummed once on the table, drawing every eye. "We are immortals. We have all the time in the world. This is a solid plan, Joey. Execute it well. I expect updated goals and projections in my inbox by the end of the week. Dismissed."

Joey exhaled, nodding quickly. They might have been lovers in bed, but she was his queen in everything else, and being queen made her the ultimate power in the den. She reveled in that power, the ability to do anything and kill anyone without question or consequence.

Speaking of killing, her thoughts returned to the elvish prince, hot anger building in her chest.

"That fucking elf prince," she uttered. "I want to take another stab at killing him. This time, do not use zombies. Have a Nyo do it to make sure the job is done. Boris has underestimated the prince, and I really, really want that elvish scum dead," she mumbled to herself as she left the room.

She had a feeling the elf was behind the magical disruption, but even if she was wrong, even if he had nothing to do with it, having him dead served her interests. One less threat. One less variable she couldn't control.

"I will take care of this personally."

The words came from behind her, already fading.

She wanted to tell him to delegate it, but her assistant dragged her to her next meeting. The conference room door closed behind her, cutting off Joey's voice.

Being the queen of her vampire den was a hectic job.

CHAPTER TWENTY-EIGHT

Brenda stretched her arms wide in the light from the setting sun. Her lungs expanded fully for the first time in days, pulling in cool evening air that smelled of flowers and dry earth instead of damp stone and torch smoke. The weight that had pressed against her chest since entering the darkness under the mountain lifted, and she rolled her shoulders, decompressing her back.

The path descended through scrub brush and scattered boulders before opening into the valley below. A river cut through the lowlands, its banks thick with vegetation. Beyond the water, the land rose again into rolling hills that met another mountain range, hazy and purple in the distance.

"It's so good to be out of the mountain," she said after making sure Odel was out of earshot.

Valor glanced over his shoulder and nodded once. "It may have taken longer than expected, but we have our dwarf...and the next steps for our quest."

As they made their way onward, Brenda replayed the events

since Lixi had announced they needed the asshole unicorn named Bob.

They'd had a goodbye ceremony, a short one, according to Valor, that had felt anything but short to Brenda. Odel's mother kept touching her son's face and his shoulders, adjusting his collar like he was heading off to his first day of school rather than a heroic quest. Odel's father stood with his arms crossed, clearly fighting to maintain dwarf stoicism.

During the ceremony, they had been presented gifts, each item wrapped in cloth and offered with both hands, accompanied by words of dwarvish blessings.

Brenda received a short, golden, incredibly sharp dagger, which she'd already cut herself on twice. Odel's mother told Brenda that every dwarf girl coming of age got such a dagger and wished her to gain some weight so she, too, could come of age soon. Brenda's eyebrows had climbed toward her hairline before she could stop them, but she had managed what she hoped was a grateful nod for the honor of receiving the gift, together with the backhanded compliment about her apparent lack of weight.

Odel had been given a wonderfully crafted, folding war hammer that he could keep in a pouch and expand at a moment's notice. He was already very proud of it and kept talking about the honor of having such a unique device as they hiked out of the dwarven kingdom.

They had presented Valor a ring with a shield engraving, which he examined carefully and appreciated deeply. He had thanked the dwarf king and queen several times for the generous gift. Brenda hadn't wanted to be nosy or make the ceremony longer than it had been, but she had decided to ask Valor later why this ring was so special.

Lixi had been given a crown. It was a tiny work of art with fine details that Brenda found remarkable given the dwarves' large, rough hands. It matched the tiny wand Lixi carried constantly. Lixi had loved it so much she promised to sleep with it on her head at all times and to never take it off.

After the gifting ceremony, they'd spent another three hours listening to Odel's mother play a trumpet in their honor and Odel's dad singing a song of glory for their quest.

Brenda's legs had gone numb after the first hour. Her polite smile had felt frozen on her face. She'd caught Valor shifting his weight at least a dozen times, while Lixi had been sound asleep on his shoulder snoring ever so slightly. After they'd been dismissed, the walk out to the exit of the dwarf city was long, uneventful, and physically easy, which surprised Brenda.

When the group reached the open air, Brenda brushed dust from her sleeves and paused. Things were different. She flexed her fingers and bent her elbow. No stiffness. No ache. She rolled her shoulders experimentally.

The persistent tightness that had lived between her shoulder blades for the past five years was now gone. She touched her lower back, expecting the familiar twinge when she straightened. Nothing. Her body felt like it had before the time gateway spell, loose and easy and pain-free. She glanced down at her hands. The fine lines across her knuckles were still there, the slight looseness of skin unchanged. She touched her face. The parentheses around her mouth remained, but underneath the surface that time had marked, her body hummed with youth. Something had returned her vitality, even if it hadn't changed her appearance.

The other peculiar thing she noticed was that her surroundings looked...different. At first, she blamed the many low-light days in the dwarf city for the change. She'd decided her eyes probably just needed time to adjust, but as they walked and the sun lowered toward the horizon, the strangeness intensified instead of fading. Plants had a faint shimmer around them, like heat waves in reverse. She blinked and rubbed her eyes. The shimmer remained. A soft blue glow outlined every leaf, every blade of grass. It pulsed gently, almost like breathing.

A small rodent darted across the sand, and it left a trail of blue light in its wake, the aura clinging to its body like phosphorescence. She stopped walking, staring. The entire desert was alive with subtle blue light she'd never seen before.

She also noticed her companions. Something about them had changed as well. Valor marched with his shoulders back, his movements more graceful than usual, almost dance-like. When had he started moving that way?

Odel's shoulders had broadened somehow, or maybe it was his posture. He hefted their equipment like it weighed nothing. Even tiny Lixi seemed brighter somehow, her wings catching light and throwing off prismatic sparkles. They all radiated energy, health, vigor, like someone had turned up the saturation in a photo editor.

"A little like superheroes," Brenda thought to herself. She chuckled quietly.

A stream flowed in the valley below them, and a certain flat spot looked more lush than anywhere along the bank.

Valor pointed. "We should camp there for the night."

All agreed, and the hike down was a lot easier than the hardship of the climb up that Brenda remembered from their search for a way up the mountain.

Odel moved through the chosen campsite with practiced efficiency. He stomped the ground in specific spots, as if testing it, then directed them where to place their packs. His hands shaped the shrubs somehow, pressing and molding them until they formed firm, springy platforms. He arranged stones in a circle for a fire pit in a position to block the wind. Within ten minutes, they had three sleeping areas and a miniature one for the fairy, a cooking space, and a clear path to the stream. Better than any setup Brenda remembered from girl scout camp where counselors had done most of the work.

"Not a lot of free dry wood. We need a lot of dry wood. This is going to be a cold night," Odel kept mumbling to himself. The trees were green and young on this side of the river.

Valor paced near the fire pit, muttering quietly. His hands moved in small gestures, as if rehearsing an argument. He didn't look up when Brenda passed.

Lixi was nowhere to be found, so Brenda strolled down to the riverbed. The trees grew denser as she approached the water, their blue auras brightening with proximity to the stream. The colors were more vivid here, deep greens of the leaves, rich browns of bark, and everywhere that soft blue glow pulsing like gentle breathing. The temperature dropped as she got closer, the air taking on weight and moisture. On the other side of the river stood a big dry tree, its branches bare, and she noticed it wore no blue aura at all. Dead wood. Odel might find it useful to chop for the night. She'd have to point it out to him when she got back.

A large fish broke the surface of the stream, water droplets catching the last rays of sunlight as it arced through the air. Its blue aura blazed brighter in the open air, leaving a trail of light like a comet. It splashed back down upstream. Then another leaped and another, each one trailing blue luminescence. Brenda caught her breath. She'd seen fish jump before but never like this, never wrapped in living light that made each movement into art.

"Aren't they amazing?" a small voice asked from her shoulder.

Brenda jumped, but Lixi sat on Brenda's shoulder and ate a bigger-than-her-own-head donut, seemingly unfazed by the abrupt movement.

"What do you think of your new powers? Aren't they

wonderful? I haven't felt this good in six hundred years!" Lixi asked casually, as if they were talking about the weather.

"What? You feel it too?" Brenda was shocked no one had brought it up during their earlier travel.

"Of course I do. It's the most wonderful feeling in the world. I will give up entire worlds for more of this feeling." Lixi smiled like she was sipping the best hot chocolate in the universe, or at least eating the best donut.

"Why aren't Odel and Valor feeling it?" Brenda asked, ignoring the comment about the worlds she didn't understand. She didn't want to sidetrack the easily distracted fairy.

"Some races feel a bump in magical energy differently than others, and I think men feel it less than women." Lixi raised her eyebrows, as if saying "If you know, you know."

Lixi leaned closer, lowering her voice. "Dwarves are resilient, but have the adaptability of rocks. Elves are beautiful but kinda slow learners. You can't have it all, unless you're a fairy."

Brenda raised an eyebrow. Lixi nodded, dead serious.

"So, how did our magic energy get this bump?" Brenda asked.

"Well, just like in real life, sometimes things have unintended consequences. We cast a very powerful spell and failed. The thing is, we didn't fail miserably like last time. We just failed a little. While I suspect most magical creatures felt a temporary decline in their power, I think we got what appears to be a permanent bump," the fairy said cheerfully.

"Much of what you say does not make sense, Lixi." Brenda turned to watch more jumping fish with blue auras.

"That is okay, Brenda. You are still one of my favorite mortals." Lixi took a big bite of her donut. "Want to see what you can do with your new magical power?" she asked with a mouth full of food.

"Sure," Brenda said hesitantly. Her head was full of questions, but conversations with Lixi were so many times like that.

"Yay! Let's do it." Lixi sprang to her feet on Brenda's shoulder. "Remember your eensy-weensy fireball trickery?"

Brenda's jaw tightened. She thought her fireball spell was glorious. It was the only offensive spell she knew, and it had dealt serious damage during the fight with the gnome robots.

Before she was able to give Lixi a piece of her mind, Lixi continued. "Up until now, you could only cast it in its basic rudimentary form. This meant you couldn't control the size or heat of it. I want you to think of a ball the size of a watermelon rather than a tennis ball and try to think of a heat explosion rather than fire." Lixi pointed at the dead tree on the other side of the river. "There, hit that tree. Instead of burning it, try to blow it up into pieces. Odel is complaining he can't find firewood? Let's bring him some firewood," she said with a smirk.

Brenda pointed to the tree, holding her hand wide as if she was holding a watermelon.

"Less heat, more wind power," Lixi whispered straight into her ear.

Brenda took a deep breath. Heat bloomed between her palms. The fireball materialized, growing larger than she'd ever made before. Five times larger. It swelled from the size of her fist to the size of her head then kept growing. The flames were different, too, pale yellow instead of deep red, dancing and writhing like they couldn't quite contain themselves. The light cast flickering shadows across the river. She could feel the power humming in her hands and vibrating through her bones. With a sharp exhale, she released it. The fireball shot forward in a blur of yellow light. It struck the dead tree dead center. The impact was tremendous. The trunk didn't burn so much as shatter, exploding into two dozen pieces that flew in all directions. Some splashed into the river. Others tumbled across the sand. The edges glowed orange, barely singed. Brenda stared at her hands. They were shaking.

At the edge of her eye, Brenda saw Lixi cast her own spell, putting out the small fires on the big chunks of wood with a frost wind spell and lifting about two dozen pieces of wood across the river toward them.

"Good job, Brenda," Lixi said.

Brenda's face broke into a grin she couldn't contain. Her chest felt full, almost painfully so, and she had to look away to hide how much those simple words affected her. When was the last time someone had praised her like that? Meant it like that?

"If we manage to cast Valor's spell, this will be a party trick compared to what you'll be able to do," Lixi whispered in her ear.

The idea was enticing.

The wind shifted, carrying a fine mist from the river. Brenda wiped her face with the back of her hand at the same moment Lixi did, their movements mirror images. They caught each other and laughed.

"Lixi, can I ask you a question?" Brenda had been so looking forward to a time when she could be alone with the fairy.

"You just did," Lixi said, flying over to face Brenda, "but I am feeling generous, so you are getting our two-for-the-price-of-one deal." She smiled like a used car salesman.

"What is the Great Treaty?" Brenda asked, ignoring the joke.

Lixi's casual munching stopped. The donut hung forgotten in her hands. Her wings stopped mid-flutter, and she dropped an inch before catching herself. Her jaw fell open, and her eyes went so wide Brenda could see white all around the irises.

"Where did you hear that term, girl?" Lixi asked, her voice serious.

Brenda wondered if she would come to regret the question.

"When you asked if me and Valor ever had...sex? Remember? I was truly sick just thinking about him that way," Brenda said.

Lixi nodded but didn't release her stare.

Brenda continued. "Well, when I felt sick like that, I saw the words 'The Great Treaty' flash in my vision very faintly. I have this thing that when people cast magic, I can see the type of magic they cast."

"Yes, yes, it's called Detect Magic. It's a passive ability," Lixi said, all technical. "You want to tell me you actually detected the Great Treaty magical spell? Well, I'll be damned." Lixi folded her arms mid-air. "Girl, you have the strongest and most intuitive detect magic ability I have ever seen in a mortal."

Lixi flew in close to Brenda and looked at her pupils like an eye doctor. It felt too close and too personal, but Brenda resisted the urge to zap her with her hand.

Then Lixi zoomed to her ear and poked her finger in. Enough. Brenda waved the fairy away. "Lixi, stop it. Respect my personal space, please." She cleared her throat. "So, tell me, what is this Great Treaty?" she asked, trying to move the conversation in the right direction.

Lixi was back on her shoulder. The sun was setting, and a cool breeze stirred the grass. Lixi settled herself more comfortably, crossing her tiny legs. They both looked at the horizon for a few seconds, and when Lixi finally spoke, she sounded different. Tired. Old.

"A while back...I am not talking about last week, more like a few hundred thousand years ago...there were great magical creatures in this land called titans. They were created from a combination of different powerful magical and non-magical creatures together. They collected magical powers of all elements and ruled this world with an iron fist. They enslaved elves and dwarves alike, butchered humans, and attacked any fairy who came to this land. When the titans fell, like all things do, the leaders of the elves, humans, dwarves, and other magical creatures gathered together to work out how to govern themselves. They could have created a paradise. They were given the opportunity to start fresh, but then everything turned south, and they fucked it up." Lixi had her story-voice again.

Another fish jumped in the river, its splash echoing across the water. The blue trail it left behind faded slowly.

Brenda exhaled slowly. Lixi's story-telling tone had a quality to it, something that made everything else fall away. It calmed her and made her sleepy. She wondered if that was where the term fairy tale came from.

"The races couldn't agree on the fundamentals of the new world," Lixi continued, the setting sun glowing in her eyes. "Greed, fear, and self-interest prevented them from reaching an agreement. They almost left the gathering without signing anything, and personally, that would have been better than the agreement they did actually reach."

Lixi looked at Brenda as if waiting for her to guess. Brenda fought the urge to do so. She wanted Lixi to tell the story in full.

Lixi sighed, clearly not happy that Brenda didn't participate in her game. "The only fucking thing that all the race leaders were willing to agree on was that they didn't want titans to be created again. They created a powerful magic, similar to Mass Manipulate but a million times stronger. That prevented the races from intermixing. Each race kept their magical element affinity. Because sex between the races was prevented, creatures with mixed elements couldn't be created. They called that spell..." She pointed at Brenda, her eyes firm as if telling her, "Say it."

Five seconds passed. Lixi was still gesturing at Brenda.

Brenda finally agreed to play the game. "The Great Treaty."

"Exactly!" Lixi looked extremely pleased. "And since then, the bees are with the bees and the birds are with the birds. From time to time, you hear about exceptions, but they are very rare. Mortals are way too obsessed with who sleeps with whom. Super fucking boring and a big miss on everyone's part, if you asked me. The only way to change the Great Treaty is to get the leaders of all the relevant races to sign an amendment to that agreement." Lixi folded her arms again. "Good luck with that!"

The sun was halfway into the mountains already.

"Thank you for the story," Brenda said quietly.

"You're welcome." Lixi looked at her hand as if there were a watch on it. There was not. "Oh, dear, how quickly time passes. We are almost late. Let's go talk to a grumpy old elf king." Lixi flew away back to the camp, accompanied by the two dozen pieces of wood flying on an invisible wind carrier.

Brenda envisioned Valor's reaction to hearing his father being called "a grumpy old elf king" and chuckled.

CHAPTER TWENTY-NINE

Tanya wiped her mouth with the back of her hand, smearing blood across her cheek. The bedroom reeked of iron and sex. She'd done it again, eaten a whole human alone, and now he sat like a stone in her gut. She would need to go out on a run or a flight later tonight to burn off the excess calories.

The room was a disaster. Blood spattered the white walls. The head had rolled into the corner, his mouth frozen open. The silk sheets stuck to her thighs, tacky with drying blood. Her jaw ached from tearing through muscle and bone.

Her dinner was a young blond called Tom. He had wanted to become a Nyo. She had found him in one of her nightclubs and had taken him home. After two orgasms, she had ripped his head off and devoured him. She did not "listen to her body" like the book she was reading told her to. *Intuitive Eating for the Modern Woman.* She'd stolen the book from a victim's purse last week. It had a sunset on the cover and talked about "honoring your hunger cues." The author had clearly never torn someone's head off and kept drinking anyway. She had known she was full and still kept drinking his blood until he had become an empty sack of meat.

"Fucking Joey," she said.

Tom's head stared at her from the corner of the room.

She'd called Joey six times and texted him twice. Nothing. She'd gone to his place, but his apartment was empty. She'd called his phone, but it was off. None of the club managers had seen him.

Even Viktor, his sparring partner, just shrugged. "He said he had something important to do for you."

Joey, her right-hand Nyo in bed and work, was gone.

For the life of her, Tanya could not remember asking him to go anywhere. He had taken care of so many things for her and kept her from freaking out or drinking too much, like she had tonight. Joey had his routines—morning sparring, afternoon security checks, evening rounds of the clubs. He would bring her coffee every night at sunset and remembered which blood type she preferred. He'd been more reliable than her phone alarm. He was her vampire version of a naive but adorable golden retriever, a shining light in her dark soul.

So where the fuck was he?

"Damn it, Joey! Where are you?" She screamed in frustration. Spit and blood sprayed from her mouth.

Taking Joey as a lover had been Boris's idea. He had said she needed the outlet, that physical activity was an important part of keeping a leader sharp. At first, it had shocked Tanya, even angered her, but Boris calmed her fire.

"Mortals are obsessed with who sleeps with whom," Boris had said, watching her with his ancient eyes. "They build cages around their lovers. Possession. Ownership." He'd smiled at her. "We are creatures of passion, Tanya. Passion is better when shared. Love many. Own none."

She'd thought he was giving her permission to cheat. Now she understood that he'd been teaching her freedom.

When she had been a human, men had owned her body, decided who touched it, when, how. Ivan had beaten her for smiling at the DJ. As a vampire, her body was hers alone. She shared it whenever she wanted, with whomever she wanted. No more possessive bullshit.

"Silly Joey, what have you done?" she murmured, her voice soft. Blood still covered her hands. She picked at the flesh stuck under her fingernails and flicked the pieces onto Tom's chest.

So what if Joey wasn't the smartest? He often misunderstood directions and confused things, sure, but intelligence was overrated. What mattered was that he was a wonderful tool—super athletic, a master swordsman, bodyguard, fantastic in bed, loyal as they came, and an operational engine who got things done.

Tom's headless body lay beneath her, young and fit. Beautiful before she'd ripped his head off. He had been so eager to become a Nyo.

She laughed. "Too bad for you."

Humans were a dime a dozen. With the US going to shit and the global economy crashing, people wanted an alternative. People were coming from all over the world to join "The movement." They believed Nyos would save them, lift them out of their pathetic mortal lives. Idiots. It was incredible that humans had run the show on this planet for so long. A bunch of losers, all of them.

"Like sheep to slaughter," Boris's voice echoed in her mind.

She would make that happen. Most humans would one day go to a harvesting factory and become food for the Nyos. She could see it clearly—vast warehouses full of sedated humans hooked to machines that kept their hearts pumping. Clean, efficient, humane even. No fear. No pain. Just harvesting. Better than cattle.

A selected few, the lucky and the brave, would become Nyos. Not too many, as Nyos never died of old age. You always wanted to keep an eye on the population. At most, ten percent of the human population should ever be turned, or else you risked starvation, and vampires were not nice when they were hungry.

"They deserve it." She spat on the body beneath her.

Tanya tried not to recall much from the time she was human. It was a dark, harsh, and sad part of her life. She had put all the horrible memories in a box and closed the lid. Sometimes she still felt the cold tile of the club bathroom floor against her cheek, still heard men laughing on the other side of the door. She shoved the memory back down.

Nyos were the future. They were stronger, braver, ruthless, but not cruel. They killed for need and did not torture their prey like humans did. They did not cause them unneeded pain for their own pleasure.

Not like she'd done to Tom. That was different. That had been hunger, not cruelty.

Nyos were a better ideal for what people thought of as "strong humans." Nyos were the next step in evolution. Nyos would inherit the world. It was inevitable. She would make sure of it.

Tanya had a plan, and Joey was a part of it.

So where the hell was he?

She decided to go back to the club and pick another boy to eat. The club would be packed by now. It was Friday night. Bodies pressed together, sweat and perfume and alcohol. The bass so loud it drowned out heartbeats. Easy pickings. She'd find another Tom, another eager boy desperate to become immortal, willing to do anything she asked. They always were.

She still had the tight body of a ballerina anyways. The diet could wait for tomorrow.

CHAPTER

THIRTY

Brenda hid a yawn. She was ready for bed, and this was getting nowhere. Their fire had burned down to red coals, giving off soft light and heat. Her ass ached from sitting on the ground for the last hour. They were all waiting, watching Valor.

The firelight caught the tension in Valor's face. He stared into the flames without blinking, holding the palms of his hands in his lap. His shoulders hunched forward like he was bracing for a blow.

The quest had not been successful so far. He kept opening his mouth as if to speak, then closing it again. Brenda counted three false starts so far.

"Are they on yet?" a voice whispered from behind her shoulder. Brenda felt the tiny weight of Lixi perched on her back, her wings tickling the nape of her neck. Lixi never hid from anyone. What was she afraid of?

"No, the king is not answering," Odel said in a whisper. He straightened as he spoke, his massive frame going rigid with attention. He wore the same awestruck expression Brenda had seen on pilgrims' faces in documentaries. His voice always softened to a whisper around Lixi. It was weird to see the bulky creature that looked like an industrial mini fridge bow to a creature the size of a dragonfly.

"As long as he doesn't call his mother, we're good," Lixi whispered in Brenda's ear.

Another five minutes passed. Valor's breathing had gone shallow. He kept glancing at the space in front of him where the sphere should appear and then back to the coals. Brenda noted how long-lived creatures tended to take their time.

Valor exhaled slowly through his nose. "I will need to call my mother then," he said after another five minutes of waiting for his father to answer.

"Oh shit." Lixi sounded like a teenager caught smoking.

Two seconds later, the air in front of Valor rippled like water. A shimmering sphere formed, expanding outward with a soft chime. The coals flared brighter for a moment. Inside the sphere, a royal, tall, slim figure stood in view, clear as a window. She was dressed in a wonderful white-and-green gown that matched her white hair and green eyes. She looked like a beautiful lady, no more than twenty-five years old. You could not mistake her for anything other than a royal queen.

"My son. It is good to see you. How fare you?" she asked with a warm smile. The queen's voice made Brenda shiver, like when she listened to soft music she loved. She sounded more tired than Brenda remembered her, but her presence still commanded the space.

"I am well, Mother. We had quite an adventure in the dwarves' mountains. I will tell you all about it in detail when I come home, but time is of the essence. My quest is not complete. I did everything Father said but failed to cast the spell he gave me." Valor's voice cracked. His lip twitched.

"That's unfortunate. Your father is not well. We all fell sick last night, all elves and all magical creatures with us. While most of us are back to normal, it hit your father gravely. He fell asleep and has not woken since." The queen's voice was even and calm, but the corners of her mouth turned down. The light in her eyes dimmed, like clouds passing over the sun.

The blood drained from Valor's face so quickly Brenda thought he might faint. His hand shot out to grip the log beside him, his knuckles going white. He looked at Brenda then to Odel.

"Mother, last night we attempted to cast the spell Father asked me to. We all fell terribly sick as a result of the failure. Do you think this caused everyone to get sick?" Valor asked.

"I do not know. Failure to cast spells at high levels can cause unpredictable events at large scale, but I have never heard of a failure event at this scale. Do you know why you failed?" Her voice was not accusatory. She sounded to Brenda like a lab professor asking their student if they knew why an experiment had failed.

"According to Lixi, the fairy member of our band, the spell was a higher level than ten. She says we need a unicorn to enhance our magical capabilities to be able to cast this spell. How did Father not know about this? I didn't even know there was such a high level of spells." Frustration crept into Valor's voice.

"Lixi...do you mean Lixiva Orera, the Crown Princess of the fairies, has joined your band? Bring. Her. Forth." The queen mother's voice was now demanding, and her words rang with power.

Brenda's pulse jumped in her throat. There was no mistake that this was an order.

There was a flash of light behind Brenda that left afterimages dancing in her vision. Heat washed over her back. A deep, sad exclamation followed, the sound vibrating through Brenda's chest.

An unbelievably beautiful woman stepped out from behind Brenda. Brenda's heart kicked hard against her ribs. The woman had a grown-up version of Lixi's small-form face, but she was as tall as Valor. She was light green in skin and white-green in hair. She radiated in a way that made Brenda's eyes refuse to blink. She wore a tunic of silver and diamonds and a matching crown on her head. She still had wings, but they were bigger now, shimmering, dragonfly-like, folded behind her back.

Brenda's jaw dropped. Lixi was the most beautiful person she had ever seen.

"Queen of the Elves." Lixi performed a curtsy that somehow managed to be both respectful and defiant. Brief, controlled, like a nod between equals who happened to have different titles. Her voice was like music.

Brenda's eyes teared up. Beside her, Odel made a choked sound. Tears streamed down his weathered face as his massive body dropped to the ground with a thud that shook the earth beneath them.

"Lixiva Orera, Crown Princess of the fairies. What new chaos are you planning this time?" the queen asked with a flat voice.

"None, Queen. I learned my lesson," Lixi said. She stared straight at the queen, meeting the elf's gaze head-on.

"The unicorn will be the judge of that," the queen said.

Lixi nodded, keeping her eyes on the queen's gaze.

Brenda shuddered. She could not fathom having a staring contest with either of them.

"Why have you been summoned? Are we at a crossroad again?" the queen asked.

"It appears so. I would not be here otherwise. Although, truth be told, I am still trying to recover my memories, so don't blame me if this is all a big mix-up that the asshole of a unicorn has come up with again."

For a second, Brenda could hear the mischief-Lixi she loved, and she had to fight back a smile despite the tension.

"Well, last time you got involved and played with fate, we got five hundred years of misery, and I lost all my sons but one!" Power crackled through the queen's words.

Brenda cringed, the queen's force pressing against her chest. She saw Odel lower his head, and even Valor looked like a child caught in the middle of an adult fight.

"You know it was not all me." Lixi faced the queen with a calm voice that shocked Brenda. "I was punished for my vanity. I do not know what happened after that. Your husband, as well as Kador, shared the vanity, and we were all punished for it."

There was a long silence.

"I know that is true," the queen said finally. The pain in her voice was so raw Brenda felt tears well in her own eyes. She wanted to comfort her somehow, but the queen wasn't really here. Just an image in a sphere, untouchable and distant.

The queen's stare hardened. "Lixiva Orera, a member of the fairies is required to complete the quest my son is on, a quest dear to me and to the elvish king. Did you accept the quest with a pure heart and good will?"

The words "Detect Lie" flickered into existence in the corner of Brenda's vision, blue letters against the darkness. *Oh, that's interesting.* She'd gotten used to these notifications, but this one made her pay attention.

"Yes," Lixi said. "I have accepted this quest in good faith and with a pure heart. I also swear to protect your son and this band with my life." Lixi's voice sounded like a young girl again.

The queen's stare softened ever so slightly. "So be it. I am very worried that fate brought you back to our life this way again. Chaos and mayhem follow your path, even if you are pure-intentioned, but we have no choice other than to power forward. One thing I know is that time is short."

Lixi nodded again and curtseyed. She darted behind Brenda with surprising speed. The flash of light came again, briefer this time, and the heat was less intense. More like relief than the anxious power from before.

Brenda's shoulders shifted as she almost looked back to check on Lixi, but the queen continued, commanding her attention.

"Valor, your quest did not fail. It is amended. Go seek the unicorn, cast the spell with its aid, and return to the elves victorious. Do you accept it?" the queen asked, almost ceremoniously.

"Yes, Mother," Valor said.

Warmth bloomed in Brenda's chest, spreading outward through her limbs. Grit. Resolve. Will. The feelings weren't hers, but they settled into her bones like they'd always belonged there.

"We will head out at dawn. Lixi said she might be able to find him," Valor told the queen. He looked at Brenda, then Odel, who had managed to pull himself to his feet. They nodded to each other, a silent agreement.

"Your father had visions of the unicorn and many other creatures heading west. Before he fell ill, he was obsessed with trying to find why that is. Your father's visions spoke of a place called 'the city of angels,' where all the human wizards are gathering. I also had visions of that great city, visions of pain and war. I am sensing a lot of death in that city. Remember, as an elvish prince, it is your duty to always prevent unnecessary deaths. If your quest takes you there, then stop the slaughter. Farewell, my son." The queen sounded ceremonious again.

"Yes, Mother. Farewell." Valor touched the edge of the sphere with two fingers. The image rippled like disturbed water, then collapsed inward with a soft pop. The coals dimmed back to their normal glow.

"Oh perfect. A goddamn side quest." Lixi was back in her tooth-fairy form, perched on Brenda's shoulder. Her tiny arms crossed, and her wings buzzed with irritation.

Brenda did not like the sound of going on a side quest at all.

CHAPTER THIRTY-ONE

The knock on the Oval Office door was soft, but James dreaded it nonetheless. Timon entered, placed the envelope on his desk with both hands, and stepped back. "Your anonymous test results, Mr. President."

His gaze stayed fixed on the eagle and shield carved into the wall behind James. Not nervousness, only calculation. The Kildare Organization didn't employ the curious. It employed the professional, the discreet, the loyal. Timon had mastered all three.

"Thank you, Timon. Cancel my next meeting."

Timon nodded once and left.

James was on his way back from his security briefing when Timon had caught up to him. Now he sat behind the Resolute Desk and stared at a single sheet of paper that could destroy everything he'd built.

The Oval Office's cream walls and blue carpet radiated presidential authority. The flags stood at attention behind him. Through the south-facing windows, sunlight painted golden rectangles across the floor. Everything was perfect and controlled, exactly as he'd orchestrated since consolidating power.

Everything except the medical report trembling between his fingers. The paper rustled faintly with each small shake of his hand.

Magical Genetic Profile: POSITIVE

The words blurred. He set the paper down on the polished wood, his hands leaving faint moisture marks on the finish. Outside the bulletproof windows, the Rose Garden bloomed in afternoon light, utterly indifferent to the irony crushing him.

He wasn't just leading the war against magic. He was the enemy.

It'd been a little over a month since he'd assumed control over this country. While America thought it was a democracy, it was no longer one. James's power was absolute now.

Previous presidents had struggled with Congress, negotiated with lobbyists, and compromised with political opponents. James didn't. When he wanted legislation passed, it passed. When he nominated judges, they were confirmed. When he restructured agencies, they were restructured.

The Senate majority leader was Kildare. So was the minority leader. The Speaker of the House. The Chief Justice. The heads of every intelligence agency. Believers. People who understood that humanity's survival mattered more than democratic process.

It had taken less than two months to complete the transition. Retirements, resignations, strategic appointments. All legal. All legitimate. Democracy hadn't died in a coup. It had faded quietly in committee rooms and closed-door sessions, replaced by something more efficient. Something necessary.

James now controlled both the visible government and the shadow organization that had protected humanity for centuries. All the power he needed to win the war against magic.

This morning's briefing. The Situation Room. His inner circle around the table, the same people who'd engineered the transition. He'd stood at the head, hands flat on the polished surface.

"All this power was given to us on a silver platter. Legal and just. This sick and decrepit democracy didn't die in war. It faded away in a forgotten hospice."

The words had landed in silence. His inner circle, the architects of the transition, had simply nodded. The American people would still believe in their republic, would still vote, still debate. They just wouldn't realize their choices no longer mattered.

The word POSITIVE burned in his mind.

James stood from the desk and walked to the windows, the medical report still in his hand. The show went on. He pressed his palm against the bulletproof glass. It was cool and solid, designed to stop a sniper's bullet. Outside, he could hear the muffled sounds of the city, life continuing normally while his world tilted.

He was the enemy? A wizard?

His reflection stared back at him, distorted by the security glass. He looked the same—graying skin, bald head, sharp features, the calm expression he'd perfected over decades. Nothing on the surface revealed what ran through his blood.

At the very least, he had the blood of the enemy in him.

He turned from the window and paced back to the desk. His fingers traced the edge of the Resolute Desk, the wood worn smooth by generations of presidents who'd faced their own crises. None quite like this.

James sat back down, the leather chair creaking softly, opened the top drawer of the Resolute Desk, and pulled out a small object he had found there a day ago. It was a gift one of his predecessors had received from the President of the Republic of Indonesia. It was a canine tooth, yellowed with age, mounted in a brass display case. *Panthera tigris balica.* The Bali tiger. Hunted to extinction by humans for sport and farmland. The last known specimen had been shot in 1937.

He turned the case in his hands. The brass felt cold, the edges smooth from years of handling. The predator's fang was sharp behind the glass.

Magic was an enemy of humanity not because it was evil but because it demoted ordinary humans from their top position in the food chain. If you are not the strongest creature in an ecosystem, then you are food. If you are not the alpha species, you are a resource to be used.

James was not as fanatical or as stupidly cruel as his predecessors were. He was logical. For him, religion was a tool, Kildare teachings were a tool, his people were tools. It all served a single purpose that James deeply believed in and cared about —the survival of humanity.

No cost was too great. No action was too cruel. Nothing else mattered.

He set the case down on the medical report, the extinct tiger's tooth covering the word POSITIVE.

He closed his eyes. Kador's prophecy haunted him. *Catalysts of fire, water, air, and earth will come. They'll cast the last spell to end the time of man.*

Four magical casters. Kador had prophesied about them six centuries ago, had seen them in whatever vision had driven him to destroy magic. The prophet had tried to prevent their gathering, had sacrificed himself and unleashed a plague that had killed millions, all to stop four specific individuals from casting one spell.

The spell that would end humanity's supremacy.

James didn't understand the significance of "fire, water, air, and earth." The words felt symbolic, metaphorical, like the obscure religious language that filled most of Kador's writings, but the core message was clear enough. Four Catalysts existed. When they gathered, they would cast a spell that meant humanity's extinction. Not subjugation. Not coexistence. Extinction.

James guessed he had pieces of the puzzle. The elf prince had appeared in their time. The Witness had already been awakened. Two of the four Catalysts were already active, already gathering power in Redrock Springs. Two more existed somewhere, but Kador's cryptic prophecy offered no way to identify them specifically.

His finger traced the brass edge of the case. The tiger tooth glittered in the light, a relic of an extinct species. That was humanity's future if the four Catalysts succeeded. Extinction. The same fate that had claimed every apex predator when a more powerful species decided they were in the way.

Kador's book suggested that elves considered themselves "good," but that meant nothing when they held absolute power. One day, they could decide that humans were "evil" and eliminate them. They might have logical reasons. They might even be right by their own moral framework.

It wouldn't matter. As long as they were more powerful, it would be their choice to make, not humanity's.

Kador had seen this coming and had done everything in his power to prevent it. Now it was James's turn to finish what the prophet had started. He had to find every Catalyst, all four of them, and stop them before they could complete whatever apocalyptic spell Kador had foreseen.

But that was not the only threat to humanity.

James returned the case to the drawer and stood, unable to stay still. The office felt too small suddenly, the walls too close. He crossed to the built-in bookshelf and ran his finger along the spines until he found what he wanted, an old copy of the Kildare manifesto, its pages yellowed and brittle. The leather binding creaked as he turned to the page he'd read a hundred times.

Kador's own words, transcribed centuries ago from the original. *I have seen what we become. What I have become. Magic makes gods of mortals, and gods forget why mortals matter.*

The human wizards were the other threat. They were dangerous to humanity because they looked like humans. Kador had studied human wizards for decades and concluded they should be classified as non-humans. For one, they lived much longer and rarely reproduced. Powerful human wizards were childless, ageless creatures who resembled humans, but as time passed, they slowly forgot how to be human and finally lost all loyalty to the human race.

No, for humanity to prevail in the long run, ordinary humans had to be at the top of the pyramid.

James traced the faded ink with one finger. Kador himself had been a powerful wizard who still remembered what it meant to be human. The legend said that he fell in love with someone so beautiful it unfroze his heart, but then his love broke his heart and made him realize his human heritage. Armed with that grief and knowledge, Kador had made the ultimate sacrifice.

He destroyed magic but not before founding the Kildare Organization to ensure it would never return. Fully aware the spell would kill him, Kador had secured humanity's place as the dominant species. Humanity had grown and thrived, exactly as the prophet had foreseen.

James closed the book carefully.

Kador was a wizard who wanted to save humanity above all things. *Just like me.*

James set the book back on the shelf. His hands were steady.

The cold dread that had gripped him when he'd first read the test results was gone, replaced by something colder.

Clarity.

He wasn't the enemy. Quite the opposite. James was walking in the footsteps of his prophet. The irony was almost beautiful. A wizard who would destroy magic. History repeating itself not as tragedy but as necessity.

James returned to his desk. He picked up the medical report and walked to the fireplace. The gas flames flickered behind ornamental logs.

He was the modern wizard who would end all magic. He would be the hero who secured humanity's future, just as Kador had done six centuries before. He would destroy magic, even if he needed to sacrifice himself in the process.

He dropped the medical report into the flames. The paper caught immediately, curling and blackening. The smell of scorched paper filled his nose, and something in him settled. The word POSITIVE disappeared, consumed by fire.

There would be no other copies. Timon would ensure that. The lab would have an accident. The technician would find other employment far away.

James Webber, President of the United States, was human. Fully human. The test had never existed.

But James Webber, Director of Kildare, knew the truth, and he would use it.

It was the only right thing to do.

CHAPTER
THIRTY-TWO

Lixi always thought marshmallows were humanity's greatest invention. They were unique to this world. She'd seen it all, in many other worlds, from flying cars to hamburgers, but she'd never found marshmallows. It was one of the universe's greatest mysteries.

Brenda pulled another marshmallow from the bag and skewered it on a stick, the puffy white confection larger than Lixi's entire head. The fire hissed and popped, sending tiny sparks spiraling into the darkness. Brenda held the marshmallow over the flames until the outside crisped golden-brown, then split it down the middle with her fingers. She handed half to Lixi without a word. The fairy took it, the warm sugar leaving sticky trails on her tiny fingers. Around them, the night pressed close. Nobody spoke.

Lixi decided to take the high road and not complain that nobody had thanked her for spending a full three milliseconds flying to a gas station two hundred miles away and acquiring the delicious marshmallows.

Valor examined his dwarven ring, his finger tracing over the shield insignia carved into the ring's face. Lixi noted that the shield on the ring glowed faintly blue. Strange. Valor didn't seem to notice, his mind obviously elsewhere.

Odel's hands worked at a piece of wood, shaving curls into the fire. He'd glance at Lixi, hesitate, shave another curl, and then look at her again. It kept going for a long while, and he was running out of wood.

After a while, she got tired of the dwarf's gaze. "What?" she snapped, making a face and sticking her tongue out at him. "What is it?"

"Lixi, are you the daughter of the fairy queen?" he asked.

"Hm, yes, I think it slipped my mind. You have to admit that aside from Brenda, we're all kids of royalty." Lixi bowed, trying to lighten the mood.

Her friends didn't seem impressed with her wonderful humor this time.

"Lixi, there seems to be a lot of context you're not sharing with us that might be helpful for our quest. I'm asking you to share it with us," Valor said in his serious royal elf voice. By the weight of his voice, Lixi could tell he'd been keeping that bottled up for a while.

The Quest magic tugged on Lixi's mind. Using the Quest bond had been a sneaky move. Lixi knew what he was doing. He was trying to use the bond of the Quest spell to make her tell all her story and secrets.

"Well, as I told your mother, my memory is still playing tricks on me. Memories come in and out. They're hard to pin down." She tried to avoid his gaze. A log shifted in the fire, sending up sparks. The night had grown colder.

They all continued to peer at her in silence. The kind of uncomfortable silence that demanded an answer. Lixi's wings fluttered. This was not going to go away that easily.

"Okay, let's start from the beginning. I'll share what I

remember, but don't blame me if it's wrong or contradictory," she said. "This isn't my first quest."

"Wait," Brenda interrupted. "Back in the dwarf mountain, you said you didn't remember what happened with King Valor and Kador. What changed?"

Lixi's glow flickered. "The Quest magic is helping. The more we're bonded, the more I borrow a little bit of magic from each of you, the more I remember. It's..." Her wings drooped. "It's not always pleasant. Some memories I kept buried for good reason."

A heavy pause settled over them. Brenda nodded slowly, understanding in her eyes.

Lixi felt the past wrapping around her again. It was like water circling a drain.

"Valor, when your father came to the fairy world accompanied by his friend Kador, they were seeking power. They were young and proud, and they demanded my mother help them in their quest to increase their magical power," she began.

Valor's eyes hardened, and his jaw tightened. For a moment, she thought he might interrupt, but he stayed quiet, just nodded for her to continue. Maybe he was maturing.

"King Valor and Kador explained that raiding parties of undead, trolls, and goblins were coming from the north more and more often, that humans didn't want to fight the wars anymore and were growing apart from their magical allies. The humans wanted stronger magic to be able to destroy evil for good," she continued. "My mother was unhappy with that demand. One does not demand anything from one of the most powerful beings in the universe. She did what fairies do when they're faced with unreasonable requests—she granted their wish, but not in the way they wanted. She ordered me, her daughter, to join their quest. I don't remember much, but I guess I was young and eager for adventure, and she promised me that this would benefit the fairies greatly. After I joined the quest and we bonded as a band, my mother gave us a scroll that was too powerful for us to even read. She said that if we cast the spell in the scroll successfully, both the elf king and human wizard would be able to cast spells far beyond their imagination."

Lixi fell silent. The fire crackled, breaking the quiet.

Brenda added another log to the fire, keeping her eyes fixed on Lixi all the while. Finally, she said, "Go on, Lixi. There must be more."

Lixi sighed, then looked at Valor over the fire. "Your father and Kador took me to their world, your world, this world. I was sick for many days. I was weaker than I'd ever been before, and I thought that I would die. Everything smelled like shit."

The foul smell of the human world still singed Lixi's nose and mouth. Lixi sniffed and nearly choked. The stench had never disappeared. Had she just gotten used to it? Had she forgotten how bad it smelled? How could she explain what it felt like?

Valor cleared his throat, the sound harsh.

Lixi shot him an irritated look before she went on. "You see, fairies aren't meant to live in this world. Magic is too weak here to sustain us. It feels like you're a stupider, weaker, drunker version of yourself without proper magic. But after a few weeks, I adapted. I became stronger, yet not even half as strong as I used to be in my land. The quest continued."

Lixi felt the memories flooding back. "We spent days, weeks, and years on the scroll, slowly unlocking its powers. At first, most of the words weren't readable. Using magic, we adapted and adjusted the scroll to be readable by anyone. Then we started understanding the mechanics of the scroll, the deep transformation of physical laws, changes at the smallest particles and waves of existence. We still couldn't cast the spell. It was locked to us and to everyone else in this world. Or so we thought at the time," she continued. "We were ambitious and proud, and the fights in the north became more and more frequent. Magical creatures that drink human blood, trolls that break farmhouses with a single blow, thousands and thousands of goblin raids..." Her voice grew weary.

The moon appeared behind a tree, and the air became chillier.

"We had two breakthroughs. The first was the Elements system discovered by your father, Valor. He found out that while each race was dominant in a different magical element, bonded creatures from different races can amplify each other's magic regardless of its magical element. This enabled elves to amplify dwarves in their earth magic, for example." Her voice grew excited as if the discovery had happened yesterday.

"After that, the king lost a little of his interest in the scroll, stating that his discovery was a valid solution to our problems. He advocated that if they all worked together, they could amplify each other's magic and beat evil for good, but Kador and I still wanted to crack the code and cast the scroll, and the king didn't mind."

She peered into the fire for a long moment.

"Kador was incredibly passionate about unlocking the scroll," she added. "My mother's challenge and the wish for powers of his own drove him to try every knowledge spell he had in his spell books no matter how risky they were. One day, he invoked a dangerous spell which raised a lost powerful creature from the dead, a barbarian king from his ancient tomb. When Kador asked him how to unlock the scroll, he said that he didn't know anything about that, but in his time, unicorns were the creatures to ask about such things. This was the second breakthrough."

Lixi took a deep breath, but the story continued.

"Kador started to study unicorns. It appeared that, at one

time in the past, they had been as common as a wild horse. As time passed, unicorns had been hunted for their powerful horns by greedy wizards, and many had left this world, never to return. Kador thought that this was one of the reasons this world's magic was so fragile. Unicorns were a powerful creature that anchored the magic and solidified it in this world."

Her voice broke a little. The memories became really uncomfortable from this point.

She shook her head. This was a bad idea. "I feel hungry for something else. I'm going to get us some cupcakes!" she said cheerfully.

As she started to vanish, she felt Valor use their bonding magic, even before she heard his voice. "Lixi, we need to hear the rest of it."

That magic tug again. She sighed. "Okay, be that way! After Kador discovered that a unicorn could unlock the scroll, he shared that discovery with your father, and I think your father became excited again. We went on a quest to find the unicorn. We were all determined to get the unicorn to unlock the scroll and to help us cast the spell within it."

Brenda leaned forward. Odel stared at Lixi, transfixed. Valor remained completely still.

"It was a long and dangerous quest. We had a lot of false hopes and dead ends, but finally, we found a unicorn. Oh, how much I wish we hadn't found him." Her voice hardened, and her glow dimmed. "The unicorn told us that he saw through our pride and wish for power. He saw everything through our souls. He saw the intentions of the fairy queen and the intentions of the evil forces from the north. He laughed at all of us. He was such a fucking asshole."

Lixi's glow flickered with the memory.

"The unicorn didn't stop there. He gave your father and Kador two impossible futures to choose from. He unlocked the scroll and showed them what would happen if they cast the spell and what would happen if they didn't. Two outcomes they couldn't accept. He held them frozen in time until they decided which fate the world deserved." Her voice dropped to almost a whisper. "This tortured them to no end. I couldn't see them suffer like that, so I cast my most powerful wind spell at the unicorn. I made him lose his concentration for a split second and helped the elf king and Kador escape." Her glow pulsed brighter for just a moment, pride breaking through. "The unicorn's wrath turned to me. He was furious I made him lose his hold on my two friends. He took my memory, broke my time, and condemned me to five hundred years of being a tooth fairy."

Her wings folded tight against her back, making her look smaller. The fire seemed to dim, or maybe it was just her light fading.

"That was the last I saw of your father or Kador. With time, I heard snippets of what had happened. I learned magic was broken. I heard that many magical creatures died. My broken mind, my time glitches, and bad memory couldn't process all of that." She now looked at Valor with a sad look. "Your father never came to help me, nor did Kador. They left me, broken and unaware."

The heavy, uncomfortable silence pressed against Lixi's chest and made breathing hard.

Brenda's finger found Lixi's shoulder, barely a touch, but it steadied her. Odel had stopped carving completely, the wood seemingly forgotten in his lap. The fire popped, sending sparks spiraling up into the dark.

"I'm so sorry," Valor said. The words came out raw. "I wish I could say I'm surprised. My father..."

Why am I not telling them the whole truth? What is true? Don't play dumb. They should know it all. Wait, why is Valor's ring glowing?

A scream tore through the night. Not human. Not an animal. Something in between, a sound that made Lixi's wings freeze mid-flutter. It came from the darkness behind Valor, where the firelight didn't reach.

Then steel whistled through the air. A blade, long and curved, cut toward Valor's throat faster than Lixi could shout a warning. Lixi was sure the sword would go right through and behead the young prince, but a glow appeared on his skin, and the ring on his finger rang and flashed as if the sword had hit it dead center. The collision threw a fountain of sparks into the air.

They all sprang to their feet and faced the enemy. The figure looked like a tall pale man, dressed in dark clothes, wielding a long, dark, samurai-style sword, which he masterfully held. The figure took position and grinned.

Lixi recognized the toothy smile. "Vampire," she called out.

"We prefer to be called Nyos," the figure said in a Canadian-accented English.

The vampire moved toward Valor again, impossibly fast. Valor fumbled, trying to summon his sword. Odel threw himself between them, his axe swinging in a wide arc. The vampire twisted almost elegantly, and his blade opened Odel's biceps to the bone. Blood sprayed. Odel grunted but didn't scream. The axe dropped from his fingers. Lixi knew the dwarf wouldn't be able to use his arm until her major heal spell could heal him...if the dwarf didn't die first.

"You son of a bitch!" Brenda's hand shot out. She grabbed a fistful of loose earth from beside the fire and hurled it straight into the vampire's face. Dirt and ash exploded across his eyes.

Lixi's glow brightened with amusement. Leave it to Brenda to find the most practical solution.

The vampire staggered back, clawing at his face.

During those two precious seconds of blindness, Valor's

sword finally materialized in his hand, the blade glowing faint blue. He lunged forward, but his form was sloppy and desperate.

The vampire's eyes cleared. Two strokes, so fast they blurred together, and Valor's sword was knocked wide. The vampire's foot shot back without him even looking, catching Brenda in the face. She went down hard.

The vampire changed tactics. No more testing. He drove forward in a blur of strikes, each one targeting Valor's vitals, each one crashing against the ring's shield. Valor gave ground, his face pale, his sword seemingly forgotten in his hand. Strikes fell in rapid succession. The shield held through the first wave, then flickered. White spiderwebbed cracks shone across the air for a split second. The next blow punched through, and blood welled on Valor's cheek. The vampire inhaled, clearly savoring the scent. He was far too distracted to notice the fairy-sized threat floating near his ear.

"Undead, return to dust where you belong," Lixi whispered. Her wand touched the vampire's neck, right where his pulse should have been.

The drain hit Lixi immediately. Death magic always felt like something rotten sliding down her throat, coating her insides with wrongness.

The vampire screamed. The sound tore from him in waves, like a thousand voices shrieking at once.

Brenda's hands flew to her ears. Odel dropped to his knees. Valor just stood there, clearly too terrified to move.

The vampire's eyes went wide. His mouth worked, trying to form words that would never come. The first breeze was gentle, barely enough to stir leaves. It peeled away his cheek in a stream of ash. The second breeze took his jaw. By the third, there was nothing left but dust scattering into the darkness.

"Motherfucker," Brenda said. She was still on the ground,

blood streaming from her nose where the vampire had kicked her. Her hands shook.

For a long moment, nobody moved. They stood in the wreckage of their camp, breathing hard, the fire casting flickering shadows across their faces. Odel clutched his ruined arm, blood seeping between his fingers. Valor's sword disappeared, and he looked like he was about to drop to his knees.

Lixi's wings drooped. The death magic still sat heavy in her stomach, but she forced herself to move. She hovered above them, raised her wand, and let her healing magic flow. White light washed over Odel first. His arm knitted itself back together, muscle and skin sealing over bone. Then Brenda's nose straightened with a wet crack. The cuts on Valor's face closed. Not perfect. The small wounds would still ache, but they'd all live to fight another day.

Lixi bowed in the air. "You're welcome."

Valor looked at her with a thankful smile, then turned to Brenda. "We have to go. The city of angels, the one my mother mentioned...have you been there?"

"Why?" Brenda asked, still pressing the heel of her hand against her tender nose.

"We can't stay here. That vampire..." Valor glanced at the pile of ash already scattering in the wind. "Unless he was a complete idiot, he's not alone. There will be more, and they'll probably have zombies too."

The words settled over them like a weight. Lixi's glow dimmed. They'd been found. More were coming.

"How much time do we have?" Brenda asked.

"Not enough," Valor said.

Lixi watched them make the decision wordlessly. Brenda climbed to her feet, still shaky. Odel tested his healed arm. Valor looked at each of them in turn.

"The city is called Los Angeles," Brenda said finally. "I was there once years ago. There's a place I remember. I think I can visualize it well enough for the spell."

"You think?" Lixi asked.

"I hope," Brenda corrected.

They didn't have better options.

They gathered their things. Valor extinguished the fire, Odel covered their tracks, and within minutes they were ready. Hands joined, eyes closed, the spell wrapped around them, and the campsite disappeared.

CHAPTER
THIRTY-THREE

Tanya doubled over as Joey's death slammed into her. The bond they shared as maker and made shattered like glass, and his final scream echoed in her skull. He was dead. Not dormant, not injured. Actually gone.

For a split second, she saw through his eyes, spying an elf prince holding a sword, blood dripping from his cheek. Then nothing.

The green-haired girl licking Tanya's neck jerked back, her eyes wide. The girl was one of these brainless wannabes, so stupid she wasn't even worth turning into a zombie.

Tanya's fangs extended, her fingers curled, and somewhere in the back of her mind, she registered that she was shaking. Not with fear. With the need to tear something apart.

Tanya strangled the girl until her eyes popped out, then threw the body into the mass of dancing bodies. It hit the floor. Nobody noticed, all of them too lost in the music, the drugs, the flesh pressed against flesh.

The club was underground, all black walls and strobe lights cutting through smoke. Tanya shoved her way through the crowd, the stench of sweat and blood filling her nostrils as she headed for the restrooms.

A wannabe with facial tattoos smiled at her, inviting her to dance. Tanya pulled the thin knife from her boot. Throat opened, body dropped. Another blocked her path. The knife slid in and out. The Nyos parted for her, recognizing death in her red eyes. The humans didn't, not until it was too late. She killed every non-Nyo in her path, their blood hot and useless. She stabbed a young guy waiting for the restroom straight in the forehead. Bone cracked. The knife stuck, and she had to yank hard to free it, his body twitching as she did.

She entered the restroom. She knew Misha was here.

"Misha! I need you!" she screamed.

"I am here, Tanya," came the voice from the booth. "Can it wait?"

The restroom booth door was locked. She tore it off its hinges, barely registering the resistance. Two gothic dressed girls kissing in the corner of the restroom looked up just as the door hit them, severing both at the torso.

In the now exposed restroom booth sat Misha, her Chief of Staff, one of the first vampires she'd ever turned. He was taking a dump, his phone in one hand. When the door exploded outward, he didn't even flinch. He just looked up at her, his red eyes flat and calm, like she'd knocked instead of ripped the door off its hinges. He didn't blink. Just met her eyes and waited.

"They killed Joey." Tanya's voice cracked.

Misha pocketed his phone. "Who?"

The bass from the club rattled the stall walls. The music was so loud that Tanya couldn't think.

"Oh, fuck that." Tanya turned and shoved back through the doorway. She needed everyone out. Now.

The DJ was fat with dark greasy hair plastered to his scalp. His skin glistened with perspiration under the booth lights. He didn't see her coming until she was on the platform. Then he tried to push her off, his sweaty hands shoving at her shoulder.

"Who the hell are you? Get off!" His voice was high and indignant, like she was interrupting his important work.

She grabbed his hair and yanked his head back. With her other hand, she dropped the music to nothing and maxed out the mic. Her years of DJing made it easy.

The club went quiet and heads turned.

"Everybody out." Her voice boomed through the speakers.

The Nyos turned immediately, moving toward the exits.

The wannabes grumbled, booed, and kept dancing. The DJ squirmed in her grip, trying to pull free.

Tanya brought the knife to his throat. It took more effort than the others. His neck was that thick. The blade sawed through skin, muscle, and cartilage. Blood sprayed across the DJ booth. His head came free with a wet sound.

"Everybody out!" She held his head up by the hair, blood dripping onto the turntables.

That got their attention. The stampede for the exits was immediate, screaming and panic and bodies pushing bodies.

It took less than a minute for the club to empty. Tanya stood alone in the sudden quiet. She could hear everything now—the hum of the speakers, distant sirens, her own breathing.

She walked back to the restroom. Misha was still sitting on the stool.

"They killed Joey!" Tanya's voice cracked. "The fucking elf and human wizard bitch!"

"I'm sorry, Tanya." Misha's eyes dropped to her hand.

She followed his gaze. She was still holding the DJ's head. Her fingers were cramped around his hair, her knuckles white. His hair slipped through her fingers as she dropped it. It hit the tile with a wet *thunk.*

Her legs gave out. She slid down the wall, landing hard on

the dirty restroom floor in front of Misha's stool. Her hands were shaking again.

"I can't do this without him." Tanya pressed her palms against her eyes. "I'm so fucking tired of humans! I can't smell them around me any longer!"

"You don't have to."

"Joey loved the Nyo idea. He didn't like the messiness of vampires. He grew up thinking wooden stakes killed vampires." The words kept spilling out, like if she stopped talking, she'd have to feel the crippling sadness of losing him.

"A common myth." Misha's voice stayed level and patient. It was like he had all night to sit there and listen.

"They killed him, Misha!" Her voice rose to a scream. "They utterly destroyed him. Nothing I can do can bring him back! I want revenge!" Spit flew from her mouth. Her nails scraped through the tile, gouging the concrete beneath like it was soft earth.

"We can do that." He was still calm, still waiting.

"I'm done with the Nyo crap. We are two thousand vampires strong. The plan has run its course. You hear me?"

"I hear you."

"Turn all the wannabes to zombies. Close every Nyo office. The professionals who helped us? Turn them all to vampires. I don't want a single living human who knows how we work." She wiped blood from her chin. "Then we vanish. Delete everything. Social media, events, all of it. Gone."

Misha's dark eyes studied her face. "Yes, Tanya." He nodded once, accepting it all.

"I want more than zombies! Boris mentioned stronger allies. Darker allies. He said if we ever needed them..." Her voice rose again. "I want them now!"

"I'll set up a meeting with Boris to talk about it. Tomorrow night. It's morning in Europe right now."

Her vision blurred. She blinked, and tears spilled over, hot against her cold skin.

"They killed Joey. Beautiful, shiny, happy, sexy, dumb Joey." The words came out as a whisper.

Misha said nothing. He just sat there, giving her the space to share her pain.

"I want all elves dead! All dwarves dead! All fairies expelled!" She grabbed the DJ's head and slammed it against the floor. Again. Again. "I want humans in cattle houses or dead on spikes!"

"It's a beautiful vision," Misha agreed.

Tanya stopped. The head was barely recognizable. She hauled herself up from the floor, exhausted. Everything hurt. "I'm heading out to sleep. I'm so fuckin' tired." She grabbed what remained of the head. "Do it all."

"Yes, Tanya, that's the plan. Good talk." Misha's voice followed her out.

On the way out, she dumped the DJ's head in the trash. That was the only place humanity deserved.

CHAPTER
THIRTY-FOUR

Teleportation still creeped Brenda out, even though she'd already done it. One second, they were in an Arizona desert. The next, they were in California. No transition, no sound, no blue light, nothing.

"Hollywoo," said Lixi.

Brenda followed her gaze up to the sign. "It's Hollywood," Brenda said. "The 'D' just fell off."

Except it hadn't fallen. Someone had blown it off.

The white letters still gleamed against the brown hillside, but where the "D" should have stood, twisted metal jutted from scorched earth like broken bones. The explosion had peeled back the letter's face, leaving jagged edges that caught the evening light. Black soot stained the hillside in a wide arc below the damage, and the trees closest to the blast were skeletal, their branches reaching skyward like charred fingers. The acrid smell of old fire still clung to the air, mixing with the dry-sage scent of the hills.

The rest of the place looked worse. Below them, Los Angeles had turned into a sprawl of canvas and plastic. Tents covered the roads in tight rows, spilling onto the highways like a patchwork quilt stitched from desperation. What used to be six lanes of freeway was now a corridor of makeshift shelters stretching as far as she could see. Blue tarps, drab olive camping tents, and even cardboard lean-tos packed the asphalt. The fading evening light caught hundreds of small fires flickering between the tents. Makeshift cook fires sent thin columns of smoke into the darkening sky, and here and there, battery-powered lanterns glowed like fireflies.

Down in the valley sat a massive tent, easily the size of a warehouse. A line of people snaked away from its entrance, hundreds of them waiting as the evening started to cool down.

"We can't go there looking like this," Brenda said. "We look like a group from a Dungeons and Dragons club that went too far."

"What's Dungeons—" Odel started.

Lixi cut him off. "She means you look like a dwarf, Odel. You are four feet tall and three hundred pounds wide. These humans will run away screaming, or at least ask us some hard questions if we come up looking like this. I've had to hide myself for years. Only human kids are smart enough to understand the supernatural."

"Supernatural?" Brenda asked.

"Yes, natural and super awesome like me," Lixi answered with a wink.

"I will disguise our appearance," Valor said, clearly unimpressed with Lixi's joke.

Brenda remembered Lixi once commenting he was kind of dry, and she chuckled softly.

Valor murmured a word and gestured with his hand. The air shimmered, and blue light washed over Valor's, Lixi's, and Odel's figures, like cobwebs brushing against their skin.

Odel gasped and grabbed at his beard. "I can feel my face,

but..." He turned his hands over, staring at them. "This is very strange. Very, very strange."

"You look like a beer-chugging biker," Brenda said. The illusion had softened his dwarfish features into something rough but human.

Valor's ears were rounded now, his eyes brown and ordinary. Lixi had taken her grown-up form, her wings hidden.

"This feels wrong," Odel muttered, still patting his face. "Like wearing someone else's skin."

"You'll get used to it," Lixi said.

"Put your hood up, Lixi," Brenda said. "You still look better than most supermodels. You will attract attention."

Lixi did as Brenda suggested while mumbling, "I am a model, only a super awesome model."

Brenda chuckled, but Valor shook his head and sighed.

The path down was steep and rocky. Brenda picked her way carefully, watching where she put her feet. Ahead, Odel moved closer to Valor, the dwarf's shorter legs working double-time to match the elf's stride.

"So...we are not going to talk about the vampire we just fought?" Odel asked.

Valor's shoulders tensed. "We fought undead on our way to your homeland, Odel. Where there are zombies, there are vampires. This was not a surprise for us." His voice was too even, too controlled.

Brenda watched him stumble on loose gravel, his hand going to the ring on his finger. He turned it once, twice, the dwarf-forged metal catching the fading light. The shield had saved his life, but it seemed to her that his fingers moved with nervous repetition, not gratitude.

Odel caught Valor's elbow. "Valor, are you okay?"

The elf stopped walking. For a moment, he just stared down at the tent city and the fires flickering in the growing dark. His jaw worked like he was chewing words he didn't want to say.

"Yes, sorry, my friend." His thumb rubbed the ring. "Your parents' gift saved my life. If it wasn't for this ring, I would have died at the hands of that vampire. He was much better than me with the sword." His voice dropped. "I worry that I am not the right person to lead you all successfully."

Brenda's chest tightened. She wanted to tell him he was wrong, that he was exactly the person they needed.

Lixi shot past her before Brenda could speak. The fairy stood directly in Valor's path, her nose inches from his. "Valor." Her voice was sharp. "I know you are so young that walking is a new thing for you, but stop fucking whining." She poked him in the chest. Hard.

Valor blinked, clearly surprised.

"We love you and trust you and think you are the shit. You are the right person to lead us because you are here." Another poke.

Brenda glanced at Odel, whose eyebrows had climbed toward his hairline.

"You were not careful, and you need about a hundred more years of practice to be as good as that master swordsman, but you are what we got." A third poke. "None of us is perfect. We live, we fuck up, and we learn."

Brenda had never heard Lixi sound so serious. Odel's mouth hung open. Even the wind seemed to pause.

Then, as if nothing happened, Lixi continued down the path.

They walked on in silence after that. Brenda could hear their footsteps on gravel, the distant sounds from the tent city, and Valor's quiet breathing.

After several minutes, his shoulders straightened. His stride lengthened back to normal. "You are right, Lixi," he said. "I am sorry. I will learn and do better."

"Good. You better!" Lixi dropped back beside Brenda and winked from inside her hood.

They reached the line of people heading toward the big tent. As Brenda got closer, she noticed something odd. The people waiting in line had a faint shimmer around them, like heat waves rising from summer asphalt. No, not heat waves. Light. A thin, flickering glow wrapped around each person like a second skin.

She blinked, but the glow didn't disappear. It was yellow and orange, almost translucent, the light shifting and pulsing.

"Do you see that?" she whispered to Lixi.

The fairy followed her gaze. "Oh." Her eyes widened. "Interesting...I have not seen so many wizards in one place since the great wars of the north many, many years ago."

Brenda's head snapped toward her. "Wait. All of them?" She looked down the line of hundreds of people, each wrapped in that faint golden shimmer. "They're all wizards?"

"Every single one," Lixi confirmed.

The line moved efficiently, but nobody wanted to chat. Signs posted every few yards said to follow the line and wait in an orderly fashion.

Brenda tried anyway. "Hey, how long have you been here?"

The woman in front of her, maybe forty with graying hair and a torn jacket, glanced back. Her eyes were hollow with dark circles underneath. She looked at Brenda for a long moment, then turned away without answering.

A man farther up had a sleeping child on his shoulder, the kid's face pressed against his neck. His shirt was stained with something dark, and his hands shook as he adjusted his grip. When Brenda caught his eye, he stared through her like she wasn't there.

An older couple behind them stood close together, the woman leaning heavily on the man. Both had that same exhausted look, that same defeated slouch. When Brenda smiled at them, the woman's expression didn't change at all.

These people were done talking. Done with strangers. Done with everything except getting through the line and finding somewhere to sleep.

A little over an hour later, they got into the tent. Brenda could see the operation in action. Five makeshift stations with separate desks lined the tent's internal perimeter, one person working at each, trying their best to keep track of hundreds of new arrivals. A long folding table near the entrance was covered with hand-labeled folders and notebooks, someone's attempt at a filing system.

The people behind the desk wore matching gray clothes, simple outfits that gave them some sense of official authority. Each one worked through their own version of the intake process, asking questions, writing answers in spiral notebooks, and handing out tent assignments on whatever paper they could find.

The young person in front of them in line got called to the left-most station, occupied by a tall thin man who took intake notes. "Name? Great. And you've got magic, right? Yes, we all do here. Don't worry. We're keeping track of who's where in case families get separated." The voices were tired but kind, people helping people.

The woman in the center waved them forward. She was big, the kind of tall and broad that said she could handle herself in any fight. Long brown hair was pulled back from her plain, wide face, and her hands resting on the table were scarred across the knuckles.

She sat like she owned the space, her shoulders back, taking up room unapologetically. On her, the gray clothes looked less like a uniform and more like work clothes. Her voice carried across the tent even when she wasn't raising it.

"Your name?" she asked without looking at them, her eyes on the notepad in front of her.

Valor turned his head sideways at an odd angle and frowned, studying her like he was reading text only he could see. "I know you. You are Rosy Underwood. You are the first discovered human wizard. I read about how you blew your partner's head off."

How does he know that? thought Brenda. Sure, Valor had told her he had read the entire Internet a while back, but his ability to recall a single article from it was, well, magical.

The woman's pen stopped moving. She raised her eyes slowly and looked at them all. "You're a weird bunch." Her gaze moved from one face to the next, lingering. The woman's stare burned through them. "I am indeed Rosy, but you do not belong here." Her chair scraped back as she stood. "Did Scar send you?"

She shifted her weight, her left leg moving back, her hands tensing on the table. Heat radiated from her palms. The other workers glanced their way.

Valor raised his hands, his palms out. "We do not know anyone named Scar. We came here to help you."

The word Charm overlaid Brenda's vision. Valor was magically trying to calm Rosy. This felt like a risky move to Brenda.

Luckily, Rosy lowered her hands. The heat quickly vanished, and her colleagues looked calmer as well.

"Come with me to the back of the tent. We can talk privately there," Rosy said, and they followed her.

"She is magnificent," Odel murmured.

"It's so exciting meeting the most powerful human wizard alive!" Lixi whispered in Brenda's ear.

. . .

How can this ordinary-looking middle-aged woman be the most powerful human wizard alive?

CHAPTER THIRTY-FIVE

6:00 a.m.

James's body refused to move when the knock came. The Secret Service, punctual as ever.

His limbs felt like they had been filled with concrete. The presidential quarters were still dark, the blackout curtains doing their job too well.

He'd been asleep for four hours. Maybe three. The sheets had tangled around his legs like he'd been fighting something in his sleep. He probably had been.

There was no emergency. This was his life now.

He dragged himself out of bed, opened the suite's door, and let Timon and the Secret Service in.

Timon walked with him toward the restroom, quickly going over today's agenda, and handed him a cup of coffee.

James wrapped both hands around the first coffee cup, needing its heat to get his mind going. The bitter liquid burned his empty stomach.

7:05 a.m.

He was rushed to the Oval Office for his first meeting, a

security briefing. It was all very predictable. These days, everything was predictable.

James was starting to appreciate his new talents and capabilities but also hated them a little. He seemed to excel in premonition. It wasn't perfect, but he started to know, to predict, many things in advance. The words formed in James's mind seconds before they left anyone's mouth. The general would say "minimal casualties" before his mouth opened. He knew what they would say the way he knew his own name.

Timon pressed another cup into his hands. The second? Third? James drank it without tasting it, just needing the temporary clarity it brought. His hands had steadied, at least.

The inconsistency of his skill grated on him. James had tried everything to identify the pattern. Catalogued every prediction, every failure. Time of day, stress levels, blood sugar, sleep quality. Nothing correlated. Two days ago, he'd known the Chinese ambassador would request a delay three hours before the call. He'd had his response prepared, his schedule adjusted. Efficient. Yesterday, the defense secretary's resignation blindsided him completely. No warning. No preparation. He'd wasted the entire morning on useless meetings when he could have been doing something useful. No system. No pattern. Just monotony. It was nerve-racking.

The security briefing went on. Director Matthew's voice became white noise. Something about troop movements. Something else about supply chains. The words slid past James without sticking. The slides blurred together, red and green threat assessments that looked identical to yesterday's. His dreams had been more vivid than this meeting.

Oh, my night prophecies.

The only time his prediction skill was consistently accurate was in his dreams. The night visions were about everything, from mundane conversations about war tactics, reports, and press questions to visions of masses of wizards living in tents in Los Angeles. All were super accurate. The details in these prophecies were confirmed by his experiences the day after as well as satellite and air surveillance reports. He had so many dreams and was so obsessed with writing them down in the middle of the night that he didn't feel as if he was getting any rest. His temper was getting worse every day.

9:45 a.m.

James blinked. Did everyone leave? The Oval Office was empty. Only the press secretary standing in front of his desk, his hand half-raised like he'd been trying to get James's attention for a while.

James's chest tightened. The press secretary was asking if he would mind giving a short statement later today. James agreed and deferred him to Timon, who ran his schedule. The man thanked him and left. What did he want? A statement?

Timon was there again with another cup. James took it without looking, the ceramic warm against his palms. The coffee didn't help anymore, but stopping felt impossible.

He was not feeling well today. His skull felt packed with cotton. James pressed his palms against his closed eyes, watching the familiar explosion of colored dots behind his eyelids. When he opened them again, the Oval Office stretched and compressed around him like breathing lungs. Timon's voice reached him from underwater, his words rippling and distorted. The dreams kept pulling him back.

There were two other sets of dreams that James returned to every night. One set was of burning cities and mothers holding their burnt kids coming out of burnt villages. It was a recurring dream that had haunted him for a long while. He could smell the ashes and chemical smoke. The other set of dreams was of a group of wizards that was going to cause that horrible future, the Catalysts. The terror was bone deep. Every time he dreamed of this band of wizards, he was eight years old again, lying rigid in his bed, certain that someone or something breathed in the darkness beneath his bed. He could hear their whispers in the dreams, but couldn't make them out. He could feel their presence like a cold draft under a locked door.

10:15 a.m.

Timon touched his shoulder and leaned in close. “Time to go to your next meeting, Mr. President.” He spoke directly into James's ear, quiet but insistent. His hand stayed on James's shoulder, applying gentle but constant pressure. “They've been waiting, sir.”

James blinked. Timon was already moving toward the door, checking his watch, his hand hovering near James's elbow, ready to guide him if needed.

Timon walked James to the Cabinet Room. The Cabinet members were all waiting for him. They'd been here for twenty minutes, waiting patiently while he'd been zoning out in the Oval Office.

James hated being late. Hated it in others, hated it in himself even more. His neck flushed hot with embarrassment. He thanked them for their patience and sat there while they debated the need to test infants for magical traits.

His thoughts went back to the Catalysts.

The Catalysts in his dream looked like four harmless, even friendly magical beings, but James knew from personal experience that monsters hid behind perfect smiles. His father had been one of these smiling monsters. His throat tightened. His hands curled into fists under the table. Some memories you couldn't think about during Cabinet meetings. Some memories you couldn't think about at all. Even if these four wizards thought they were friendly, they were going to cause a lot of death. That was certain in James's mind. He had to stop them.

12:40 p.m.

James surfaced from his thoughts like breaking through water. The debate had ended. When? He'd heard arguments about ethics and logistics and legal precedent, but none of it had stuck. Now, the entire Cabinet sat in silence, eight pairs of eyes fixed on him. Expectant. Patient. Waiting for the decision only he could make.

"Do it. Test every baby."

They all nodded. The meeting adjourned. They all left.

The room had a big map of the US on the wall. James walked to it and pointed at southern California. "There you are!" he said to himself. Realizing he said it out loud.

For the longest time, he hadn't known where the Catalysts were specifically in the world. They were in some unrecognizable underground maze and then in a campsite by a small river. James had drawn hundreds of pictures of these underground rooms and desert landscapes. They filled his desk drawers, stuffed between official documents. Stacked on his nightstand. Hidden in the false bottom of his briefcase. Charcoal sketches of stone corridors. Watercolors of desert campfires. Every detail from his dreams committed to paper with obsessive precision. By now, he felt he knew the group personally. An elf, a dwarf, a fairy, and a woman all together, all smiling and happy. What a shit show.

The Catalysts were most capable of causing harm when they were together. According to the book of Kador, mixed wizard groups were vastly more powerful and dangerous. James had memorized page forty-seven. The illustration showed figures in a circle, their hands joined, light radiating outward. Beneath it was Kador's warning in angular script. "When the races combine their power, even the titans must take notice." James felt the menace of that evil team in his mouth every time he woke up.

Today was a breakthrough. Today, he saw them in his

dreams in a place he recognized. They were near the outskirts of Los Angeles. What did these devils want with human wizards? He could not figure that out. He knew they had purpose, and he knew he had to stop them to save humanity from the burning ashes.

12:55 p.m.

Timon was tugging at his sleeve, and another cup materialized in James's hands. Timon never asked if he wanted it. Never suggested water. Just kept the black liquid coming like an IV drip. James's stomach churned acid, but he drank anyway.

"It's time for your press meeting, Mr. President."

The press room was five minutes away.

Timon handed him the statement to read as they were walking.

James entered the press room. He remembered when this room had been chaos—shouting reporters, camera flashes like lightning, hands waving for attention. Now, everyone sat perfectly still, their notebooks open and pens poised. Not a single camera. Not a single voice raised above a whisper. Good little school kids taking notes for their class report.

The press had become reduced to a propaganda channel by a simple process. Journalists with a negative attitude were "randomly tested." All had been found positive for magical skills and had been quickly deported to LA.

James read the press statement. "The nation has never been stronger, more vigilant, and more free. Blah blah blah."

The press gobbled it up and clapped at the end of the meeting. They all left quietly.

His mind wandered again. If he could just get more sleep...

1:26 p.m.

Timon was tugging him toward the Oval Office. The cup Timon had given him had gone cold in his grip, a thin film forming on the surface. James drank it anyway and grimaced at the bitter, room-temperature dregs.

James was holding the press briefing from earlier. He looked at it, and his stomach dropped. His pen had moved with precision while his conscious mind had read propaganda to the journalists, and now, a woman's face covered the press brief. Not a quick sketch either. A portrait shaded and detailed. Individual strands of hair. The exact curve of her jaw from his dreams.

The sketch was of the female wizard member of the Catalysts, the woman wizard in his dreams, but he knew her from somewhere else too. James recognized her from the brief he had shared with Roy. The document had been titled "Suspected Witness #K25" and had photos of this exact woman. She was the Witness! The woman who helped the elf prince bring all the elves back to this world.

Now his theories were connected with facts. The elf and the Witness were two of the Catalysts.

Kador had predicted everything that had come to pass—the elf prince, the Witness, the return of magic. The Catalysts were already gathered together, about to cast a spell that would end human supremacy in the world.

James felt that he deeply understood how Kador could predict the future so well. Kador must have had the same magical powers as James had, only ten times stronger.

Am I the only person with Kador's capabilities in the world?

2:15 p.m.

Blessed Timon gave him some time for a quick restroom break, and then, James was back in the Oval Office. The next ten meetings in the Oval Office didn't really register. It all felt like a blur. People shaking his hands. People asking for decisions and favors. All so very predictable.

1:47 a.m.

He fell into bed, bracing for the next restless dream.

Did Kador have the same dreams? Had he been as tired as James was right now?

Some days were a whole lot of nothing. Meetings. Decisions. The machinery of government grinding forward. But tonight, tonight would be different. Tonight, he would dream of them again, and tomorrow, the real work could finally begin. Capture them. Torture them. Have their heads on a spike. Save humanity.

Simple.

CHAPTER THIRTY-SIX

Brenda's eyes took a second to adjust as they followed Rosy crossing the divider to the back of the tent.

The back section was dim, lit by a battery lantern on a crate that threw shadows up the brown makeshift walls of tarps and plywood. Sounds from outside bled through. The corners of the room disappeared into darkness. Metal shelving lined two walls, mostly empty except for random supplies—trash bags, bleach, tangled extension cords, and a few simple metal chairs.

Rosy planted herself in front of the shelving, facing them.

Brenda had never seen any person radiate so brightly. It was as if Rosy had an aura like the saints in European churches. The aura glowed in yellow and orange, just like Rosy's hands did once they were in the back room. Rosy stood with her weight leaning forward, her fists half-clenched at her sides. Brenda found herself unconsciously taking a half-step back, her body reading *threat* before her mind caught up.

"What the hell brings you here?" Rosy demanded.

Valor opened his mouth.

She cut him off. “You ain’t no wizards, at least not the regular kind. I felt you tried to trick me back there.”

Beside Brenda, Odel shifted his weight. His hand moved almost imperceptibly toward his belt.

Valor’s fingers twitched. Brenda recognized the gesture. He was readying a spell, running through the words in his mind.

“Next time you do it, you will meet my fists.” Rosy’s hands began to glow more orange, heat distorting the air above them. “I don’t know *what* you’re hiding, but I can tell that you are hiding *something*.”

Brenda’s muscles tensed. Her own hand drifted toward the small knife in her pocket. Ready for violence. It was shocking how quickly she’d gotten used to it. Four months ago, she wouldn’t have swatted a fly.

The air felt explosive, like lightning about to strike.

Only Lixi seemed unfazed.

“She’s scared,” Lixi whispered in Brenda’s mind. “Angry scared. Like a cornered cat.”

“Rosy, we are here to help.” Valor’s hands were open, empty, held at chest height. “We are a group of wizards sent to assist you in your ordeal. My mother is a powerful and important wizard who sensed the dangerous situation here and dispatched us to help you out.”

Rosy scowled at Valor. Her lips pulled back, baring her teeth. “Bullshit! There ain’t no important wizards. We are all shit! Not even humans in the eyes of our government.” Her voice rose with each word. “We suffered hunger, we suffered humiliation, we suffered death. No one here has money, or even if they had millions, no one will let them into the simplest supermarket. Prove to me you are no government agents or another scheme of Scar!” She raised her arms, which were now red hot.

“Okay. I will show you who we are.”

Valor murmured something under his breath.

The shimmer passed over them as their illusion fell away.

Rosy's eyes widened. Her mouth opened. She took a step back, then another until her legs hit the chair. She collapsed into it. The metal frame groaned under the impact.

"What the..." Her voice died in her throat.

The orange glow in her hands flickered out like a candle. The heat disappeared. Rosy stared at Valor's pointed ears and his cat-like eyes. She glanced at Brenda and Lixi, who remained the same, but then at Odel's compact, barrel-chested frame, massive rock-like muscles, and long beard and back to Valor. Her hands had started shaking.

"You're...you're not human," she said softly.

"I am human, Rosy," Brenda said, "but magic is waking up, and the world is getting filled with other races of magical creatures. I'm with these people to help save all magical creatures. We were sent here to help prevent more wizards from getting hurt or being killed."

Rosy sat in silence looking at Brenda. "Death..." she murmured.

Her shoulders dropped. Her head tipped back against the shelving, and she closed her eyes for a long moment. After a few seconds, she shrugged and pushed herself up. Her hands stayed cool, no longer threatening.

"What do you know about death?" Rosy words were full of exhaustion. "I have been dying most nights here. I have died more times than I can count."

"What do you mean?" Brenda asked. "Do you mean dying metaphorically?"

"I don't know what dying metaphorically looks like," Rosy said, "but dying for real sucks and ain't pretty either."

She took out her phone and played them a video.

The screen was small, the footage grainy and dark. Night vision, maybe. Yesterday's date showed in the bottom left corner. Rosy stood on a ridge, silhouetted against a lighter sky. Her hands moved in rapid succession, and fireballs erupted from her wrists one after another after another, orange streaks cutting through the darkness.

Then, there was a flash of white light.

Brenda's breath caught. Rosy's left arm, from the shoulder down, just disappeared. Vaporized. Blood sprayed black in the night vision, coating her side.

But Rosy kept firing with her right hand. She kept fighting.

Another flash.

The top half of Rosy's head was gone. Just gone. Everything above the nose. She collapsed backward, dead before she hit the ground.

Brenda couldn't look away from the small screen. She couldn't process what she'd just watched.

The tent was silent. From the outside, children's voices drifted through the canvas. Normal sounds. People living. It felt obscene against what she'd just seen.

Brenda swallowed hard against the bile rising in her throat. Rosy died last night. Brenda wanted to sit, but there was no chair close enough on their side of the room. Odel reached and held her elbow. Her vision narrowed to a tunnel. She concentrated on breathing until the world widened again.

Lixi wrapped her arms around herself, looking suddenly very young beneath the hood. "That's messed up," she said quietly.

Rosy cleaned the phone on her sleeve and slid it back into her pocket. When she spoke again, there was something almost proud in her voice. "And that was yesterday! Look at me today. I'm ready for another day to die," she said with a rusty voice.

They all looked at her in silence.

Rosy stared at her hands and turned them over, studying the palms like they might hold answers. "I don't know why I keep coming back. Don't know how it works. I just...wake up. Sometimes hours later, sometimes the next morning. Naked, usually. Cold. Confused as hell." Her voice dropped. "First few times, I thought I was going crazy. Thought maybe I never really died, you know? Maybe it was all in my head."

Odel's eyes widened. He glanced at Valor, then back at Rosy. "Miss Rosy, how many times have you died like that?" he asked in his deep, respectful voice.

"I think Odel has the hots for her," Lixi whispered in Brenda's ear.

Brenda ignored her. This was too important.

Rosy studied her hands, her fingers flexing. "More than I could count, really. There was the first time in jail, where that bitch slit my throat. I woke up that night in the morgue and almost died again from a heart attack. The police caught me when I used my credit card in a gas station and took me to a facility. I think I got so mad I blew us all up. I woke up the morning after in a garbage dumpster."

Brenda's breath caught. "You blew up a government facility?"

Rosy shrugged. "I was mad. And scared. And I didn't know what I was doing." She looked at them. Her jaw worked for a moment before she spoke again. "After that, I found a few other wizards on the streets. We were so hungry, and no one would sell us anything, even if we had money!" Her hands flared red-hot again. She took a breath, and the glow faded. "Ben found us all homeless and hungry and gave us food. He told us he was going to Washington to give the government a piece of his mind. He said that if we joined him, we would all get food and nice clothes and would never need to live on the streets anymore. Ben had a nice truck and lots of beers, burgers, and chips. We joined him very willingly. We were hungry, and he was the first person with money that was nice to us."

Lixi's expression darkened. "He was using you, wasn't he?"

"Of course he was using us." Rosy's voice went flat. "But when you're starving and people spit on you in the street, you take what you can get." Her gaze dropped to her hands. "Ben introduced us to his friends. They were all shiny and rich. They told us we were going to attack Washington for them and eliminate the government that was bad to us, that if we destroyed the government, we would have plenty of food and a place to stay. We met other wizards Ben had collected from streets all around the country. We spent a week in their big warehouse and prepared for their plan. Then they took us by bus to Washington DC. It was glorious. As much food and drinks as you can ask for."

Then she smiled sadly. "It all turned to shit after that. The police and the soldiers reacted so fast after we started the attack. Many of my street wizard friends got killed by police the moment they shot their first fireball. My squad was supposed to take the White House. They killed all of my friends one by one. I told them this would not have started if we had food to eat, but they would not listen."

"They should never have put you in that position," Odel said. His voice was gentle, almost tender. "You were just hungry."

Rosy's jaw tightened. She nodded once. "They blew me to a million fucking pieces. It was very painful," she stated without emotion. "I woke up the day after on the road next to the White House, naked and cold again. I teamed up with a few street wizards going to LA. They were homeless but gave me food and clean clothes. We headed to LA on the truck they stole, and we became real tight." She pointed back to the entrance of the tent they came from. "These are the guys in the front of the tent. We run this shit now. We raided a few stores along the way and got many tents and supplies. When we got to LA, we found out all the non-wizards left and stole a bunch more things. We've been getting a lot of new wizards every day, but we still have not run out of supplies yet. It would have all been sweet if we did not have fucking Scar to hunt us!" She spat on the floor.

"Is Scar the guy who attacked you in the video?" Brenda asked.

"That bastard? Not a chance!" Rosy laughed. "He sends his wizard minions to attack us every night. From what I heard, Scar was a gang lord a while back. He now controls most of the city with a bunch of wizard gangsters. He sent us a messenger that told us we must all work for Scar now. We sent the messenger back with one less arm. Since then, they have been raiding our camp every night. I am the only one that cannot fucking die, so I am the first line of defense. After I pick most of them off, the rest of the wizards can defend themselves, and Scar's people retreat, but he is able to recruit people pretty fast or has a lot of wizards already working for him because they keep attacking us again and again." The words came out flat and drained.

Valor stepped forward. "Rosy, would you accept our offer to help you fight Scar?"

Brenda noticed a buzz of magic surrounding Valor and echoing in his voice.

Rosy's eyes went from dull blue to almost unnatural shiny blue as her gaze locked on him. "Nobody gives nothing for free. What's in it for you?"

"No strings attached," he replied.

She didn't look convinced. "Because I don't do debts. I don't owe nobody nothing."

"You won't owe us," Valor said simply.

Rosy's face shifted. The suspicion melted first. Then, something desperate and raw broke through, and finally, something that might have been gratitude softened the hard lines around her mouth.

"Fuck yeah, I will take all the help I can get," she said.

The Quest magic pulsed through Brenda's chest. There was a brief flare of warmth and a strong sense of rightness and purpose. Acknowledged. Accepted.

"Your friends out front," Valor said, "the ones who run things with you, how many are you?"

Rosy thought for a moment. "Twelve, including me. We're the ones who kept everyone alive this long."

Valor exchanged a look with Odel.

"We can work with that," the dwarf rumbled.

"Work with what?" Rosy asked.

"We're going to teach you how to fight properly," Valor said. "All of you."

CHAPTER THIRTY-SEVEN

Tanya's fingers tapped the mouse, and she looked at her image in the conference call window. Pale skin, thin face, her hair pulled back like a ballerina. Her Canadian den had become a total mess since Joey died, so she'd chosen one of those fake backgrounds, a sterile office space the software creator thought was appropriate.

Boris was late to the call.

She took a deep breath. He would come. Her nails dug into the stone kitchen countertop.

Another two minutes passed, and Boris's face finally appeared on screen, stone walls and flickering torchlight behind him in Romania. She could see ancient tapestries faded with age on the walls behind him and what looked like bones scattered on a table just at the edge of the frame.

"Can you hear me? Does this thing work?"

Yes, that was his usual greeting.

Tanya felt her lip twitch. "Boris. They killed Joey! The elf prince and that witch! They fucking killed him, destroyed him. I don't know how they did it, but I felt it. He is gone." Tears dropped on the keyboard. She didn't care.

"Oh, Tanyushka, I heard. I am so sorry. I know you cared for him a lot," Boris said in a comforting voice. "It is a horrible thing, death. How dare they take a vampire's life! They took your love. He was so young, so beautiful. I truly feel for you, love."

Tanya sniffed, feeling comforted. Boris always knew the right thing to say. "I am done with this Nyo thing, Boris! I'm done pretending we're friendly, new-age vampires. Done with the brand. I want revenge! I want blood!"

"This is a smart move, Tanya. I am glad you are done with this Nyo thing. We are vampires and should be proud of it. We are the most majestic, wise, and benevolent creatures in the entire world. We are not a brand. We are the royal predator." He still spoke too loudly. Probably always would on calls like this.

Heat flushed through Tanya's chest. She breathed in slowly and smoothed her voice back to steadiness. "Boris, darling, you were right all along." She straightened in her chair. "I want to act now. I have two thousand vampires and more zombies than I need."

His eyes widened in true shock, an expression she'd never seen on him before, and it almost made her smile for the first time since Joey had died.

"Two thousand, Tanyushka! Already?" he actually cried out, the sound crackling through the speakers. "That is amazing!"

"Well, it was the Nyo idea. I know you did not like it, but it worked much better than the good old bite in the neck from time to time. Boris, we are ready! This is our moment." She leaned toward the screen.

"Indeed, my dear, it is our time. For too long, we have been doing what we do in the shadows. For too long, we were hunted by humans," Boris agreed with a smile.

"Boris, I need more allies for this to succeed. The Americans are still reeling from the attack on Washington. Their government is in chaos. Their new president is paranoid, and they're rounding up anyone with magic and sending them to LA. They're at their weakest, but we are still relatively small compared to their Army or even police force. I need to overwhelm them with power. You mentioned once that when the time comes, we can call upon many other dark allies to help us. I need them now."

Boris was silent for a long moment, deep in his thoughts.

Her laptop battery flashed a warning. Ten percent. She ignored it.

Tanya almost thought Boris was going to tell her it was not time again. She prepared all the counter arguments. Despite them being friendly and informal, Boris's decisions were final. Even through the screen, she felt the weight of his authority, the pull to obey that went deeper than choice.

"Yes, it is time," he said finally.

Tanya realized her whole body had been frozen as she had waited. Now, relief flooded through her. He was finally ready to go to war.

"You are right to seek allies, Tanyushka. Against the elves and their witch, you will need more than vampires and zombies." Boris's expression turned thoughtful. "There are powers in this world, ancient powers that slumber in the deep places, dark creatures that once ruled these lands before magic faded." His voice dropped lower. "Monsters. Shadow beasts. Things that have been sleeping for centuries, waiting for magic to return strong enough to wake them."

Tanya leaned closer to the screen, her pulse quickening.

"I am going to send you a scroll," Boris continued, "a summoning scroll that will call these armies from below and bind them to our cause, but I must warn you, it is a high-level spell, one that has not been cast in hundreds of years. It is far beyond your ability to cast alone." He met her eyes through the screen. "You will need another race wizard to cast it with you, a wizard who can channel different magic and enhance your vampiric powers to reach the level required. I think the gnomes will be willing to join if we promise them loot and power when this is over."

Gnomes. Tanya's fingers drummed against the countertop. She'd heard stories about them, and none of them were good. Her mother used to spit three times whenever someone mentioned them. She had thought they were just stories, but apparently, she had been wrong.

"You will need to go personally to talk to their newly anointed king. I had a strong vision that the elves just slayed their old one." A slight smile crossed his lips. "The new king will be ambitious and greedy, desperate to prove himself. Perfect for our purposes." The smile faded. "But be careful, Tanyushka. The gnomes are a wicked race. They have no honor, no loyalty. Everything is a transaction. They would sell their own children for the right price." He leaned closer to the camera, his expression grave. "Do not trust them. Show no weakness. They respect only strength and gold."

Tanya nodded. She would do whatever it took. She had a bad feeling about it, though. Her mother had said gnomes lived in underground kingdoms built on greed and treachery. Meeting with their king would mean walking into a nest of vipers.

"As king of the vampires, I have the right to request an audience with the gnome king," Boris said. "I will invoke that right and delegate it to you. Together with the scroll, I will send you a map that shows how to reach the meeting place." His old eyes looked at her with worry. "Remember, Tanyushka, the gnomes are as vile as they get. Keep your guard up."

"Do not worry, Boris. I will bring them into our fold. They will join us," Tanya said, bowing her head.

"If you win this, Tanya..." Boris leaned closer to his camera, his ancient eyes burning with intensity. "If you win this war, vampires will rule this world. No more humans at the top of the food chain, butchering everything in their path, poisoning the earth, enslaving every other living creature to feed their greed." His voice grew passionate. "For too long, we have hidden in the shadows while they destroyed what should have been ours, but if you win..." He paused. "You and I will rule over it all." His expression softened. "Do you remember what I promised you when I turned you?"

Tanya's breath caught. She remembered.

"I promised you would be my queen one day," Boris said quietly. "If you win this war, Tanyushka, I will make you queen of all vampires."

Queen.

Tanya nodded enthusiastically. She felt like a kid being offered candy. She stared at the screen, certain she'd misheard him. Queen of all vampires. Not just her den. Not just her territory. Not just North America. All of them. Every bloodline. Every ancient den. Every vampire who had ever existed would answer to her.

If she won this war.

When she won this war.

Her mouth opened, but no sound came out. She tried again, but her throat closed completely. The magnitude of it crashed over her like a wave. For Joey. For herself. For everything.

"Thank you, Boris." Her voice cracked on his name. She had to stop and blinked hard. The screen blurred. She swiped at her eyes, surprised to find them wet again. These weren't sad tears. These were tears of joy. "I will not fail you. I will not fail my people." She drew a shaking breath. "I will win this war."

CHAPTER THIRTY-EIGHT

Brenda peeked outside their tent to make sure no one could hear them before going back to her place inside. Battery-powered lamps hung from the tent poles cast warm shadows across the canvas walls. The day's heat was finally fading, leaving the air thick but breathable.

"I don't get how she could die and be revived. Not even once, let alone so many times. Is that a magical trait of some kind?" Brenda asked once Rosy had showed them to their tent and had left to gather the rest of her team.

"No, I'm not aware of any magical power that can create that effect," Valor said thoughtfully. He frowned and sat on the edge of his makeshift bed inside the large tent Rosy had assigned them.

"It's a racial trait," Lixi said plainly. "She's part fairy."

Brenda turned and looked at her. The fairy had removed her hood. Even in human form, Lixi looked airbrushed, her skin glowing in the dim lamplight with the kind of perfection that belonged on magazine covers, not in dusty refugee camps.

They waited in silence for Lixi to continue.

"She clearly has fairy blood," Lixi said, as if it were common knowledge. "No other creature I know of is indestructible, other than maybe dragons, and no one's seen those bastards in thousands of years. She doesn't look like a dragon, but she definitely gives out fairy vibes. Believe me, I have a wonderful fairy radar," she concluded with a decisive nod.

"That's why she's so glorious," Odel said, the words barely above a whisper. A tiny smile tugged at his lips, his eyes glazed and distant.

"How can she be a fairy?" Brenda asked, deliberately focusing on Lixi instead of the smitten dwarf beside her.

"Your guess is as good as mine," Lixi said with a shrug. "There were stories of hidden, forbidden relationships between humans and fairies. Sometimes fairy genes carry through the generations, lying dormant like some magical recessive trait. Maybe these genes reactivated when magic came back to the world. I read magical textbooks that theorized magic in humans is actually a manifestation of fairy blood from way the hell back, millions of years ago, when things were...different. Rosy might be an outlier of that manifestation."

"Sounds like your guess is better than mine, Lixi. I didn't have a clue how any of this could even happen," Brenda commented, surprised by Lixi's seriousness.

"She'd be perfect if only she had a beard and maybe if she was three feet shorter," Odel said, pulling at his beard.

Brenda leaned toward Odel, catching his glazed eyes with her own. "Odel," she said softly but firmly. "This is not the time. Focus."

The dwarf blinked, color flooding his cheeks as he seemed to remember where he was. He cleared his throat and dropped onto his bed, suddenly very interested in the worn leather of his boots.

"Okay then, if she is a fairy, do you think she's aware of that?" Brenda asked.

"Clearly not," Valor said. "She's exhibited a lot more magical power than her purely human wizard friends, but Rosy strikes me as a person who accepts the facts of life without asking a lot of questions."

"Yes, not the sharpest tool. It must be the human half of her," Lixi said with a smirk, shooting Brenda a sideways glance.

Valor sighed, but Brenda was glad he didn't take the bait. This was just Lixi being Lixi. After a moment, he continued. "Let's keep it to ourselves right now. Our main objective is to give these wizards the means to defend themselves and to take care of their basic needs without help from us or others. I'll take care of that once Rosy comes back with her team." He glanced at the tent entrance.

Brenda chewed her bottom lip, waiting for the rest of Valor's plan.

"Then we need to take care of this Scar guy. That's going to be a little more complicated. If what Rosy said is true, he has a lot of firepower." Valor turned to Lixi.

"With proper preparation, we'll be able to take care of them easily," the fairy said. "I can handle that."

After they unpacked their stuff, Brenda heard movement outside. She gave Valor a long look. This was it.

They stepped out of the tent to find Rosy briefing a cluster of people, their faces curious and guarded in the lamplight.

They headed to where Rosy stood. Brenda noticed a young woman with a healing burn scar across her jaw, an older man with salt-and-pepper hair, and a teenager who couldn't have been more than sixteen clutching a backpack like it held everything he owned. Rosy glanced up and motioned them over without pausing her briefing.

"We are here for one reason and one reason alone." Rosy

planted herself in the center of the circle, making eye contact with each wizard in turn. Her voice wasn't loud, but it commanded attention. "We have magical power, and because of that, we've been thrown out of our homes, rejected by society, and forced to migrate here. We are human beings and deserve to be treated better!" The last words came out fierce, and several wizards nodded, their expressions hardening. "We also suffer because of the crime gang's endless attacks on us. We will not surrender to Scar and his scum wizards!"

The response was immediate, a cry of approval that rippled through the group.

"I found allies today, strong wizards who can help us better use our power. I ask you to listen to them. I trust them, and you all know that I either trust you completely or not at all. I picked every one of you because I believe in you. I ask you to believe in them in the same way." She gestured toward Valor's band.

The group of wizards exchanged glances, a silent conversation passing between them, and then, one by one, they nodded. Brenda watched in surprise as suspicion melted into acceptance. Whatever Rosy said here was law.

Rosy pointed to Valor, who nodded back at her.

"Thank you, Rosy," Valor said.

Brenda watched him step into the circle and felt that familiar mix of admiration and slight intimidation. He moved like true royalty, not arrogant but confident. The effect on the wizards was immediate. Hard expressions softened as they all fixed their attention on him. When his eyes swept the circle, each wizard he looked at seemed to straighten reflexively.

"My name is Valor," he said. "I am a master wizard. While this doesn't mean anything to you right now, think of it as the highest level you can achieve in magic mastery in this world."

He said the last three words while looking at Lixi, who nodded in agreement.

"My friends and I will train you to become effective and powerful wizards. You'll be able to defend yourselves from attacks." His voice carried an otherworldly resonance.

Brenda watched the wizards hang on every syllable; they needed hope.

"You'll be able to create food, to heal the wounded, to fix and move objects, and to attack in many more ways than your current limited fireball."

A few wizards grinned at each other, excitement sparking in their eyes.

He looked at Brenda, and she heard his voice echo in her head, that peculiar mental touch she still hadn't quite gotten used to. *"This will be new to you too. Pay attention."*

"I must correct one thing that Rosy said." His tone shifted, becoming more formal. The circle seemed to sense it, the excited murmurs dying away. "You're not here because of your magical powers. You're here because you are magical creatures. Magic is part of your being." Valor paused, letting that sink in.

The wizards shifted uncomfortably. The teenager's grip on his backpack tightened.

Valor nodded once. "Many years ago, humans used to discover that one in every thousand children was a wizard. That wizard child would be sent to learn how to use their magic to benefit the world. They would rarely bear children. He or she would have a longevity measured in centuries rather than decades."

The woman with the burn scar touched her jaw again. This time, her expression was filled with wonder rather than self-consciousness.

"This child would no longer be considered human." Valor looked at each face in the circle, giving them time to absorb the words.

Brenda examined the gathered wizards, expecting shock,

denial, anger. Instead, she saw something else. The older man with salt-and-pepper hair nodded slowly, realization hitting his face. A few others exchanged glances, not of horror but of recognition. These people had been betrayed by humanity, cast out, and hunted. Being told they weren't human at all...it seemed to make sense to them in a way Brenda hadn't anticipated.

"Nothing like a good 'us versus them' speech to bring people together," Lixi muttered from beside Brenda, low enough just for her to hear. "Humans kicked them out, so now they're not human. Clean break. Mortals do love their divisiveness." She paused, watching the crowd. "Doesn't make it any less effective, though."

"From this day forward, you will be members of a proud new family of wizards," Valor said. "You will serve to benefit this world with your great powers, and you will not use your power for evil. Do you all take this oath?" His voice rang with authority.

Silence held for a heartbeat. Then, one voice spoke. "Yes." Another joined. "Yes." The circle erupted in a chorus of affirmation that echoed between the tents. Not a cheer but a promise, a commitment, a choosing of sides.

Valor's smile was warm and genuine. Pride shone in his eyes. "Wonderful. Now let's teach you how to master magic."

This time, the cheer that rose up was pure joy, loud and fierce and unrestrained. Fists pumped in the air. Voices raised in triumph. Even the most guarded faces broke into grins. The sound echoed through the camp, carrying into the night.

These weren't just refugees anymore. They were wizards, and they were united.

CHAPTER THIRTY-NINE

The words on the security briefing document swam in and out of focus.

James blinked hard, trying to force his exhausted brain to focus on the lines of text, but they kept sliding away from comprehension. His left eye twitched, a nervous tic that had started yesterday and wouldn't stop. Nightmares and sleep deprivation were a bad cocktail.

"Sir, the tunnel was completed as requested." The lieutenant paused, her throat working as she swallowed. "We had several casualties digging it so fast." Her voice caught, then steadied. "But we're done."

The lieutenant was tall and athletic, her lieutenant's bars still shiny enough to suggest recent promotion. A muscle jumped in her cheek, and she shifted her weight from foot to foot. She looked at James with an expression he couldn't quite read, something hungry and desperate, like she needed him to tell her something.

Is she trying to get my approval for something?

The conference room was too warm, packed with bodies

generating heat faster than the overtaxed ventilation system could handle. Fluorescent lights hummed overhead, casting everything in a sickly white glare that made James's headache worse. The smell of stale coffee mixed with nervous sweat hung in the air. Twenty-seven people crammed into a space meant for fifteen, their chairs scraping against tile whenever someone shifted position.

James's mind kept drifting back to his nightmares and the group of wizards. He could see them standing in a circle—an elf, a dwarf, a human, a fairy, and a...horse. The horse was a weird addition James couldn't understand. It was a dream, after all, so maybe it was his imagination. The band was chanting their spell, and his dream immediately cut to the familiar images of burnt cities and babies. He knew these events were connected. He knew the spell was the cause. He knew he had to stop it.

"Sir, should we attack the elvish settlement as planned?" the lieutenant asked in a voice that said she was already expecting a resounding yes. It seemed she was waiting for him to congratulate her or at least give her the go-ahead.

"No. Don't do that." James motioned for her to move on to the next topic.

The lieutenant looked confused, glanced at her notes, and then back at him.

He sighed. His only wish was to sleep again, to get more clues about where and when exactly that dreadful band of wizards was going to cast that spell.

The entire conference room fell silent. The shift in the atmosphere was physical, like all the oxygen had been sucked out of the space. Chairs stopped creaking. Papers stopped rustling. Twenty-seven faces turned toward James in perfect synchronization, a wave of confusion, shock, and barely suppressed anger rippling through the crowd.

Something was wrong. What did they want from him?

"Mr. President," Secretary of Homeland Security Marie Ortega said. Her voice was gentle and careful. "We've been planning this attack for days. It's been the sole thing you told us to focus on. We lost many men digging as fast as we could as you directed. We've stopped everything in preparation for this attack."

The context was helpful to James. Truth be told, he wasn't sure what this discussion was about. Now, he understood why people were questioning his indecisiveness. His team members were true professionals. They'd given him everything they had and expected him to be at his best, but he'd failed them.

He took a deep breath. He was on edge, and he didn't care to show it. "I want to thank you all for the hard work and sacrifice," he said to the room, immediately sensing the tension decrease. "We do want to attack the elves, but not right now."

Questions exploded from every direction, voices overlapping.

He raised his arm, and they all fell silent. This was still the best team in the world.

"I've received intelligence of an upcoming catastrophic attack on the US." He didn't wait for their follow-up inquiries. "A special group of wizards has been spotted in Los Angeles. Wizards of non-human descent. We think they're planning an attack on humanity with the help of the displaced human-descended wizard population."

"How long do we have?" someone asked.

"Unknown," James said. "Could be days. Maybe hours."

James needed to stop the spell from happening, and knowing what, when, and where were critical for that. Everything else was a distraction.

What if the elvish prince decided to cast the magic as soon as he heard about the invasion of the elvish village? What if he headed back and the attack failed and then he cast his horrible spell in the safety of the elvish settlement? There were too many variables, and James wanted to limit them as much as he could.

The room burst into a cacophony of worried voices again.

Matthew, the head of the NSA, looked at him questioningly. His expression remained neutral and professional, but James could see the calculations happening behind those sharp eyes. The man was supposed to be aware of everything happening in the US, and this was news to him.

Of course it's news to him. I just made up the idea of intelligence coming in. Too late to go back on this.

"Before the attack on Washington, I had a small team of special agents go undercover and move to Los Angeles to mix with the wizards." James's mouth had gone dry. He reached for his coffee glass and took a sip, buying himself a second to think. "They were not to report back unless something really bad was about to happen. Yesterday, they reached out to me." It was all a lie, every word, but he kept his eyes steady on Matthew's face, willing the man to believe him.

Matthew's gaze narrowed.

James stared at his head of the NSA. Matthew was a Kildare operative with over ten years of experience. He trusted James. They had risen through the ranks together. At least that was what James hoped.

"Matthew, I'm sorry I didn't tell you about this. I totally forgot about that team after the attack and only heard from them on the way to this meeting. I'm almost as shocked as you are. I expected them to be dead."

There was a long silence as people looked at Matthew for a cue on how to behave.

"Mr. President," Matthew said, "you don't have to apologize. We're all here to serve the same cause. If we need to defer plans and resources to meet this new threat, so be it. We trust you, sir."

Tension drained from the room.

"Very well." James knew he'd dodged a bullet by more luck than brains. "I'll need a special ops team on the ground in LA as soon as possible. They must not be detected. As long as we haven't finished the work there, we mustn't attack the elvish settlement."

"Why not carpet bomb LA or nuke it?" Marie Ortega asked.

"That's too risky," Matthew answered. "We know the elvish settlement has a protective dome around it. We assume it will protect them from direct attacks. It would be stupid to start a war we don't know how to finish. You saw what wizards can do when they have nothing to lose. We might not win this war if we don't play our cards right." His calm voice left no room for debate.

James nodded. Good! The man was playing along.

"Ladies and gentlemen, if the elves and potentially other unnatural forces collude with these morally depraved wizards in Los Angeles, it will be disastrous not just for the US but for the world. I want secrecy on this. Make no mistake, we are at war. This needs to happen now. No questions asked." James directed this comment at the Army and other non-Kildare operatives in the room. He knew exactly who in this room was Kildare and who wasn't. The distinction mattered now more than ever.

"Yes, sir. We will have that assault team on the ground within the next few hours," Ortega said.

"Thank you, Marie." James pressed his fingers against his temples. The room swam, exhaustion making everything feel distant and unreal.

As people left, James noticed that Matthew studied him with a serious frown.

James's eye twitched again, harder this time. That look. What did it mean? Was Matthew questioning him? Doubting him? The thought wormed its way into James's exhausted brain and wouldn't let go. He couldn't afford doubt, not now, not when everything depended on secrecy.

His mind skipped ahead, planning without his permission. Matthew would need to have an accident. Something natural. A heart attack.

The thought should have shocked him, should have pulled him back from the edge, but exhaustion had worn away the parts of him that used to care about lines he shouldn't cross.

Yes, a heart attack would be best.

CHAPTER FORTY

The fireball came at her fast.

Brenda threw up her hands, her heart lurching, and the shield spell burst from her palms a half-second before impact. Heat slammed into the translucent barrier. Even through the magic, it felt like opening an oven door directly onto her face. Sweat poured down her back, the borrowed training shirt clung to her skin like a second layer.

Around her, the sounds of training echoed through the scrub brush and dry grass—Odel's deep voice barking orders, the sharp crack and hiss of spells colliding with shields, and the occasional grunt when someone's defense failed and they took a hit.

They'd chosen this nearby hiking trail because it was hidden from the tents. She was glad it was close enough that she wouldn't have to drag herself too far when this torture session finally ended. She kind of regretted asking to join Rosy's team training, but it was too late to chicken out now.

"Shields up!" Odel's voice boomed across the training ground, deeper than seemed possible for his height.

The dwarf paced between trainees with his arms crossed over his barrel chest, his braided beard swinging with each sharp turn. He was born for drill sergeant work.

"Switch up! Freeze!" He was clearly enjoying working them into an early grave.

No time to think. Brenda let her shield collapse and immediately reached for offensive magic. The switch felt like changing gears in a car while still moving, the momentum of one spell fighting the pull of another.

Across from her, her sparring partner dropped his attack and threw up his hands to shield.

The ice bolt formed slowly, the water magic resisting her human affinity for fire. Brenda gritted her teeth and forced it, pulling the cold into her palms until frost spread across her fingers. The bolt took shape, crackling with frozen energy, and she hurled it at her opponent's shield before it could melt.

Her opponent's shield caught the ice bolt with a flash of blue light. The frozen magic shattered on impact, shards dissolving into cold mist. Fast. He was always faster than her at the switch, his shield solid before her attack would even finish forming.

Brenda shook out her hands, trying to warm her fingers. Ice magic fought her every time, but Valor had insisted they master it anyway.

"Paralysis can help you win battles," he'd said right before letting someone hit her with an electric bolt that had locked every muscle in her body for ten minutes.

The memory of being paralyzed on the ground made her more careful and more willing to push through the discomfort of water magic.

"You're learning faster than I expected," Lixi had told her that morning. "Foundational magic always comes quick—shields, basic attacks, simple elemental work. You'll hit walls later when you start getting into the complex stuff. Enjoy the easy wins while they last."

Now that she was two days in, Brenda could feel what Lixi meant. Every session brought new competence, new control. The magic responded faster now, more reliably. She still had a long way to go, but the improvement was undeniable.

"Take a break," Odel shouted.

Brenda's legs nearly buckled with relief. After four hours of constant magical combat, every muscle in her body was screaming.

She stumbled toward the edge of the training ground where water bottles and towels waited on a flat rock, her hands still tingling with residual cold from the ice magic.

Lixi sat on that same rock in her human form, watching the trainees with an amused smirk. "Isn't magic wonderful?" she asked, leaning back against the rock with an empty water bottle dangling from her fingers. In a tight pink t-shirt that had a sparkly magical wand printed on it, and short white tennis skirt, Lixi looked like any other twenty-something lounging in the California heat.

Brenda took the bottle, too tired to answer, and cast the Conjure Water spell. Cold, clean water filled the bottle, condensation beading on the plastic immediately. She drank half of it in one long pull.

"Yes," she finally managed between gulps, "it is."

Lixi stretched, completely relaxed. "I will never understand why anyone would want to limit this. Magic is literally the essence of everything."

Brenda was too exhausted to get into a philosophical conversation about magic's place in the world. Her legs were still shaking, and all she wanted was to sit down, drink more water, and maybe never move again.

"Did Valor come back from his surveillance?" she asked instead.

"Yes, he is in the tent with Rosy." Lixi leaned back, eyeing Brenda. "If you want to join them, you should shower first. You stink."

"Lixi, that's rude! I spent the last four hours sweating my ass off learning magic," Brenda protested.

"Yes, it's very noticeable," Lixi said, waving her hand in front of her nose theatrically.

Brenda glared at her. Some friend.

She pushed herself to her feet and headed toward the tent where Rosy and Valor were meeting. She'd shower after she found out what was happening.

Brenda ducked through the tent entrance, grateful for the shade even if the air inside was still hot. She breathed in the scent of canvas and damp earth, a welcome change from the ozone smell of combat magic.

Valor and Rosy's voices carried clearly in the enclosed space. They stood facing each other across a folding table, and from the tension in their shoulders, this wasn't a friendly debate.

"I will not kill those wizards for you, Rosy." Valor's hands were flat on the table, his voice firm. "And you shouldn't either. They're not evil. I can tell."

"They're Scar's minions!" Rosy's fist hit the table, making maps jump. Her face was flushed. Whether from anger or the heat, Brenda couldn't tell. "They didn't have any problem killing me!"

Last night, Valor had replaced Rosy as the first line of defense. Instead of killing the attacking wizards, he'd electrified them and let them retreat. Apparently, Rosy hadn't appreciated his mercy.

"They're probably terrified of Scar." Valor's voice stayed gentle despite Rosy's anger. "They're slaves, Rosy. I can feel it. I can't kill non-evil creatures when I have another choice. It's not in my nature."

Elves couldn't harm non-evil creatures, something built into their fundamental nature. Valor had explained it to Brenda once, how vampires and zombies registered as corrupted evil, so there was no moral conflict in destroying them without hesitation. Humans were untouchable, though, unless they'd already chosen evil. It clearly frustrated Rosy, but Brenda was starting to understand the distinction.

Rosy's jaw clenched, but she nodded. "Can you at least take care of Scar?"

"Yes." Valor straightened. "I found where he's staying. I'll take a team and confront him before evening."

Both of them looked up when Brenda moved closer.

Rosy's expression shifted, the anger cooling into something more even-keeled.

Brenda stepped toward the table. "Are we going to fight Scar?"

Valor's expression turned grim. "Not if we don't have to, but probably. When I got close enough, I could detect his alignment. He's evil, Brenda—the real kind of evil."

Brenda nodded. Humans were neutral by default, capable of choosing good or evil or anything in between. Unlike elves, who were born good, or vampires, who were corrupted into evil, humans had free will, for better or worse.

"We'll move before sunset," Valor continued, turning his attention to the maps spread across the table. "Scar's wizards usually attack us around dusk. If we leave an hour earlier, we can reach his stronghold while they're still preparing." His finger traced a path on the map. "The element of surprise is our main advantage. He doesn't know we've found him."

Rosy leaned over the table, studying the route. "What about his offensive spells and weapons?"

"Lixi will cast protective wards on the team before we head out." Valor's hand moved to gesture as he spoke, fingers waving in the air, the way he always did when explaining magic. "They'll render us practically invincible against conventional weapons and most basic offensive spells. Not perfect protection but enough to get us close." He straightened. "Once we're in range, I'll disable his wizards without killing them. Then we take Scar alive if possible and bring him back to face justice."

"And if it's not possible?" Brenda asked.

Valor's expression darkened. "Then we do what we must."

Brenda liked the plan. She stepped closer to Valor and examined the map.

Valor coughed. Then, he looked at Brenda with what was probably meant to be a warm smile, but it faltered immediately, and his nose wrinkled.

"Brenda, my dear," he started carefully. "We will need to move in stealth tonight. We can't risk detection." He paused. "You'll need to shower first."

Brenda stared at him. "Are you serious right now?"

"It's really bad," Rosy added.

"Rosy!" Valor looked scandalized.

Brenda's face went hot. "Oh, for fuck's sake! Lixi said the same thing. Fine! I'm going to shower!" She threw her hands up and stormed out of the tent.

Behind her, she heard Rosy say quietly, "I feel bad."

"You should. You made it worse," Valor whispered back in a harsh voice.

Lixi's laughter greeted her outside, high and delighted. "Told you!"

"You're all assholes," Brenda muttered, heading for the showers.

CHAPTER FORTY-ONE

The air tasted of mold and rot, thick enough to coat the back of Tanya's throat. The cave hall was dark, filthy, and enormous. Water dripped somewhere in the darkness above, each drop echoing off slick stone walls.

The trip had been long. The new gnome palace, also called *this shithole*, was in a mountain ridge in southern California. Tanya hadn't felt comfortable in her bat form, but it was the fastest way to travel unnoticed. Boris had made it sound intuitive and easy. Well, it was not intuitive nor easy for her. It had still taken more than two days to get here. Now in her human form, her back muscles ached.

Tanya walked through a side entrance toward the center of the hall. Her shoes squeaked against the sticky floor with each step. Hundreds of gnomes filled the carved dirt seats, their voices a constant chittering hum. The wealthier ones sat closer to the throne, their clothes only slightly less filthy. Dice clattered. Food scraps littered the floor. The smell of unwashed bodies mixed with the garbage and grease stench.

The hall was fashioned like an amphitheater, round with

seating for thousands carved into the dirt walls. At the center sat a massive throne made of deep purple amethysts, blood-red rubies, and murky green emeralds, all jutting at odd angles like broken teeth.

On the throne sat the new gnome king. He was barely four feet tall but grotesquely wide, his bulk straining against the crystal chair. His skin had the grayish pallor of something that lived underground, and his eyes bulged, too large for his face. Thick fingers clutched a sandwich, grease dripping into his lap. He smirked while motioning her forward.

Tanya kept her face blank, fighting the urge to roll her eyes.

"Velcome, velcome," he said while chewing. "You traveled a long vay. Ve are not used to visitors. Pardon our lack of ceremony."

"I am Tanya of the Vampires, delegate of Boris, King of the Vampires. I seek Luc the Conqueror, King of the Gnomes," Tanya said, using the words Boris had taught her. She could almost hear his voice in her head, patient and precise as he'd made her repeat the formal phrases until she had them perfect. This ceremony ensured she would be recognized and addressed with proper respect.

"Yes, yes. I am Luc the Conqueror." The gnome king licked his fingers.

"I have come to invoke an ancient debt. King Boris calls upon the gnomes to honor the blood-debt owed from the battle of Shuchan, when vampire strength saved gnome lives from elvish blades. He invokes your sworn friendship and calls upon your honor," Tanya said in a booming voice.

Luc the Conqueror eyed her up and down. "Vell, I don't know about friendship or honor." He laughed like a madman. Pieces of sandwich spat from his mouth.

The audience around her burst into laughter.

"Regardless of your commitment to honor and friendship with the vampires, you still owe us." Tanya's voice didn't waver.

Her shoulders remained squared. She knew the gnome king wouldn't be receiving her audience if he wasn't bound by the debt to the vampires.

She took out a pouch and a scroll. "The pouch is full of gold. As a token of our friendship, you'll receive it after you cast the scroll with me." She lifted the pouch and shook it.

Gnomes were very good at detecting precious metals by their sound. The room filled with wows and whispers.

The gnome king licked his lips. "Very vell. Come over, my beautiful delegate. I am so happy Boris did not come himself. It vill be a pleasure to get to know you," he said in a sleazy tone.

Tanya stepped closer to the king's chair. The crowd of gnomes cheered. She took the scroll out of its box. Light burst from the ancient parchment, casting sharp shadows across the amphitheater walls. The temperature dropped. A low hum vibrated through the stone beneath their feet. This was a very powerful scroll. The crowd's chittering fell to awed whispers.

"Vhere did you get this scroll?" the king asked. He licked his fat lips.

"Boris had it forever. It's a scroll to awaken our darkest friends." She paused. "Where did you get the sandwich?"

The question caught him off guard, which was what she'd intended. Show him she owned the conversation.

He looked at the half-eaten sub in his hand. "Ve captured some humans on the vay. Ve started eating them, but they convinced us they could get us better food. Each time ve release some of them to go and get us things, if they do not come back, ve just eat some of their friends. This time, they got us these sandviches. They are actually better than human meat. Do you vant a bite?"

Growing up a hungry kid in Romania, Tanya had eaten some funky things. She was not that kid anymore.

Without moving a single muscle in her face, she gave him an Eastern European look of pure disgust. "I'll pass." Her voice was cold as stone.

She reached the bottom of the stairway leading to the king's high chair. Luc walked down, still holding the greasy sandwich. He rested it on the dirty steps and shooed away some cockroaches. Then he tried to wipe the grease from his hands on his shirt. After that wonderful ceremony of cleansing, he gave her both his hands.

Tanya took a deep breath, suppressed her gag reflex, opened the scroll, and laid it on the ground. She took the gnome king's hands and started chanting the scroll, following Boris's instructions exactly. The words felt wrong in her mouth, ancient syllables that tasted of ash and iron, but she kept reading. Power surged through her palms, cold, dark red, and electric. The scroll's light intensified, casting harsh red shadows across the amphitheater. She felt the clarity of the magic, the elegant simplicity, the terrible force of something that should never have been written down. Luc's voice joined her, shrieking like nails on a chalkboard. It was unbearable to hear.

Two dark shadows materialized in the hall, growing more solid with each word she spoke. A troll towered at least ten feet tall, its body thick with corded muscle beneath stone-gray skin. Tusks jutted from its lower jaw, and its eyes burned like hot coals. A goblin stood barely four feet high, but what it lacked in size it made up for in menace. Its skin was a sickly green. Its fingers ended in black claws, and its mouth was full of needle-sharp teeth.

Tanya stared at them, waiting for fear to hit. It didn't come. Instead, she felt a strange kinship. These were monsters, but they were going to be *her* monsters.

"You called?" the troll said. His voice was rough as if he was not used to talking, his words vibrating through the stone floor.

"Yes, I summoned you. We are heading to a war to end all wars against the elves, dwarves, and the humans. The humans have proven themselves unworthy of this world. They multiply like locusts, consuming everything in their path. They destroy the natural order, poison the earth, and wage endless war upon themselves. They are a plague that must be cleansed. Magic will return to those who understand its sacred purpose. Humanity's age is ending. Remember your promise to fight in the last battle," she said, stating the memorized words.

The words rang true in her mind. Humans had hurt her, used her, discarded her.

Let them burn.

"Yes. We remember," the goblin said, its voice like grinding metal. "We pledge our legions to your cause. Thousands of goblins, orcs, and liches will answer your call, skilled in ambush and slaughter. We lust for human flesh, it has been too long since one of your kind has summoned us. We are ready, we are hungry." Its eyes glittered. "Worthy or not, humans taste delicious."

The troll stepped forward. "Battalions of trolls who cannot be stopped by blade or arrow will serve at your request. We bring war machines forged in the deep places, siege towers that walk on legs of iron, and catapults that hurl fire and destruction. Our army has crushed kingdoms and razed cities to ash many times before. You can now summon us at will, our vampire mistress."

They bowed and disappeared.

Tanya pulled her hands from the disgusting gnome king's grip.

He opened his palm, signaling for her to give him the pouch of gold. When she did, he grabbed her hand and pulled her close. "Stay here! Be my vife. Ve vill rule over the entire vorld," he whispered in her ear. His breath reeked of rotting meat and something fermented.

She tried to pull away, but he was surprisingly strong. "Let me go!" Memories of men grabbing her like this flashed through her mind.

"I vill not." He licked his lips again, pulling her closer.

She moved without conscious thought, vampire speed rendering her nearly invisible. Her knife sang free from its sheath. One clean slice, and the gnome king's smirk froze on his face. His head toppled, bounced once on the crystal steps with a wet thud, and then rolled down toward the crowd, leaving a dark trail. His body remained standing for one impossible moment, his hands still outstretched, before crumpling.

"Fuck. Look what you made me do. I promised Boris I'd be on my best behavior," Tanya said to the rolling head, the eyes wide and surprised.

The crowd screamed. Bodies surged forward, gnomes shoving and trampling in their rush toward her. The sharp ring of swords clearing scabbards mixed with pounding feet as the guards charged, murder in their bulging eyes, short swords at the ready.

Tanya's body compressed, bones hollowing and reshaping with familiar pain. Wings erupted from her shoulders. She launched into the air as a bat and shot through the cave entrance into the night sky.

She'd killed before. This was just one more body. The fact that it bothered her less each time, well, that was a problem for another day.

On the return flight, she thought about the fact that it probably *was* her best behavior after all. The quest was a success. Boris would be happy...or at least not that mad.

CHAPTER FORTY-TWO

This time, it was not a drill. Fire slammed into Brenda's shield from the left, then the right, then straight ahead. Each impact sent heat washing over her skin. Fireballs whistled past her ears and exploded against her shield with hollow thumps. Sweat stung her eyes, and the air tasted like ash and burnt copper. The effort of maintaining the magical barrier made her head ache.

The plan had been simple. Odel was on tank duty, standing in front of the band and attracting the fire. Dwarves were resilient to heat. Generations of forging in hot furnaces had made their skin hard and resistant. Lixi was boosting the dwarf's natural capability with her own shield spells. Brenda's job was to spot the wizards shooting their fireballs at Odel and point them out to Valor.

The problem? A lot of the firepower was aimed at her as well.

They were walking through a sketchy neighborhood that had been rough long before Scar's human-wizards had arrived. Single-floor houses squatted behind chain-link fences, bars on every window. Scorch marks blackened the pavement where firebolts had missed their targets. One house had its front wall blown out. Pit bulls and rottweilers lunged and strained against their chains, barking at the magical battle like it was just another Tuesday disturbance. Cars stripped for parts sat on cinder blocks in driveways. Broken glass glittered in the brown lawns.

Brenda ground her teeth and kept her shield up. It was not hard to deal with these low-level offensive attacks, but it required a lot of painful concentration. Her face must have turned red with the heat, and the steaming shower she had taken was long gone.

She glimpsed Lixi, who didn't even flinch when a fireball passed within inches of her. Fireballs kept missing her for some reason. Odel, by contrast, drove forward like a boulder in a stream of fire, letting the fireballs wash over him without giving an inch.

Valor was the only one on offense. Brenda couldn't split her focus from the shield, and Lixi had refused to limit herself to stunning spells, so she stuck to defense. It was working. Valor threw electric bolts with precision, rendering wizard after wizard unconscious. Each wizard who targeted Odel gave away the enemy's position, and Valor's lightning found them before they could fire twice.

"Keep going!" Valor called as the fire intensified, scorching the dwarf's beard despite the heavy shield protection Lixi was giving him.

Brenda ducked behind a rusted pickup truck. Her hair was plastered to her skull with sweat. Pain exploded along her left forearm. The shield had failed for a split second.

She looked down and immediately wished she hadn't. Blisters were rising on her skin, angry and red, some already weeping clear fluid. The smell of her own burnt flesh made her stomach lurch.

Lixi appeared beside her in a blur of motion, her face creased with concern. She whispered something too quiet for Brenda to catch, and the words "Minor Heal" flickered across Brenda's vision. Coolness spread through her arm, and the blisters began to shrink. The pain dulled to a manageable throb. When Brenda looked down again, her skin was pink and tender but almost normal.

"Thanks," Brenda breathed.

Lixi winked and darted away.

A fireball caught Odel square in the chest. Brenda winced, but the dwarf just grunted and brushed embers from his beard.

"Is that all they've got?" he called back, his voice surprisingly cheerful for someone being used as target practice. "My grandmother's stove was hotter than this!"

Unconscious wizards dotted the street and yards, each one having managed only a single shot before Valor's lightning found them. Brenda noted how efficient the elvish prince was, and how uneven the fight was. This time, it was a planned offensive. They had had ample time to cast protective spells and boost their defenses.

They inched closer to Scar's hideout, a shabby-looking house in a bad part of town. For whatever reason, Scar hadn't moved to a nicer house and kept on living in what looked like a crack den straight out of the movies.

As they got closer, they started hearing shots fired. This was Lixi's turn to act.

Like a child shooting imaginary enemies, Lixi lifted her index finger and pointed. Suddenly bullets hung in the air, frozen mid-flight. A shimmer rippled around them. The bullets dropped to the ground with harmless clinks, dozens of them, a rain of lead that never hit its mark. After the barrage ended, Lixi blew on her finger as if to blow out smoke and smiled mischievously at Brenda.

Wizards were scattered all across the yard, and Valor knocked them unconscious one by one, but the majority of the gunshot firepower came from within Scar's house. Brenda winced as she heard a bullet hit a wall next to her. It would be only a matter of time until one of them got hit really badly.

To Brenda's surprise, Valor shot a heavy fireball in the direction of the gunfire. This wasn't like the sputtering attacks from Scar's wizards. This was a miniature sun, white-hot and roaring. It punched through the second-floor wall and detonated. The explosion blew out every window simultaneously, glass raining down like deadly snow. The roof shattered into thousands of pieces. Tiles slid off and shattered on the ground. Smoke poured from every opening, black and thick. The entire second floor was gone.

A big man came out of the front door with an automatic machine gun. A scar ran from his temple down across his cheek, splitting his upper lip. He aimed at them and started shooting.

Lixi flicked the bullets away as if they were fireflies. When the man ran out of ammunition, he pulled a grenade from his belt and threw it at them. Lixi cast a quick wind spell, and the grenade flew far off into an empty lot. Brenda tensed, counting in her head. The explosion came three seconds later, a dull crump followed by a fountain of dirt that scattered across an already-ruined lawn.

"Scar, surrender! We will not harm you if you do," Valor called. His voice was artificially louder and more booming.

"Fuck off!" Scar quickly dashed into the house. Screams came from within.

Brenda and the team approached with care, searching for traps. Semi-conscious and groaning wizards dotted the large yard in front of Scar's den.

The door opened again. Scar came out with two small kids, neither older than four years old.

"Leave or I will fucking waste them!" Scar called. He was holding a gun straight at the kids' heads. They were shaking, tears cutting clean lines through the dirt on their faces.

"Valor?" Lixi asked in a tone that meant more than words could say.

"Do it," Valor said in an ice-cold voice.

Lixi blurred into motion. One second, she was next to Valor. The next, she was behind Scar. She touched him with her wand. When she spoke, her voice was nothing like the cheerful fairy Brenda knew. It was ancient and terrible. "Return to dust."

Scar's entire body crumbled to ashes.

Brenda had seen Lixi use that spell before, when they'd fought the vampire. It hadn't gotten easier to watch. Gray ash drifted on the breeze where a man had been standing moments ago, and her stomach churned despite knowing he'd deserved it.

Lixi could have ended this fight in seconds, Brenda realized. The fairy must have wanted to give Valor this win to boost his confidence.

The kids still stood there, too afraid to move.

Brenda stepped toward the kids with her hands extended, non-threatening. "It's all done now," she said in a calming voice. "Come to me, kids."

They stood frozen for a heartbeat, then ran. They slammed into her and held on like she was their mom. Their quiet sobbing cut through all the battle noise. Brenda wrapped her arms around them. They were safe. That was what mattered.

"This wasn't that hard," Lixi said calmly. "I would like to talk to one of these fucking wizards to figure out why they would help that scumbag."

One of the kids holding Brenda's leg screamed "Mom!" and ran to one of the unconscious wizards sprawled in the yard.

The woman wizard was completely out.

The kid held her shoulder and tried to wake her up, shrieking, "Don't be dead. Mommy, don't be dead!"

Lixi appeared faster than light next to the kid and touched his little hand, which seemed to calm him immediately.

"She is not dead. She is just sleeping very hard. Let me wake her," she said. She whispered a spell to wake up the woman.

"Samuel! You're alive, my baby boy!" the woman said the second she woke up.

They embraced in a rush of tears and desperate grasping. The woman's arms encircled her son completely, her hands checking his face, his arms, his body. Samuel buried his face in his mother's neck, his small shoulders shaking. Her lips moved against his hair, words Brenda couldn't hear but could feel—apologies, prayers, promises.

When the kid finally calmed down, the woman looked around, stared at Scar's ash on the ground and many of her wizard friends all around, moaning or unconscious.

"Thank you for saving my baby," she said. Tears streamed down her dark cheeks, her face twisted with relief and grief.

"You are welcome!" Lixi said cheerfully. Then, the fairy frowned. "Why would you fight for this idiot?"

Lixi never did waste her words.

The woman wizard pulled Samuel onto her lap, holding him tight. "At first, he was nice to us. He fed us when we could not buy food or rent hotel rooms."

Around them, other unconscious wizards were beginning to stir. One groaned and rolled over. Several called to their kids, faces wet with tears.

"After a while, he started threatening us and denying food if we did not do exactly as he said," Samuel's mother continued.

Brenda glanced at Valor, who had gone very still.

"In the last two months, he took our babies and threatened to kill them if we did not fight for him. We tried to rebel and even took over his second hideout and captured some of his crew." The woman's voice shook. "But he started sending us body parts, and we folded like paper dolls. He had nothing to lose, we had everything to lose."

A strange cry came from within Scar's home, the sound tiny and afraid.

"I sense a lot of kids in the basement of that house," Lixi said with a cool, hard certainty.

"Basement?" Odel's voice was hard. "How many?"

"At least a dozen."

Odel's expression darkened immediately. His grip tightened on his war axe. "On my way."

The dwarf was already moving before he finished speaking, his heavy boots pounding toward the house. Whatever those children had endured, it was over now.

Valor went down on one knee, his movements slow and ceremonial. "We have completed our quest," he intoned, his voice resonating with power that made the air vibrate. "The massacre of the city of angels has been prevented."

Lixi leaned toward Brenda and whispered, "Bit dramatic, isn't he?"

Before Brenda could respond, blue light exploded from Valor. It touched her, and the warmth that flooded her body made her forget about the theatrics. Her arm healed completely. The fatigue lifted. Even the headache from maintaining her shield for so long disappeared. Dramatic or not, it sure felt awesome.

Valor stood, sighed, and brushed dirt from his knee. "We will now continue our main quest to seek the unicorn and cast the spell to return magic in full force to this land."

Brenda blinked. “Don’t we get a break? I’m not asking for a week, but maybe a few hours?”

“Unicorn? Are they looking for Bob?” the kid named Samuel asked.

Valor’s eyes widened, and Brenda and Lixi exchanged glances.

The kid knows a unicorn named Bob?

CHAPTER FORTY-THREE

He is going to say he's in position, in three, two, one, James thought.

"We are in position," the sergeant said over the video feed.

James looked around the operations room, his left eye twitching. The large space was lit by both overhead fluorescents and the blue-white glow from dozens of monitors showing live feeds from every operative in the field. Equipment hummed and beeped, and keyboards clattered, but James heard it all from a distance, filtered through the roar of his own pulse.

Secretary of Homeland Security Ortega stood at the command console where the NSA director should have been. The man had suffered a fatal heart attack last night. "Sudden," they'd said. "Unexpected."

Other operations officers also sat in the room, coordinating satellite and communications.

"Status report. Do you see anything suspicious?" Ortega asked.

"Negative. The area is clear," the special ops commander said.

The headgear cameras on the screens confirmed that fact. The ops team was positioned at different angles around a small grassy field in a park on the outskirts of Los Angeles, thick trees surrounding them on all sides. They'd deployed according to James's extremely detailed instructions. Some of the team were undercover on the ground, while others were high in the trees.

James paced around the room. Six steps to the wall, pivot, six steps back. Sweat soaked through his collar. When he noticed Ortega watching him, he frowned and sat down.

"Should we wait or progress toward the city?" the sergeant asked. "We are hearing heavy fire coming from the city direction."

"No! This is where it is going to happen! I have seen it a million times!" James almost screamed.

People were looking at him. He didn't care. He didn't care about his slip of the tongue about his visions either. This was where the future of humanity would be determined. Fuck everyone in this room who stood in his way.

A small voice in his head told him he had reached his limit of sleep deprivation and coffee, but his main voice told that voice to fuck off too.

"Negative. Stay put," Secretary Ortega said on the official communication channel.

"Roger that." The sergeant's voice came through steady and professional, as if this were just another routine operation.

James's pulse hammered in his ears. The voices clashed in his head. *"This is a mistake. Turn back. Abort."* But underneath them, steady and cold, the knowing whispered, *"Twenty minutes."*

James pressed his palms against his thighs to stop their trembling.

"In twenty minutes...wait for the horse," James said, not sure if he was talking out loud or not.

Everyone was looking at him.

The voices told him some of them would have to have accidents.

His vision blurred at the edges. When had he last eaten? Slept? The fluorescent lights seemed too bright. They were stabbing into his skull. His mouth tasted like old coffee and bile.

He blinked. The clock on the wall had jumped forward. Fifteen minutes. Gone. A flash of panic. Had he been sleeping? Standing up? Ortega was staring at him with an expression he couldn't read. The communications officer had moved to the far side of the room. When had that happened? The voices were laughing. Had he missed the moment?

"Five minutes...wait for the horse," he said quietly.

The door opened. James spun, his heart still hammering. One of the analysts came in, coffee cup in hand. Returning from a break, probably.

James forced himself to breathe. His hands were shaking.

Something on the screen moved. The special ops officer's camera zoomed in. James's breath caught. Something white was moving through the trees at the field's edge. His dreams had shown him this exact moment.

"There," he said, pointing at the screen with a shaking finger. "Focus there."

The cameras adjusted, capturing the clearing and the white shape emerging into sunlight.

The special ops officer zoomed farther in on a corner of the open field. Another special ops operative was looking down from a tree. They both focused on the same object from different directions.

It was a white horse.

Ortega's eyes locked on him. The horse was there, just like he'd said.

"Command, are you seeing this?" A beat of silence. "I need confirmation on visual. Target appears to be a horse with a white coat, way over sixteen hands, but there's a protrusion from the skull, a single horn approximately three feet. Please confirm."

James moved closer to the screen until his nose nearly touched the glass. The overhead view was too distant, the angle wrong. The officer's camera kept trying to focus and failing, the image swimming in and out of clarity.

A horn...James felt ice in his stomach. He'd missed the horn. What else had he missed?

"Get more cameras on it," James said. His voice came out hoarse. "All of them. Now."

Secretary Ortega complied, and all the other screens showed different angles of the animal.

It was a fucking *unicorn*.

Pure white from muzzle to tail, not a single mark on its coat. The horn rose from its forehead, three feet of spiraling ivory that seemed to glow from within. Even through the cameras, James could see how the surface of the horn caught the sunlight and threw it back transformed, scattering rainbow prisms across the clearing.

"Are you seeing what I'm seeing?" Static crackled through the line as the officer's breathing quickened. "Should we take it down?"

"No!" James yelled. "No, no, no, no, no!" He touched the screen where the horn glowed. How could he be so wrong?

"Negative. Stay put," Ortega commanded.

"In ten minutes, they will come to meet it," James said.

His face was still inches from the screen. This close, the unicorn dissolved into pixels, just red and blue and green dots arranged in patterns. Not real. Just light. But he knew it was real. More real than anything else in this room.

If he was wrong about the horse and it was actually a unicorn, what else had he been wrong about? He needed so many questions answered. He couldn't save humanity based on dreams if they weren't accurate. He needed a carving knife and a few hours in a private room with the Catalysts bound to chairs, and he would have all the answers in the world. Yes, he was going to carve the truth out of these wizards!

"Change of orders." He looked at Ortega. "No more shoot to kill. I want them alive. I don't mind if they wound them, but I want to interrogate them. We can always kill them later."

Ortega communicated the change of orders to the field officer, who acknowledged.

The unicorn moved with deliberate grace to stand beneath the tree where the operative was positioned. It stopped and tilted its head. Then slowly, impossibly, it raised its gaze to look directly into the headgear camera.

James's breath caught in his throat. Those eyes. They weren't animal eyes. They were looking through the lens, through the satellite feed, through the screens, straight at him. The unicorn knew. It knew James was watching.

James stumbled backward, his chair clattering. His hand clamped over his mouth to stop the sound trying to escape. How? How could it know?

"It can't be," he whispered. "No, that's not possible."

But the unicorn held his gaze, unwavering, as if waiting for James to understand.

"I do not understand," James said to the unicorn on the screen.

The unicorn moved to the center of the field and stood in a shaft of sunlight. The light struck the horn and refracted, sending cascades of rainbow light dancing across the grass, the trees, and the cameras. For a moment, the clearing looked like something from a dream.

"It's beautiful," the communications officer said softly, almost reverently.

Calm in the sunlight, the unicorn lowered its head to graze.

Two minutes left. James knew what came next. He had seen it a hundred times.

"It is the end of the world," James said softly. "It is death. It is destruction. Cities burning. Mothers screaming over the bodies of their burnt children. Humanity dying." His palm pressed against the screen, against the impossible horn. "And it starts here."

The clatter of keyboards stopped. Ortega's jaw tightened. Even the analyst in the far corner had swiveled in his chair to stare.

"We are seeing movement from the south corner," one of the special ops members said on the line.

James's breath stopped. The screens showed shadows at the tree line. Multiple figures.

The unicorn raised its head, as if it had been waiting. The horn caught the light one more time, scattering prisms across the clearing like a signal.

"They are coming," James said. His voice was steady now. Calm. This was the moment the dreams had shown him. "The Catalysts are coming. Death is coming."

CHAPTER

FORTY-FOUR

"Unicorn? Are they looking for Bob?" the kid asked.

"I don't know, baby. Why don't you ask them?" Samuel's mother gestured toward Valor and Lixi.

The boy took a few steps toward Lixi, who squatted to meet his face.

"Are you looking for Bob the unicorn?" the boy asked. He was about four years old.

"Yes, have you seen that asshole?" Lixi asked, meeting the kid's gaze.

The kid frowned. "That is a bad word."

Lixi's eyes widened in shock. "What? Unicorn? No, it's a perfectly good word."

"No, the other one," the kid said.

"Which other one?" Lixi asked.

The kid squinted at her. She squinted back, matching him. He smiled.

"Lixi, stop it." Brenda kneeled down beside the kid.

Lixi sighed with irritation. Kids were so much more fun than adults, and Brenda had just interrupted her game.

"What is your name?" Brenda asked, even though she knew it already, just to break the ice. Kids were not her specialty.

"My name is Samuel. Bob told me he will have visitors, but he said they are going to be a weird bunch. He said an elf, a human, a dwarf, and a fairy. I told him there are no fairies, and he laughed," the kid said.

"Well, kid, *we* are the weird bunch Bob was talking about. He laughed at you because unicorns come from fairy land," Lixi said.

Brenda gave Lixi a shut-up look. Lixi returned the look with a frown.

"Can you take us to the unicorn?" Brenda asked, returning to the kid.

"Over there by those woods." Samuel pointed to a hill about a twenty-minute walk away.

Valor stepped forward. His face was serious and more determined than Lixi had ever seen. "Samuel, we will need you to take us there. Can you do that?"

The kid looked to his mom for permission.

She nodded and put a hand on his shoulder. "I will come with you, Samuel. Don't worry," she said. "We owe them at least that."

The group set out from Scar's safe house as word of his death rippled through the gathering crowd. Wizards from both sides clustered in the streets, their voices a mix of celebration and uncertainty.

"You saved those kids," an older lady wizard said, catching Lixi's arm as they passed. Her eyes were wet. "Thank you."

Lixi nodded, basking in the gratitude.

Odel rejoined them after a brief conversation with another wizard, and Lixi caught sight of the other kidnapped children being led away to safety.

As they moved through the streets, more people stopped

them with thanks or congratulations. Lixi even posed for a few selfies with some of the younger wizards. She smiled whimsically at male wizards who turned red when she lowered her hood for a moment.

They approached the tree line, and the noise of the gathering faded behind them. Ancient trees rose ahead, their thick canopy swallowing the voices and celebration. The temperature dropped in the sudden shade, and the air smelled of moss and damp earth. It was strange to see such old trees so close to the city. They seemed displaced, like they belonged somewhere else.

After a hundred yards into the woods, they reached an opening. A field of grass stretched before them, bathed in sunlight. In the center stood a spotless white unicorn, its three-foot horn glittering like a diamond, catching the light and throwing back brilliant shimmers.

When they cleared the woods, Lixi felt a small hand slip into hers.

Samuel was holding her hand. "Bob is wonderful. He is not an asshole!" he told her.

"Dude, don't be a snitch," Lixi said quietly as the unicorn raised his head with slow, deliberate grace.

The unicorn's eyes were an unsettling pale blue, almost white, ancient and knowing. "Samuel, thank you for bringing them to me as requested. Now run along back with your mother. You have been a good boy and will be rewarded accordingly," he said with a mouth half-full of grass.

Samuel ran toward the unicorn like he was a friendly dog in the park. He looked so tiny compared to the huge beast.

"Thank you, Bob!" Samuel said cheerfully. He touched the unicorn fondly on the snout and ran back through the woods.

There was a long silence while the unicorn finished the grass in his mouth. The group waited.

"Lixiva Orera..." The unicorn's voice was dry as a teacher

talking to a bratty student. “We meet again. I had the feeling I would see you once more in fate’s crossing. I hope you have learned your lesson from last time.”

Lixi wanted to say something snarky, but the unicorn turned to Valor and lowered his head to inspect the elvish prince.

“You are the youngest of your line. Why isn’t the crown prince here instead of you?” the unicorn asked.

“All my older brothers are dead. I am the crown prince of the elves,” Valor said, his voice clear but with a tremor on the word “dead” that only someone listening closely would catch.

Lixi’s snark died in her throat.

“That is unfortunate indeed,” Bob replied. “Your father had more kids than any other elvish king before him. I guess it was foresight that made him have so many, and not vanity as I once accused him of.” The unicorn shifted his gaze to Odel. “Crown prince of the dwarves. I welcome your honorable presence here. Do you come freely and of your own will?” The unicorn’s voice was full of respect.

That stopped Lixi cold. Bob respected someone? That was new.

Odel bowed on one knee and lowered his head. “I do, your majesty. It is my free will to be a part of this quest and a true honor to meet you. The dwarves are forever your friends.” He rose to his feet again.

“I know.” The unicorn bowed his horn, then nodded to Brenda. “Hello, Brenda, the royalty who does not think she is royalty. Poor humans only remember the past. How unfortunate.”

Lixi watched confusion flash across Brenda’s face.

“Well, you are all here, as predicted. What would you request of me? This doesn’t feel like a social visit.” The unicorn leaned down and collected a little more grass, his movements casual. He moved his head sideways, looking around at different points on the surrounding trees.

Valor stepped forward. "We call upon you to aid us in completing our quest. Help us cast this spell." He pulled the scroll from his inner pocket. It glittered in the sun. "And bring magic back to its full glory."

Time did its weird thing again. Lixi's stomach dropped as reality stretched around them. The leaves that had been tumbling from the ancient trees suddenly hung suspended, rotating with impossible slowness. The wind's whisper became a long, drawn-out sigh. Lixi could feel her own heartbeat slowing, each pulse taking forever.

"Why?" the unicorn asked.

"Because we cannot complete it without you," Valor answered.

"No. Why do you need to complete this quest?" the unicorn asked.

Valor looked confused for a moment. "Well, this quest was given to me by my father, the king of the elves. It is a quest to bring magic back to its glory, to make the world magical again, to make all magical creatures thrive."

"I know your father well. He came with the same ignorance you come to me today. While he was motivated by greed for power, you are motivated by the fear that you cannot protect your loved ones without it. I do not know which motivation is worse." The unicorn chewed lightly on the grass he picked, looking placidly at Valor.

"Wait, I-I am not here to..." Valor sputtered.

"Your father failed at this quest in the past. Do you know that? He came to me with this scroll many centuries ago and, in the end, failed to execute the spell. Do you know why?"

There was a long silence. No one answered. Lixi barely breathed.

"No," Valor said quietly. "Why did he fail?"

"Consequences," the unicorn said, continuing to munch on the grass. "He and his friend could not deal with the consequences of this spell. You see, this spell is a world-altering spell. It changes the essence of your planet, the rules that govern it, its mechanics."

"What are the consequences?" Valor asked plainly.

Valor's innocence struck Lixi. He truly believed in good, truly thought he was on the right side.

A cold shiver of memory hit her from hundreds of years ago, when she was young and had felt she was on the right side.

Time buzzed around them. Lixi noticed that the leaves had almost stopped moving. She felt the power radiating from the unicorn like heat from a forge, bending reality to make time slow so much. Why would he do that?

An external thought came to her, like a voice in her head from another magical being. *"Lixiva Orera, your presence is requested."*

Who the fuck...Valor's mother?

What does she want?

Lixi forcefully ignored it, refocusing on the conversation in front of her.

"You are at a fate crossing. You might have known that, or else you would not bring a fairy princess with you, or maybe you are so ignorant you did not even know that," the unicorn stated. "Two futures are standing before you. Both paths are harsh and painful. You must choose which path you take, and you must do it now. Time will not continue till you do."

Time stopped around them. All magic stopped. Their visual illusions were gone, and their magical shields were down, all sucked into the power needed by the unicorn to stop time.

"The first path is inaction. If you do not cast this spell, magic dies. It will be a long and sad road. It will take decades, but in the end, magic will disappear from this world. All magical creatures will die or go dormant forever. All that you love will be gone. Moreover, nature itself will be gone as humans harvest this world to its death."

The vision slammed into Lixi's mind—elves falling to the ground in forests gone gray and lifeless, dwarves digging mass graves deep inside their silent mountains, human wizards dying in endless hospital beds as magic faded from their bodies. Endless cities of metal and smoke consumed the world. She tried to close her eyes, but the vision held them open. Around her, she heard gasps. The others were trapped in the same nightmare.

"You have witnessed the destruction of magic before, haven't you?" the unicorn asked.

"Yes, I have. It is horrible. It took most of my people. It took all my brothers," Valor said quietly.

"Well, let's talk about the other path." The unicorn paused for a bit. "The other path brings magic back, but not quietly. It returns in full force. On this path, all magical creatures are revived. Some are good. Many more are evil. Magic will alter this world beyond recognition, and with it comes war. An ancient battle between good and evil. In that war, there is one clear loser. Humanity."

Images of burnt cities filled their minds, the heat palpable even in the vision. Human mothers clutched children already turned to ash. Towns were consumed by fire that never stopped, white-hot flames turning the land to smooth black glass. Broken roads, bridges torn apart, skyscrapers crashing to the ground... The smell of burning flesh and wood filled Lixi's nose, making her almost gag.

Brenda doubled over and vomited, the scent of it sharp in the air. Odel grunted and covered his mouth with his hand.

Valor stood frozen beside her, all the color gone from his skin, his hands clenched so tightly his knuckles were white.

"No matter which path you choose, you will not be purely good from now on. Each path condemns good people to death, and you must choose now," the unicorn said.

There was a slight tone of satisfaction in his voice that made Lixi's jaw clench. Now she remembered exactly why she believed the unicorn was such an asshole for all these years.

"This is impossible," Odel growled.

"It is what it is." The unicorn went back to chewing grass.

Lixi felt a tug in her mind again, like hooks pulling at her consciousness from inside her skull.

Valor's mother's voice was urgent in her head. *"Your presence is demanded."*

Lixi needed her full mental strength not to be yanked out of the present conversation, her hands clenching into fists with the effort.

The unicorn sighed. Lixi knew no one could stop time forever. Leaves started falling slowly again around them.

"I cannot choose," Valor said. It was not a false claim. It was a fact.

"But you must, and time is running out," the unicorn said in an emotionless voice.

The crack of gunfire stretched out, distorted by slowed time. A bullet punched through the unicorn's body. Red blood bloomed across his white fur in slow spirals. The unicorn's breath caught, his eyes wide.

Another shot. The bullet slammed into Odel's stomach. The dwarf grunted, nearly collapsing before catching himself with his axe, blood spreading across his shirt.

"I will be dead in a few seconds," the unicorn said, his voice tight with pain. "You will not be able to cast this spell without me."

"I cannot make that decision!" Valor screamed. In the same instant, a bullet tore through his shoulder, blood spraying across his face.

Lixi reached out instinctively but stopped herself. Watching her friends get shot, bleeding in slow motion, was pure torture. Her fists clenched. She was helpless. The minute she stopped resisting the mental pull, she would be plucked out of this place. Valor's mother was summoning her away. Her entire being screamed not to be blinked out of here.

"I can choose." The voice came from behind Valor, strong and clear.

Brenda stepped forward. She held Odel's hand in one of her hands and Valor's hand in the other, her jaw set with determination. A bullet went slowly through the side of her forearm, blood running down to her wrist, but she didn't flinch.

"Brenda, this is not the right decision. There will be grave consequences. Fate does not..." Valor rasped.

"Fuck fate! We need this magic to fight another day. I cannot lose you all. Lixi, close the circle of magic. Let's cast this spell!" Brenda screamed.

Lixi used the last shred of her consciousness to take Valor's hand and to touch the unicorn's side with her other hand. Odel nodded to Brenda and put his free hand on the other side of the unicorn.

Oh, no. This is a horrible idea. What have I done? The thought hit Lixi with sudden clarity.

The scroll blazed with golden light and unfurled itself, floating free. It hung in the air for a heartbeat, then dissolved into particles of light that swirled around them like a galaxy. The world erupted in brilliance, golden and white and blinding.

Words rose from their throats without conscious thought, ancient syllables in a language that predated humanity, predated Lixi herself. The sounds resonated through her chest and vibrated in her bones. Their voices wove together in perfect harmony, five distinct tones becoming one unified chant. Magic poured through them like liquid fire, hot and cold at once, connecting them in a way that felt permanent and fundamental.

The air crackled with power. Light streamed from their intertwined hands, brilliant threads weaving between them, forming patterns that hurt to look at.

Then, time restarted.

"Lixiva Orera. You are summoned by the royal power of the elvish queen. Your presence is mandatory in witnessing the passing of the elvish king." Valor's mother's voice crashed through Lixi's mind like a tidal wave.

Now, there was nothing in Lixi's power to resist the royal summoning.

The world ripped apart. As her consciousness was torn away, she reached for Valor even as she faded. "I am so sorry," she whispered to him.

Her body vanished, pulled across space and time, but her mind clung to the bond for a few precious seconds longer, witnessing what came next through Valor's senses.

Through his eyes, she watched the unicorn's body explode into a thousand pieces, white fur and red blood scattering across the grass.

Through his body, she felt bullets punch through him from different directions, hot metal tearing flesh.

Through his ears, she heard Brenda and Odel scream in pain. Then, there was silence, followed by a faint sound of people speaking above their bodies.

"Area secured. Subjects disabled. Bring the chopper. We are bringing them in."

Then it all went dark.

EPILOGUE

Og felt a shiver go through his heavy scales. It was a strange feeling, one he had not felt in thousands of years. The weight of the mountain pressed down on his back, and his scales had gone as cold as the stone itself. When he flexed his claws, rock crumbled to dust between his talons.

It was a shiver of anticipation. Warmth crept through his stone-cold body, going from the tip of his long tail to the spikes on his head.

"Maca?" he tried to say, then projected the thought around him.

"Hmm," was all he heard back.

Somewhere in the deeper darkness, her massive form shifted, her scales whispering against stone. Her tone was cuddly but not happy. It was a "hmm" that said she was still deep in sleep and trying to wake her would not be a good idea.

He'd learned that lesson the hard way when they had first started their relationship. His friends had laughed when he'd told them about the extreme wrath he'd encountered when he'd woken her from a deep sleep. Now that she was mother to his child, she needed all the rest she could get. He could hear their son's tiny snores echoing softly between Maca's much deeper breaths.

Still half asleep himself, Og sniffed. The usual scents of the deep cave surrounded him—ancient water seeping through limestone, the metallic tang of iron veins, and the dust of undisturbed stone.

But something strange flavored the air. Magic tasted like ash and hot rocks on his forked tongue, the way it had so many thousands of years ago. Like smoke from a raging wildfire. It was unmistakably there. Magic was back again. Strong. Enough to fully wake him up.

Og had doubted this day would ever happen. Magic had not been strong enough to sustain his kind for so many millennia, not since this world had been all fire, when volcanoes had lit the night sky and dragons ruled the skies. Those had been glorious times.

There was something else, though, something more sinister and worrisome than magic returning. Time was being manipulated. To a creature who had lived through millennia, who could feel the patient turn of ages, this was agony, like claws scraping against the world's bones. It tasted bitter in his mouth and burned his nostrils like acid.

Had fate created another Time Welder? That bastard!

Manipulating time was a terrible sin.

He needed to know more.

Og took in the entire world in a way only his kind could. He moved his consciousness to the recent past and observed the history of the last two thousand years. Wars. Empires rising and falling like tides. Humans were trying to study time but failing to understand the basic concepts. The elves had a better grasp and had recently time-traveled to the present, but they had not broken the time continuum. Neither species had manipulated the future.

Yet.

No, something much more powerful and older than the humans and elves was about to break the world. A fight for control over the next era of this land was starting. Change was coming, and powerful forces were pulling their strings.

Og did not like that. He did not like that at all.

The dragons would not let the world break. The dragons would not let any power, no matter how strong, change the course of time.

If Maca were awake, she would have rolled her eyes and made fun of him for referring to themselves in third person again. She always did. He still thought it was cool.

Seeing the past was easy for Og, but it was hard for him to see the future. Maca was much better at that than him. He knew, though, with absolute certainty, that they would be called upon to save the world from breaking.

It was only a matter of time.

Soon, it would be time to join the fight, and when dragons returned to the world above, the mortals would learn what it meant to wake an ancient power.

War was coming, and Og was ready.

ACKNOWLEDGMENTS

To my wife, Deby Shevat, who supported me from the moment I said "I have this idea for a book," all the way through to publication.

To my sons, Daniel and Jonathan, who read draft after draft without complaint. Your patience never wavered, even when you could probably recite entire chapters from memory.

To my editor, Bokerah Brumley, who took a rough manuscript and helped me shape it into something I'm genuinely proud of. Your patience with my learning curve was extraordinary, and this book wouldn't exist without your guidance.

To my alpha readers: Nimo Naamani, Tal Sarig-Avraham, Nicole Zoltack, Rotem Boker Michaeli, Eli Klaiman, Anat Ben Yosef, Yochay Kiriaty, Gal Shtokhamer, Shirley Marom, Kate Reading, and Lindsay Galloway. Your feedback made this book immeasurably better. Every note, every question, every suggestion pushed me to dig deeper.

And finally, to everyone who picks up this book and gives Brenda, Valor, Odel, and Lixi a chance. Thank you for taking this journey with them. I hope you enjoy reading it as much as I enjoyed writing it. See you in book three.

Fun fact: People who write great book reviews online or share good books with friends live longer, happier lives.

WHAT'S NEXT?

Continue the adventures of Brenda, Valor, Odel, Lixi, and other beloved characters in book Three, *The Time Welder* (Book Three of The Time of Magic series), available at TheTimeOfMagic.-com/bookthree

WANT MORE?

Join our community, explore The Time of Magic lore, and discover other books at TheTimeOfMagic.com

ABOUT AMIR SHEVAT

Like my characters, I'm far from perfect. I'm dyslexic and dysgraphic, learned English as my second language, and spent my career in tech before turning to fiction. I probably worked on several of the pieces of software you use every day. I'm a D&D enthusiast, food lover, and compulsive traveler who's endlessly fascinated by humanity's contradictions. My stories explore what happens when flawed people face extraordinary circumstances, because the most interesting characters are the ones who struggle beautifully with being human, even when they are wizards.

www.ingramcontent.com/pod-product-compliance
Lightning Source LLC
La Vergne TN
LVHW041111080826
845145LV00007B/1772

* 9 7 8 1 9 7 1 2 9 5 1 0 7 *